JOHN DOE

TERRELL VERNON HICKS

All characters appearing in this work are fictitious. Any resemblance to real persons, living or dead, is purely coincidental.

Cover Photo by Piotr Marcinski/Courtesy of Shutterstock, Inc.

DEDICATION

For Sybil.

"Let go of the past

and the past will let go of you."

~Author Unknown

The following story takes place during 2011-2012.

ACKNOWLEDGMENTS

First and foremost I must give thanks to the Creator for giving me, blessing me, with the talent of writing.

To my Grandmother: having you in my life from day one has been simply awesome. I love you and thank you for always being my biggest supporter in more ways than one.

To my angels in heaven, my mother Sybil and my grandfather, Vernon, I miss you and I love you.

My editor Maggie Farrand, this is only the beginning.

To my bestie, Saleia, thank you for being the greatest friend in the world.

To my relatives, BPD family, and friends, thank you for all of your love and support.

To my readers, thank you.

♦ ONE ♦

Dr. Charlotte Tate tilted her head, uninterested in what she was listening to, even though her face said otherwise. It had to. Her 15-year career as a psychologist required its neutral expression as she sat across from one of her patients, Sarah Dickinson, a woman whose progress after a year and a half seemed to be moving at a snail's pace.

Dr. Tate shifted in her chair trying to reengage her attention back onto Sarah who seemed to be sucking the energy from the room with her long, drawn out talking. She checked the time on clock behind Sarah. *Fifteen more minutes of this. I'm going to have to cut this short. I can't take too much more of her today,* she thought to herself, taking a deep breath. She could feel her body drifting further into boredom with each word Sarah spoke about her broken relationship with her mother. Dr. Tate cleared her throat hoping it would cause Sarah to take a break, but it didn't.

"Have you tried talking to your mother, Sarah? Telling her exactly how you feel." Dr. Tate interjected.

"Every time I try she always brushes me off and brings up my sister and what she's doing or what her kids are doing. She doesn't care about me. She never has." Sarah wiped away tears. "I was the mistake. I was the child that wasn't supposed to be born. Sometimes I wish I never was."

3

For the first time in a year and a half Sarah had spoken words that hit Dr. Tate in a way she hadn't felt in quite some time. So much so that she leaned forward, wanting her to repeat her previous statement. "What did you say?"

"I said I was the mistake. My parents were satisfied with my brother and sister and didn't want any more children. And oops, here I come. I was the accident."

"I'm sure you weren't a mistake or an accident Sarah. I'm sure your mother loves you very much."

"Telling your child you wish she had never been born on more than one occasion is a great way of showing you love her."

Dr. Tate looked at the clock again. "I'm actually going to end our session a little early today, if you don't' mind," she said standing up.

"Ok. Sure." Sarah took her co-payment from her wallet and handed to Dr. Tate as she stood up.

Dr. Tate took the payment and walked her over to the door. "See you next week."

"Okay."

"Take care."

"You too, Dr. Tate."

Dr. Tate watched Sarah until she got to the elevator doors and then went back inside her office, shutting the door. "Whew Lord! I don't how much longer I can do this. I mean, damn, it's been a year and a half and it seems like we're getting nowhere." She shouted, knowing that her office door had twice the thickness of standard office doors for patient confidentiality.

She felt her frustration level on the rise and sat down at her desk. *Calm down. Inhale. Exhale. Inhale. Exhale.* As boring as the sessions with Sarah usually were, she couldn't shake the words Sarah spoke out of her head. *A mistake.* The same words her mother spoke about someone whom she loved years earlier. She grabbed a yellow W.B. Mason pad from the drawer she had designated just for them. A back-up in case her iPad malfunctioned. She wrote:

September 8, 2011
10:00am

Sarah again! It has been a year and a half now since I began sessions with her and it seems as if she wants to talk more about her past than move on from it. I've given her numerous tools to help her move forward and it seems like she doesn't want to use them and it's beginning to become frustrating. And not even with just her. My career in general. Lately, I've been wondering if I even want to continue being in my profession. I feel stuck. Bored with it. It's been fifteen years and I still don't feel fulfilled.

But today's session with Sarah did bring you into my mind. Not that I haven't thought about you. I wonder about you. I wonder how you are, if you're married now, with any children of your own. I often think about looking for you, but like I said in my previous letters, I wouldn't know where, or how, to begin. There's not much I know about you. Let me stop, I'm starting to sound like Sarah. You've heard me say that too many times before. You know, I'll never stop loving you. You will always be in my heart. I love you, B.B.
Charlotte.

She slowly put down the pen looking at yet another written letter. It had been 31 years since she had last laid eyes on him and the not knowing him still hurt more than the events of the day he left. She folded up the short letter and placed it in an envelope and wrote the date on the front.

There was a tap on the door and her eldest sister Kenya peeked inside. "Hey Girl, you ready?" She asked walking in further, her curvy frame hugging by every inch of her gray business suit.

"Yeah, just let me grab my purse." Charlotte dabbed the corner of her eyes with a tissue not wanting to smear her makeup, looking in the mirror on her desk. She was good. She grabbed her purse from the drawer and tucked the envelope inside. "Where's Tamara?"

"She said she's going meet us there."

"Figures." She closed the drawer and walked from behind her desk. "Ooh, I like that suit. Where'd you get it from?"

"Macy's." Kenya answered.

"I like it. It looks good on you."

"Don't it?" Kenya posed.

"I figured we'd go to Darryl's since it's closer." Charlotte said.

"Good. Since my lunch time will be shorter than usual today."

"Big case?"

"No, too many little ones."

"I have to stop at the bank first if you don't mind."

"That's fine."

Charlotte locked the door as they stepped out of the office.

Charlotte walked into the Westinghouse Bank, its interior was old and wide like the banks used as sets in Hollywood gangster films. She smiled and waved to one of the associates she had come to know well since she opened the account ten years ago. This account was private, one not shared with her husband. Its value too sentimental to shared with anyone, especially him. She walked up to the bubbly, brunette teller who greeted her with a big smile like she always did, reminding Charlotte of a Crest commercial.

"Need to make a deposit, Mrs. Watson?" asked the teller.

"Yeah."

The teller placed her "next window" sign on the counter and walked Charlotte past the gate guarded by two big security men. "How is everything?"

"Everything is well. How's your little boy?" Charlotte asked as they walked into the vault room that housed numerous safe-deposit boxes.

"He's doing good. Now that we got his diabetes under control, he's doing real good."

"That's great," said Charlotte

"Here we are." The teller unlocked the case and pulled out the three long boxes and sat them on the silver table. Charlotte lifted the cover off of the first box and it was completely filled with envelopes. She took the cover off of the second and it mirrored the first. She lifted the cover of the third box and it was on its way to becoming like the previous two. Some envelopes had discolored over time. She took the envelope from her purse and placed it inside the box and stood there marveling at them all. She couldn't believe how many she had written. Ten-thousand, three-hundred and ninety-nine letters. One envelope for each day of her life since 1980. They were her diary. Her story. And she hoped for the day when she would share them with the one person who needed to read them.

"All set?" asked the teller.

Charlotte cleared her throat. "Yeah."

She walked out and the teller covered the boxes and placed them back in the safe deposit box, locking it. Charlotte walked back through the bank questioning herself as she did after every deposit: Did she really want to find him after all these years?

"Everything okay?" Kenya asked standing up.

"Everything's fine. Let's go."

♦ TWO ♦

Boston • October 1979

Fourteen-year-old Charlotte Watson sat on the front cement steps of her brick tenement in the Orchard Park projects watching the neighborhood kids play in the courtyard. The section for which she, her mother and her two older sisters resided was the hangout, where the other residents within the multi-building housing development came to hang. She continued to watch the children, most of whom she knew, play as a group of mothers, whom her mother called "loose lips", sat on the stoop across from her discussing the word on the street.

It was a clear, warm, Spring-like day and Charlotte was shivering inside like the temperature was twenty below. She was scared. Nervous, sitting there alone trying to imagine what her mother's response would be to what she had to disclose. Her mother was a woman of conviction - strong and stern who believed in the word of God. She didn't spread the words of the Bible to every set of ears that she came in contact with, but Sunday attendance at Twelfth Baptist every week was mandatory.

Charlotte looked down at her palms and rubbed them against her jeans trying to remove the perspiration. She wasn't your average stereotypical teenage nerd. She was a non-glasses, beautiful, bright bookworm who wondered where her logic went

8

when she decided to close her books one afternoon and open her thin-long legs to the Captain of the basketball team. She was the golden child. The one whose pedestal stood a little higher than her two sisters Kenya and Tamara at least in her mother's eyes.

Kenya was a replica of their mother, but dark and tall like their father. Fierce. Smart. 5-foot-9 and 18 years old her curves were beginning to fall into the right places catching the attention of most, if not all, of the boys in her senior class, but between work, school and college preparation, she barely had time for the boyfriend she was seeing so little of now.

Charlotte let out a sigh of relief noticing that the car pulling into the parking lot didn't have her mother behind the wheel. The anticipation was dreadful. The mystery of not knowing whether or not her life was going to cease to exist was electrifying, but not in a good way.

Sixteen-year-old Tamara stepped out of the building slurping an orange popsicle and sat down next to her. Tamara was the second oldest and took pride in how she looked to herself and to others, loving the spotlight whenever it shined upon her. Spending more than the allotted time in the bathroom causing her sisters to bang and yell outside of the door for her removal. "Don't y'all know beauty takes time," she'd shout from inside the bathroom, leaving her sisters as steamed as she did the bathroom mirror after her long, over-the-top sung showers.

"Did Mama get home yet?" She asked slurping on the popsicle.

"No," said Charlotte coldly.

"What's wrong with you?"

Charlotte didn't answer, just let out a breath, hoping her sister got the hint to leave. She loved her, but Tamara's mouth was bigger than Grand Canyon and Charlotte knew her business would be all over the projects faster than a speeding bullet if she told her of her plight.

"Fine then. Keep it to yourself. I don't care." Tamara slurped on the melting popsicle. "Tell Mama I'll be at Paula's if she's looking for me."

Charlotte kept quiet as Tamara walked away. She closed her eyes at the sound of squealing car brakes in the distance. Her leg began to shake and her palms began to sweat again. The sound of her mother's car brakes were distinctive. She slowly moved her eyes in the direction of the parking lot, terrified. Her mother exited the blue '73 Chevy Impala which her father left behind when he walked out, six year earlier, into the arms and the bed of another woman who was much younger than her mother.

Carol Watson was tired as she grabbed her bag from the back seat. Her day at the Department of Children and Families was long and difficult. She waved to the gossiping mothers on the stoop as she headed towards Charlotte. She was an average-heighted woman with a skin tone and the facial features that resembled actress Pam Grier whom most people that she was at first glance. She welcomed the comparison, at times, depending upon her mood.

Charlotte felt a piece of her life slip away with each step her mother took in her direction. Everyone and everything seemed to move in slow motion as she tried to keep her focus on the tree in the distance in front of her trying not to give off any hint of a problem. She swiped her index fingers under her eyes trying to remove any wetness as her mother walked up. Tamara, not far away, noticed their mother approaching her sister and quickly made her way back. Her nosy radar on high.

"Hey," said their mother.

"Hey Ma," said Tamara.

Charlotte remained silent.

"I said Hey."

"Hi Ma." Charlotte said lowly.

"What's wrong with you?"

"Nothing."

"Well, something must be wrong for you to be sitting here looking sad and...crying." She lifted her head and noticed the dried tears. "What's wrong? Come on, we'll talk about it in the house. Y'all know I don't like my business all in the street like some people around here."

Carol looked back in direction of the mothers on the stoop and waved. Charlotte got up from the stairs and walked in, her mother and sister following suit.

"Where's your sister?" asked their mother.

"At work," said Tamara.

"I thought you were going to Paula's." Charlotte said in a disapproving tone not wanting her sister around.

"I changed my mind. I'll see her later."

They entered the piss-scented hallway of their building and journeyed up the two flights of stairs to their three-bedroom apartment, one of ten in the whole complex. Carol unlocked the door and they walked into the spotless apartment. Everything neatly in its rightful place. Quietly and quickly, Charlotte made her way to the couch, sitting down, wanting to gain distance from her mother. Carol locked the door and put her purse on the coat rack, dropping her keys in the dish on the small end table near the door.

"Okay, you've been very quiet a lot around here lately I noticed. What's going on with you?"

Charlotte didn't answer.

"You better answer me when I ask you a question."

Charlotte's stomach churned as she worked up the little courage she could to answer her. She lowered her head scared. "I'm pregnant," she mumbled.

"You know I don't like it when you mumble. Come here."

Charlotte got up from the couch and walked over to her, body trembling.

"Now what did you say?"

Charlotte looked into her mother's eyes, tears streaming from her eyes. "I'm...pregnant." "Ahhh!"

Carol's slap stung her face like a bee. Tamara stood off to the side in disbelief at the words that came from her sister's mouth and the slap that followed.

"How dare you? How dare you embarrass me and not to mention this entire family with this mess?! Huh!"

"I'm sorry."

"Shut up!" Carol screamed slapping her again. And again and again. Charlotte covered her face with her hands protecting her. "How could you, huh?! How could you do this to me?!"

"Ma! Stop!" Tamara shouted running over, separating them.

"Whose is it anyway?! Whose child is that?! That Keith boy?! Huh!"

"Yes." Charlotte cried.

"Did you tell him?! Does he know?!" Carol yelled trying to catch her breath.

"No."

"Good. Keep it that way."

"Ma...I'm sor—"

"Shut up! You're an embarrassment! You better be glad you're still standing. Now get out of my face!"

Charlotte cried herself into her bedroom and closed the door. Tamara stood next to their mother like a deer caught in the headlights still trying to wrap her mind around what had just happened.

"Do something with yourself." Carol snapped at Tamara as she sat on the couch.

Tamara headed for the door.

"And you keep your damn mouth shut."

Tamara didn't respond.

"Did you hear me?"

"Yes."

"I swear Tamara if you say any—"

"I won't. God," Tamara said sucking her teeth.

"You better not."

Tamara walked out.

Carol held her head in her hands still in disbelief at the words that came out of her youngest daughter's mouth. *I'm pregnant.* The words made her head ache. She was beyond pissed. She was storming mad. And hurt. *Why would she do that?* She thought. How could the child she favored a little more in her heart than the oldest two do this to her? Those words were the last things she wanted to hear from any of her daughters, especially her.

Carol sat back on the couch wanting to hurl something across the living room, but there was nothing she didn't feel like replacing later. "Why me Lord? Why my daughter?" She leaned forward rubbing her face with her hands. Her mother, Mae Anne, was right Charlotte was like her in more ways than one.

◆ THREE ◆

"Aaaaaahhhhhhhhhh!" Charlotte lay back against the bed, beat, exhausted. It was the late summer of 1980 and she had managed to keep her pregnancy a secret from her friends and classmates, disguising her expanding body with clothes much bigger than her size. If anyone questioned her weight gain, her thyroid was the excuse. Now she sat—or rather lay—in the delivery room at Boston City Hospital, participating in a pain her young body and mind was not prepared for.

Carol dabbed the sweat from her daughter's forehead with a wet towel, holding her hand in support. She was raising her girls to be respectable young women and the fact she was now helping guide the youngest through one of the most painful experiences in her short life was not her proudest moment.

"I can see the top of the head! I'm gonna need you to push Charlotte," said the doctor from between her legs.

"I can't! I can't!" Charlotte shouted.

"You're gonna have to, Charlotte," said the doctor.

"You have to push honey," said her mother.

"I can't! It hurts!"

"I know it does, but you're gonna have to push," said her mother.

"You can do this, Charlotte. I just need one big push, okay? The baby's almost here," said the doctor. "Can you do that for me?"

Charlotte nodded.

"On the count of three. One…Two…Three!"

"Aaaaaahhhhhh!" Charlotte squeezed her mother's hand tightly, grabbing a hold of the sheets with the other, pushing this new life within her out. She fell back against the bed exhausted once again as tiny, sweet, innocent, wails emanated from between her legs.

"It's a boy!" the doctor shouted as the nurse cut the cord. "Here he is, Charlotte. Your beautiful baby boy." The doctor carried the baby over to her.

"I don't think that would be a very good idea, Doctor," snapped Carol.

"Why not?" said the doctor.

"Because we don't want him. That child is a mistake. That child means nothing to us. I suggest you take him."

The Doctor couldn't believe what she had just heard. "But Mrs. Watson—"

"I said he is irrelevant. We don't want him."

"I want my baby. I want my baby." Charlotte moaned.

"Shut up! You don't know what you want. We wouldn't be here if it weren't for you."

"Mrs. Watson, please think about what you're saying here. There are programs that can help your daughter raise this baby."

"Like what? Welfare? I don't think so. No child of mine is going on public assistance. She has already embarrassed me enough by getting herself pregnant. Welfare will make it worse. It's bad enough we have to live in the projects. So no. You can take that thing with you."

"Nurse, could you please take this precious baby with you? Clean him and take him to the nursery. Wait a minute." The doctor turned back around, her insides boiling with anger. "Can she at least name him?"

"What part of 'we don't want him' don't you understand, doctor?"

"Nurse, could you please…thank you." The nurse took the baby from the doctor.

"Mama, I'm sorry. Please don't let them take my baby!

Please! Please don't take my baby!"

"Hush up!"

The mood of the room had changed. It went from a happy, joyous, active room to a somber, quiet, atmosphere. Charlotte's cry now filled the room, bouncing from the walls like an alarm. The nurse wiped her eyes as she cleaned the six-pound, four-ounce bundle of joy and wheeled him out in a bassinet.

"I'm going to...um...take you to your room now Charlotte," said the doctor.

The doctor unlocked the bed and wheeled a distraught Charlotte from the delivery room out into the hallway, her wailing catching the attention of the nearby hospital staff.

"Now cut it out. Hush up." Carol took one of the pillows from behind Charlotte's head and gave it to her to cry into. "You're embarrassing yourself, not to mention me."

The doctor wheeled Charlotte into an empty hospital room and positioned the bed, locking it in place. "If you need anything, just buzz the nurse, okay?"

Charlotte didn't respond.

"I'm sorry," said the doctor touching Charlotte's shoulder.

"She doesn't need your pity, doctor. She did this to herself trying to be grown."

The doctor left the room without another word. Carol looked back at the door making sure the doctor or hospital staff wasn't in earshot. She grabbed Charlotte's face.

"If you breathe a word of this to anyone, ever, I swear I will do you harm. You understand me?"

Charlotte didn't answer.

"I said do you understand me?"

"Yes." Charlotte answered tearfully.

"Good." She let go of her face.

Charlotte turned her head and looked towards the gorgeous day that was displaying itself just beyond the window hoping its view would drift her away from the sorrow, the guilt, the shame that had now been forever imprinted upon her soul.

♦ FOUR ♦

The tears had dried hours ago as Charlotte lie awake in her hospital bed staring at the ceiling numb and emotionless. It had been several hours since she had given birth to her son and she wondered what he looked like. If he had that new-powdery-baby smell. If he was cold or hungry. If he knew who she was. She wanted to see him, kiss him, touch him, even smell him.

She looked over at her mother who was asleep on the small couch near the window. She watched her mother's chest expand with each inhale and fall with each exhale, waiting for her signature snore. The loud, sawing-sound snore came during her mother's next inhale and she knew she was in a deep sleep.

The floor was as cold as ice as Charlotte crept out of the bed like a prisoner quietly trying to escape their captor. She glided her feet across the floor and slowly opened the door hoping the low-light from the hallway didn't shine on her mother's face waking her up. She was in no mood to be belittled with sentences of embarrassment and shame once again.

It was 2:30 a.m., the clock on the wall at the nurses' station read as ticked loudly. The hallway was quiet and empty, Charlotte could hear a pin drop, making her over to the nurse who was flipping through a magazine behind the desk.

"Excuse me, where are the babies?"

"Through those double doors there." The nurse pointed.

"Thank you."

The sweet small sounds of newborns greeted Charlotte as she walked through the wooden double doors. They were all so precious, sweet, kind, loving, not yet affected by the world as they lay bundled up in their bassinets as if there for anyone's choosing. Charlotte looked at the names taped on the end of each bassinet searching for her last name. *Brown. Richardson. Franklin. Johnson. Watson. No Watson? Where is he?* Charlotte thought looking at the infants. If only she had seen his face, she would know which one he was.

"Cute, aren't they?" A nurse said walking in startling Charlotte. "I'm sorry. I didn't mean to frighten you."

"That's okay."

"They are so precious. I wish I could take them all home with me. Especially that one on the end over there. Poor thing. Family just left him. No name, no nothing. Just gave him up."

Charlotte's eyes widen with joy as she laid them upon her beautiful baby boy for the first time. He was so precious like an angel. She touched the window and smiled.

"It looks like someone gave him a name. John Doe," said Charlotte.

"Oh, yeah, that's just a name the hospital uses when a child or an adult can be identified or attached to a family. That won't be his name forever," said the nurse.

Charlotte didn't say a word, just stared at him beaming with love.

"Would you like to hold him?" asked the nurse.

"No, no." Charlotte sniffled.

"You okay, honey?"

"I'm fine. I just have something in my eye."

The nurse started to walk away.

"Excuse me, can I...hold him?"

"Sure. Follow me."

Charlotte followed the nurse into an area where the hospital staff and parents washed their hands before touching the infants.

"Just wash your hands in the sink there and follow me."

Charlotte swiftly washed her hands twice with the hospital-approved antibacterial soap and dried her hands with a couple of paper towels. She followed the nurse into the room where the babies were and her heart began to race. The nurse grabbed a pair of blue latex gloves from the box on the wall. A bolt of indescribable energy electrified Charlotte's young body from her head to her feet as the nurse lifted her son from the bassinet, placing him in her arms, her heart skipping a beat. Was this really happening? Was she really holding her son? Or was this a figment of her imagination? She felt the pin-size prick as she pinched herself. This was for real.

"Five minutes," said the nurse.

"Okay."

Charlotte looked down into the eyes of her son and melted inside. She thought of making a run for it, but she knew she would never make it past the double doors before the nurse noticed. Her eyes welled with tears as she continued to stare.

"You are so beautiful. Yes, you are." She said touching his hand. "You will always have a special place in my heart. I'll never forget you. Never." She wiped the tears from her eyes. "I love you." The baby moaned and she smiled. "I know. I know." *God, I wished I could take him home. I promise I wouldn't mess up in school.* She closed her eyes and prayed, hoping to get a sign that would make it possible for her do so. Nothing.

"Time's up." The nurse said walking back in.

Charlotte opened her eyes. This was the end. She would never see him again. She placed him in his bassinet, kissing him softly upon his forehead.

"A cutie, isn't he?"

"Yeah." Charlotte half-smiled not wanting the nurse to learn the child was hers. "What's going to happen to him?"

"Well, he will stay here and continue to get the proper care he needs until his family comes back to get him or social services steps in and takes him, whichever happens first."

Charlotte's heart ached looking back at her son, gradually walking away. She felt herself weakening with each step took in the opposite direction of him.

"Well, it's time to let the little guy rest."

"Thank you."

"You're welcome, honey."

Charlotte walked back through the double doors and headed back to her room, heartbroken. She stopped at the door, wiping eyes, making sure no tears or dried residue appeared in case her mother was awake. Her mother was still asleep as she slowly opened the door and quietly crept back to her bed and slid underneath the covers.

She stared back at the ceiling feeling elated, but sad at the same time. She rolled onto her side facing the door, not wanting the sight of her mother to spoil the mixture of feelings she couldn't quite explain. She had something. A moment for which no one, not even her beloved mother, could take from her. The moment of holding in her arms what her mother had deemed a mistake even if it was only for five minutes.

◆ FIVE ◆

The morning sun shined through Charlotte's hospital room window onto her beautiful round face as she shifted in her sleeping position. Carol glanced up at her from the magazine she was flipping through. Even though the previous day's events were behind them, she still held disdainful eye about her daughter. The nurse from the delivery room walked in.

"How is she?"

"She's good. Just resting," Carol said putting the magazine down and standing up.

"Good. The doctor should have her released by the end of the day," smiled the nurse. She started out of the room.

"Excuse me Nurse?"

"Yes."

"Can I talk to you out in the hall for a moment?"

"Sure."

Known to play sleep, Carol glanced over at Charlotte as she walked out into the hallway with the nurse. Charlotte shifted her position towards the door and parted her eyelids just enough to see her mother hand the nurse a piece of paper as they spoke in the distance. She closed her eyes as she noticed her mother headed back into the room. Carol slowed her pace as she noticed her daughter shifting her sleep position once again, this time away from the door. *Humph,* she thought sitting back down and resuming flipping the pages of People magazine wondering just how much asleep her disappointing daughter really was.

Charlotte looked out of the window of her mother's '73 Chevy Impala as the rain pelted against the glass. She watched as some of the buildings went by like blurs and others slowed to a crawl as they stopped at a traffic light. It was the summer, but Charlotte wasn't warm. She was raw, cold, like the rain. The traffic light changed and the buildings began to blur by once again.

"You haven't said much since the hospital," said her mother not taking her eyes off the road. "You hungry? You want something to eat?"

Charlotte didn't answer.

"I said are you hungry?"

"No." Charlotte replied parting her lips just enough so the words could flow clearly and she wouldn't have to repeat it.

"I suggest you take that bass out of your voice. God is giving you a second chance and I suggest you better take heed to it, you understand?"

Charlotte kept her focus outside of the window.

"Well, you can get yourself some more rest when you get home. The sooner you forget about it, the better off you'll be. Trust me, I know."

Carol pulled into her favorite space in the parking lot just outside her building and they got out. Charlotte made her way into the building and up the stairs to the apartment like a tortoise. She dreaded answering the questions she knew awaited her other side of the door from her sisters.

Tamara muted the television as they walked in, curious to know what transpired at the hospital since their mother didn't allow her or Kenya any visitations. Charlotte didn't make eye contact with her sister and began making her way towards the bedroom.

"Where's Kenya?" asked their mother locking the door and hanging her purse on the coat rack.

"On her way home from work." Tamara answered.

"Where's the baby?"

"Dead," Carol said coldly.

"Oh my God. What happened?" Tamara asked, eyes watering.

"I said it's dead," Carol snapped.

Charlotte stopped in her tracks wanting to turn around and speak the truth, but knew she wouldn't live to see another day if she did. The door unlocked and in walked Kenya dressed in her Burger King uniform. Her dark skin glistening from the Vaseline that covered it.

"Hey." She locked the door, noticing the silence. "Okay, what's wrong? What happened?"

The silence grew thicker as no one was eager to speak.

"The baby...it died," Tamara whispered.

"Oh, my God. Charly, are you okay?." Kenya moved to touch her.

"Don't touch her. Let her be," said Carol. "She doesn't need pity. She needs Jesus."

Charlotte felt like an outcast in her own home as she made her way towards her room and shut the door. Silence filled the room once again as Kenya and Tamara stood around looking at one another not knowing what else to say or do.

"Now that, that is over. No one, and I mean no one, will speak of this to anyone or ever again. Am I understood?" Carol said.

Silence.

"I said am I understood?"

"Yes, Ma'am." Kenya and Tamara spoke.

"Good."

♦ SIX ♦

The sun shined luminous over the grassy, quiet field that stretched for miles. The warm breeze softly caressed Charlotte's face, the grass tickling her bare feet. She smiled lifting her baby in the air and slightly from her hands catching him. His smile as bright and lovely as the sound of his giggle. She twirled feeling the happiness and love that flowed throughout her body as she held him in the air. Then...

BOOM! Carol dropped an empty bucket to the floor startling Charlotte from her beloved daydream. "Get your head out of the clouds." Charlotte sat up. "I want you to clean that bathroom and go to the store. You pick whatever one you want to get done first, but both need to be done by the time I get home from work." Carol walked away as Charlotte got up from her bed at a snail's pace. "The money and the list for the store is on the counter in the kitchen."

Charlotte took a deep breath. The thought of running away crossed her mind as it had before, but she had nowhere to go, no one to run to. She put her sneakers on and headed out of the bedroom. She knew her mother would be mad, but not this long. The tone that carried every word from her mother's mouth had a sting with it. A feeling of disgust that made her feel dirty every time her mother spoke in her direction.

Cars drove by with their booming systems as Charlotte walked to the store still wearing the same big clothes she did when she hid her pregnancy. She was once like the girls she noticed playing double-dutch on the basketball court. Vibrant, energetic, loud. Now she was dark, cold and quiet.

The bell above the store door jingled as she walked into Saul's, the neighborhood convenience store and pulled the list from her pocket. The salt-and-peppered-hair man stood behind the counter. With over twenty-five years in business he had become a staple of the neighborhood.

"Hi, Miss Charlotte," said Saul.

"Hi, Mr. Saul." Charlotte spoke not making eye contact with him afraid he'd start asking questions.

"Haven't seen you in a while?"

"Been sick."

She grabbed a shopping cart as a mother entered the store carrying her baby. The mother greeted Saul as she struggled to get a cart. "Excuse me. Excuse me. Can you hold him for me while I try to a get a cart?" The woman asked Charlotte.

"Sure," said Charlotte. She took the six-month-old from his mother's arms and he smiled. "Hi. You are so cute. Yes, you are." He touched her face and smiled. She looked into his eyes and thought about her baby boy and the peace she felt the one and only time she held him.

"What's his name?"

"Mason."

"How you doing, Mason?" He grabbed her finger as she gently touched his nose. "How old is he?"

"Six months." She smiled as she watched Charlotte interact with her son. "I'll take him now."

"Oh, sorry."

"That's okay. He likes you." The mother placed him in the shopping cart. "You'll make a great mother one day."

Charlotte smiled.

"Thank you," said the mother walking away.

"You're welcome." Charlotte responded lowly.

"You okay, Miss Charlotte?" Mr. Saul asked noticing the sadness in her eyes.

"I'm fine, Mr. Saul." Charlotte pushed the cart and started looking for the first item on her mother's list. She thought about going back to the hospital. *Forget it, he's probably gone already.* She continued shopping.

* * *

Charlotte increased the speed of her pace as she made her way down the pathway to the front door of the building hoping Tamara didn't see her from the courtyard. She was fragile and in no mood to deal with her blabber-mouth of a sister. She struggled with the main door not wanting to drop a single bag from her hands. She managed her way inside and up to the apartment hoping the door was unlocked as Tamara often left it. Something their mother couldn't stand.

Yes, it's open, she thought as pushed the door opened and kicked it closed putting the bags on the kitchen counter. She went into her bedroom she shared with Tamara and stretched out across her bed and grabbed a pillow. She could still smell the baby from the store on her clothes. It smelled soft, happy. She wondered if seeing and holding that baby was God's way of further punishing her, showing her what she could have been.

She sat up against the wall, still clinching the pillow, feeling the urge to cry. Nothing. She felt dry and empty like the Sahara desert. Kenya walked by and noticed her sister sitting on the bed and stopped, walking in.

"Hey, what's wrong?"

"Nothing. I'm fine." She said without looking at her sister.

"You sure?" Kenya sat down on the bed beside her, rubbing her back.

Charlotte turned her head towards the window and wiped her eyes not wanting her sister to notice the tears gathering at the bottom of her eyes. "I saw this cute baby in the store today. His mother let me hold him. You should have seen him he was so cute." She kept her vision on the window, wiping more tears. "What's wrong with me?" She looked at her sister. "Why does Mama hate me so much? I told her I was sorry. Why won't she forgive me?"

"Mama doesn't hate you." Kenya held her close. "She just needs time, that's all. Besides you're not the only one to have sex."

"You too?"

"Of course."

"How many times have you done it?"

"Enough. Charly, listen, even the smartest people have slip-ups. I slip-up all the time. Not quite as big as yours, but I do."

They laughed.

"I miss my baby," said Charlotte.

"I know." Kenya said hugging her. "Come here." She took her by the hand into her room and shut the door. "Are you going to do it again?"

"Do what?"

"It."

"You mean have sex?"

"Yes."

"No. Never again."

"Well, if you do…" She reaches in her top dresser drawer, pulling out her secret stash of contraception. "…you need to take one of these."

"What is it?"

"They're birth control pills."

"Birth control pills?"

"They keep you from getting pregnant."

"Does Mama know you have those?" Charlotte whispered.

"Yeah. She took me to get them. So, if you think about doing "it" again, just take one of these." She put them back in the drawer and closed it. "And make sure Keith wears a condom next time."

"He was wearing one the last time."

"What happened?"

"It broke."

Kenya let out a breath. "Well, just let me know when you take one, okay."

"Okay."

"I'm your big sister and I'm here for you, okay."

"Okay. Ken…"

"Yeah."

"…can you do me a favor?"

"What?"

"Can you clean the bathroom for me before Mama gets home?"

♦ SEVEN ♦

Charlotte and Tamara were getting ready for the first day of the new school year as their mother walked in, dressed in a white blouse and a black skirt. "Tamara, I need to talk to your sister alone." She stepped aside and Tamara walked by. Carol closed the door and stood in front of Charlotte who was trying to not let her nervousness show.

"Don't think you're gonna use your little accident as an excuse to let your grades slip." She grabbed her daughter's face and held it tight. "If your grades slipped below a 'B-' I will break you, you understand? Keep your head in those books and away from that boy. You got it?"

"Yes, Ma'am." Charlotte said tearing up.

"Good." She let go of her face and straightened her clothes. "Have a good day at school." She walked out of the room.

Charlotte let the tears falls from her eyes as she shook her head in frustration. She had grown tired of her mother's treatment towards her since she revealed the pregnancy. She snatched her backpack from the floor and walked out headed to the one place that would get away from the Evil Queen even if it was only for six and a half hours.

It had been almost three weeks since Charlotte had left the hospital and she now walked the graffiti covered halls of

Eastwood Central High in the herd of students, hoping no one she knew noticed her. She felt like an immigrant new to a foreign land. She felt as if everyone's eyes were on her and she was the topic of their private conversations even though she wasn't.

She kept her head down and tried to stay in the middle of the herd. She had gone the whole summer without seeing any of her friends and was hoping not to bump into them. Especially Miranda. She wasn't in the mood of explaining how eventful her summer had been because, like Tamara, Miranda too had a mouth that didn't hold secrets very well.

It was almost the start of first period and she still hadn't seen the one person she desperately wanted to see. She wondered if he even came to school as she opened her locker to grab her mathematics book. He normally didn't attend the first day. She hadn't seen or spoken to him the whole summer. She missed the touch of his arms around her waist. The scent of his father's cologne that always seeped from his neck. She hoped he hadn't change and became the stereotypical high school jock and moved onto someone else.

"Charlotte! Charlotte!" Seventeen-year-old Keith Tate shouted in the distance as he made his way through the crowd of students. He was tall, thin and dark like the night sky. His big, bright smile showing almost every tooth in his mouth. He wasn't your average high school jock who was only good at putting the ball in the hoop. He was a strong 'C+' student, whom wasn't very fond of math, which Coach Fields knew when he asked Charlotte to help him prepare for an exam that would keep him on the Eastman Eagles varsity team roster if he passed it.

Charlotte tried, but couldn't, stop her heart from racing whenever she knew they were meeting. The idea of her having the smallest of body contact with her secret crush kept her concentration unstable. Her speech becoming slow and low every time he moved in to get a better understanding of the material. She laughed at his off-beat jokes during their walks home. The more time they spent with together the more smitten Keith became, keeping his feelings hidden until their last day of tutoring when he kissed her. Now he stood before her at her locker feeling rejected, having not spoken with her the whole summer.

"You could've called and told me you didn't want to see me anymore?" Keith said.

The familiar scent of his father's Brute cologne tickled Charlotte's nose as she breathed it in.

"Huh? What?"

"I called your house and your mother told me you never wanted to see me again and to never call her house again. I mean you could've told me yourself that you wanted to break up with me, Charlotte."

"What? I never said that."

"The whole summer no call, nothing."

Charlotte looked away. "I was sick." She lied. "I never told her to say that. I swear." She grabbed his denim jacket.

He looked into her brown eyes and knew she wasn't lying.

The school bell rang.

"I'll see you later."

"Okay."

They kissed.

"Well, if isn't Romeo and Juliet," said Miranda, Charlotte's friend, as she walked up. She was fifteen and fast. The total opposite of Charlotte. "We need to talk. Excuse us, Keith."

Charlotte looked back as Miranda pulled her away. Keith made a funny face and she smiled.

"So, how was North Carolina?" asked Miranda

"North Carolina?"

"Yeah, your mother said you were spending the summer with your Aunt and Uncle in North Carolina."

Charlotte let out a breath disgusted. "Not so great."

"Well, I got something to tell you."

"What?"

Miranda looked around making sure no one was in ear-shy of what she was about to mention. "I'm pregnant."

"What! Are you serious?" Charlotte said pulling her to the side.

"Yeah. I've been waiting the whole summer to tell you."

"Does Danny know?"

"Yeah, he knows. He trying to say it's not his, but it is."

"What are you gonna do with the baby?"

"I'm gonna keep it." Miranda touched her stomach.

"Your mother's gonna let you keep it."

"Yeah. We can't afford an abortion, so she said she's going to watch it while I go to school."

The school bell rang again alerting students that the next period had begun and hallway conversations were over.

"I'll see you later," said Miranda.

"Okay."

Charlotte wanted to drop to her knees and scream right there in the middle of the hallway. It felt like a slap in the face that Miranda was allowed to keep her baby. Why Miranda? Why not her? What was wrong with her? Why wasn't God allowing her to keep her baby? She covered her mouth with her hand, feeling herself about to hurl. She ran into the girls' bathroom around the corner and burst into an empty stall, releasing her vomit into the toilet. She reached up and flushed the toilet and sat back against the stall door and cried.

♦ EIGHT ♦

Charlotte looked out the window at the buildings and the people as they passed by while she rode the bus. Miranda's words about keeping her baby played over and over in her head like a broken record. A passenger pulled the string that lined the bus just above the windows, sounding the bell, and yelled "next stop".

The bus pulled over as it reached the next stop and the passenger got off and a few others got on. The doors closed and the bus moved again. Charlotte looked on as the bus passed people were getting patted down by the police while others stood on the corners talking among themselves. The bus stopped at a red light and the bus driver looked back.

"Young lady. Young lady," said the bus driver.

Charlotte looked up.

"You going to the hospital, right?"

She nodded.

"Well, this is your stop. I don't go directly by the hospital, so you're gonna have to get off here."

Charlotte got up and walked to the front of the bus.

"Come back here in about twenty minutes okay and stand across the street. Right over there..." He pointed. "...and I'll pick you up. Okay?"

She didn't speak, just nodded. He wondered if she was a

mute as he opened the door and she stepped off the bus.

"Across the street, okay."

"Okay."

He smiled, closed the doors, and she watched as the bus drove away. She headed towards the hospital. The thought about seeing him made her beam with joy. She looked around at the enormity of the main entrance of the ambulatory care section of Boston City Hospital as she came out from the rotating doors. She was scared, but determined, walking up to one of the security guards sitting behind the information desk.

"Can I help you?" The security guard spoke.

"I'm looking for where the babies are."

"You mean the maternity ward?"

"Yes."

"Take the elevator to the tenth floor."

"Thank you."

She walked over to the elevators and waited watching the numbers above each of the four elevator doors stop at every other floor. A pair of elevator doors opened and she walked in amongst the crowd and the doors closed. She reached to press the tenth floor button and realized it had been pressed.

The elevator seemed to move at a snail's pace as it made a loud buzz sound at each floor it arrived at or passed. She watched the numbers above the elevator door illuminate as it made its way towards the tenth floor. *"Ninth floor."* The automated voice spoke as the doors opened and the last few riders stepped out. Charlotte glanced over at the woman still in the elevator with her and wondered if she, too, was going to the maternity ward.

The elevator buzzed and the doors opened and the woman stepped out ahead of Charlotte and went in the opposite direction of the maternity ward. Charlotte's nerves were on high. *Forget it.* She quickly turned back around to get on the elevator and the doors closed. "Shoot." This was it. She needed to do this. See him again. Even leave with him. But where would she go? What would she do? She didn't know and she didn't care. She wanted him. Or at least see him one more time and know if he was okay.

She turned back around and followed the arrow on the posted maternity ward sign across from the elevator. She walked down the short corridor, which seemed like a mile, and up to the two nurses who were talking and laughing amongst themselves behind the nurses' station. Her heart beating a mile a minute.

"Can I help you?" asked the brunette-haired nurse looking up from her large framed glasses.

"Hi, I'm looking for a baby that was born here last month."

The nurse grabbed the log book from the corner of the desk.

"What's the baby's name?"

"I don't know. He doesn't have one."

"Well, he must. What baby is born without a name sweetheart? What's the mother's last name?"

"Watson."

The nurse flipped through the pages of the log book and scrolled through the last names that began with a "W".

"You said last month?"

"Yes."

"What date?"

"August 5th."

The nurse continued scrolling through the names. "I don't...see...anything...here. Nope. No children or mother listed with the last name of Watson. Sorry."

"Are you sure?" Charlotte's eyes began to water.

"Yes, I'm sure."

"Can you check again? Please?"

"I've checked. There is no child or mother listed in our records with that last name. I'm sorry."

"Wait a minute," said the other nurse. "Are you talking about that baby with no name that was born here around that time?"

"Yes." Charlotte said anxious.

"Oh, I'm sorry, but he's no longer here anymore. He was taken."

Charlotte's heart dropped into the pit of her stomach as if the nurse's words had suck what little life was left inside out. "Do you...do you know where he is?" Charlotte asked on the verge of tears.

"Sorry, I don't know."

"Thank you." Charlotte walked away.

"What baby you talking about Elaine?"

"The one Doctor Coleman was telling us about. You know, the one Nurse…"

Charlotte felt weak as she walked the short corridor back to the elevators. Tears streaming down her face regardless of how hard she was trying to keep them in. She pressed the down button and looked up at the numbers. She was broken. Dead inside. Like her heart had been ripped straight from her chest once again. She just knew she was going to see him again. Hold him again.

The elevator wasn't moving fast enough. She pressed the button again. And again. She wanted out. Off the floor. Out of the hospital. Out of her hurt. Out of the sadness that had now spread throughout her body like a disease. The elevator doors opened and she rushed in, pressing the first floor button. She wiped tears from her eyes, but more fell. She pressed the first floor button again hoping it would increase the elevator's speed, but it didn't. She wiped more tears as she watched each number light up as the elevator passed the floors. She didn't want it to stop or anyone else to get on. She wanted out. As far away from the hospital and the world as she could possibly go.

The doors of the elevator opened and she bolted like an Olympic sprinter almost knocking down a woman waiting to step in. "Excuse you!" the woman shouted. Charlotte reached the street and ran to where the bus driver had told her as if a victim running from her attacker. She stood at the bus stop and tried to catch her breath. She hoped she hadn't missed the bus, for the walk home would be too much to bear with the sorrow she now carried in her heart.

* * *

She walked up the two flights of stairs to the apartment door feeling drained, lifeless. She hoped no one was home as she unlocked the door and walked in. She rolled her eyes noticing her mother on the phone. The last person she wanted to see, especially today.

"I'll talk to you later." Carol quickly hung up the phone not wanting Charlotte to hear the conversation. "How was school?"

Shouldn't you still be at work, Charlotte thought to herself as she walked past her mother towards her bedroom not responding.

"I said, how was school,"

"Fine."

Charlotte walked into her room and slammed the door. She dropped her bag and stretched out across her bed, grabbing her pillow. A gush of air blew into the room as her mother burst opened the door.

"Look, let me tell you something little girl, I know you had an eventful summer, but you will change that little attitude of yours before I do, you understand?" Once again, Charlotte remained silent. "I said, do you understand?"

"Yes, Ma'am."

"You're really trying my patience. You really are," she scoffed. "Let it go or I will do it for you. Slamming doors in my house…" She closed the door.

Charlotte threw her pillow at the door wishing she had the balls big enough to stand up against her mother like Kenya, but she didn't. And even if she did, she probably wouldn't. She grabbed another pillow as her thoughts returned to her son. Who had him? Where could he be? And why didn't the hospital have any record of her as his mother? She tried to wrap her 14-year-old brain around the situation.

John Doe. Why didn't I give the name "John Doe"? She thought to herself sitting up. "I need to go back. Maybe they could tell me where he is." She stopped thinking about what the other nurse said the night she saw her son for the first and last time. "It is not even a real name." She sighed and then cried accepting the fact that her baby boy was now gone. Never again would she be able to touch him, smell him, see him, hear him. He was now a memory. A moment officially in her past. Even if the past was only a few weeks ago. She grabbed her journal and pencil from her bag and wrote:

36

September 8, 1980

Dear Baby Boy,

I hurt as I sit here in my room thinking about you and where you might be. I went back to the hospital today and they said you were gone. I've been asking God to keep you safe wherever you are. I can still hear you crying sometimes. Just like you did when you were born. I miss you so much. I wish Mama would have let me keep you like Miranda is keeping hers. I don't care what Mama said. I know I would make a great mother.

I told Mama I was sorry, but she doesn't want to hear it. She said she will never forgive me, but I know she would if you were here. If she could just see your cute little face like I did through the window at the hospital. I wanted to tell your dad today, but I was afraid what Mama might do if she found out. She keeps telling me I embarrass her and it hurts me because I love her. I just want her to forgive me. I didn't mean to embarrass her or the family. One day I'll have more kids and show her that I'm not an embarrassment.

I know one day we'll be together again. I just know it. Pastor said that for us to get what we want we must pray for it. Well, I'm going to keep praying for you to come back to me every day until you do and I promise I'll write to you every day after school. I promise.

Charlotte

◆ NINE ◆

Present Day • September 2011

Darryl's Corner Bar and Kitchen was filled with its usual afternoon lunch patrons. It was where Charlotte and her sisters spend their second and fourth Thursday afternoons catching up on work and family matters that weren't discussed during after-church Sunday dinners.

Charlotte and Kenya walked in and Tamara waved them over from the table near the back. They noticed and headed in her direction. Tamara had grown into an exceptional, still nosy, materialistic mother of three who still cared more about appearances than reality itself.

"Hey." Tamara stood and kissed her sisters on the cheeks.

"Hey," said Charlotte

"What's up? What's going on?" Kenya asked as they sat down.

"Nothing. What's going on with you two?" asked Tamara.

"Nothing," said Kenya.

"Same here. Did you order yet?" Charlotte asked. "I'm starving."

"No, I was waiting for you two."

Kenya picked up the menu from the table. "Let me see what I want to eat."

"I'm going to go with the Darryl's Corner salad with grilled chicken," said Charlotte looking at the menu.

"You order the same thing every time," said Kenya.

"Because it's good and I like to eat healthy," said Charlotte

"I think I'm going to go with the hearty beef chili," said Kenya.

"Really? You want to be passing gas all through the courthouse. You know you and beans don't get along," said Tamara.

"I know, huh. Maybe you're right. I guess I'll get a corner salad too."

"Might as well make it three."

The waiter walked over and they placed their order. He took their menus and walked away.

"Well, since nobody else has anything new going on. Marvin was just named the new marketing director of Harper Hill," said Tamara of her husband of nineteen years.

"Wow. That's great," said Kenya.

"Yeah," said Charlotte. "Well, I know you're happy, Tamara. More money for you to spend."

"Whatever."

The waiter brought their salads and placed them on the table and they thanked him.

"I think I'm going to quit practicing," said Charlotte

"What?!" Kenya said holding her hand to her mouth trying to keep her food from falling out.

"Really? Why?" Tamara asked.

"I don't have the passion for it like I used to. Fifteen years and I don't feel fulfilled. My life doesn't feel like it's fulfilling. I mean I got the husband, the kids, the career and I still feel like I'm failing...at life, being a mother. You know what I mean?"

"I know exactly what you mean," said Kenya.

"Sometimes I feel like screaming," said Charlotte.

"What you need is a vacation," said Tamara.

"I know. If you're not helping a patient, you're doing something for the kids. I mean your children are teenagers now, I think they can take care of themselves," said Kenya.

"Yeah, I know. I'm just...I don't know."

"Maybe you should talk to someone," said Tamara with a

mouth full of salad.

"Really, Tamara? I'm a therapist. You really think seeing one is going to help me."

"Well, you never know. Everybody needs help at some point."

"Maybe she has a point," said Kenya.

"Well, maybe this will pass this little funk I'm in."

Charlotte knew it wouldn't as she touched around the salad with her fork. She knew it was more than just her career and home life that was plaguing her. An old itch had been sparked by Sarah's words and maybe the time had come for her to scratch it.

♦ TEN ♦

"The cancer has returned. I'm sorry we weren't able to catch it in time, Barbara," said the gray-haired Doctor. The word, although familiar, were still hard for Barbara Robinson to hear. This was her second bout with the ovarian disease and she knew the fight this time was going to take every little ounce of energy she could muster.

She sat there quiet trying to let the words sink in. Was this really her end? Was this thing, this disease that had risen once again, going to be the cause of how her sixty-plus years on the planet were going to end? The last words of the Doctor kept ringing in her mind like a bell. *Catch it in time.* What did that really mean exactly? It wasn't as if the disease was throwing itself at them. How can you catch something that never wanted to be caught? She shook the thought from her mind remembering what her mother always used to say. Dwelling on the inevitable always brings you closer to it.

"We could try another round of chemo," said the doctor.

"No, I don't think I can handle another round of chemo this time. It took a lot out of me five years ago. I don't think I have it in me do it again." Losing all of hair during the last round of chemo, she was no mood to forgo her beautiful mane again. She sighed. "Is there anything else we can do?"

"Well, you're still on the list for a bone marrow transplant.

41

We can begin the process of checking family and friends to see if they're a match."

"Okay. How long would you say I have?" Barbara asked curious.

"Now, you know I don't do that."

"I know. An estimation? Maybe."

The doctor let out a breath. "My best advice would be live each day like it's going to be your last."

Barbara smiled. "Thanks, Irene."

"I'm here for you whenever you need me, okay." She touched her hand. "You're gonna beat this again. For good."

Barbara smiled again. "You are coming to my retirement party, aren't you?"

"Wouldn't miss it for the world."

"You've always been so good to me, Irene."

"You've always been an awesome nurse and person." She smiled. "Generate a list of all of your family and friends so we can get started on trying to find a match."

"Okay. I'll start that tonight when I get home."

Barbara smiled as her Doctor and friend for over 30 years exited the room. Barbara had met many people over her 30-year career as a nurse, some of them colleagues, and others whom she had treated during their visits, but none were like Dr. Irene Hollis. Barbara loved her spirit, her heart. The genuine love she had for her patients. The passion she had for helping people. Something Barbara had grown to love more after meeting one day in the hall through a mutual colleague.

Barbara sat there in the abyss of quietness trying to think of the people whom she could contact about being a marrow match. She stared down at the blank screen of her cell phone, which she had taken from her purse, afraid to call the one person who was first on her mental list of marrow prospects. The one person with whom she had a relationship that was more damaged than a pot-hole-filled city street, her youngest son.

She pressed the power button and the screen of the cell phone illuminated. She dialed the number and pressed talk. She knew he wouldn't answer. He never did. She rolled her eyes as the voicemail prompt came on.

"Hi, it's me. I know you probably won't return my call. You never do. I know that this is a stretch, but I need your help. I was wondering if you would give my doctor a call. Her name is Dr. Irene Hollis and she really would like to speak to you. I was wondering if you would get tested to see if you're a bone marrow match. Anyway, when you get the chance give Dr. Irene Hollis a call. Her number is 617-555-3472. Thanks. Bye."

She removed the phone from her ear and hung up. She took a deep breath and got down off the examination bed. She put her phone back in her purse, grabbed her jacket and walked out. She smiled and waved at a couple of the nurses behind the desk. She didn't know them, but seen them in passing sometimes during her shift.

She walked to the elevator and pressed the down button and looked up at the arrows above the door waiting for the down one to light up red. The elevator doors opened and she stepped in, pressing the ground floor button. As the elevator made its way towards the ground floor, she thought about all the things she had never done, but always wanted to do. If this was going to be her last act, her bucket list had now become deep and long like a barrel.

The elevator reached the ground floor and the doors opened once more and she stepped out. She walked through the large silver rotating doors out onto the street. She held her jacket together as a gust of wind blew by, chilling her. Eddie Robinson, Sr., her husband of more than forty years sat in the car, just beyond her, reading the newspaper. She stopped in the distance and let out a breath as Dr. Hollis's words once again played in her head. How was she going to survive this second round? Was she meant to survive it? She stared at the ground trying to decide her next move. She looked up, her eyes stopping on her husband who hadn't taken his attention away from the newspaper, not even for a quick glance of his surroundings, and it hit her. If she could survive him, she could survive anything.

"Eddie, you promised you wouldn't hit me, don't hit me please! No, no, no! Noooooo!" Barbara screamed as his fist connected with her face, not once, but twice. Her ears rung loud as if a bomb had exploded in her head. Slowly, she tried to move away from him, the blood streaming from her nostrils had begun to cover more than just her top lip.

"Ahhhhhh! Eddie, please! Stop! Stop!" She cried as he dragged her across the floor by her hands into the living room.

"Shut the fuck up! Shut the...fuck up!" He tossed her on the couch. "Huh?! Huh?!" He pulled his back into a fist and she quickly covered her face, turning her head another direction. "When I say I want something done. I want it done the way I want it done *when* I want it done." He stepped back. "And I want this cleaned up by the time I get back, you understand?" She didn't answer and he took a half-step towards her.

"I understand." She answered quickly, knowing another punch or slap would come at her like a freight train if she didn't.

"And go on clean yourself up! You look a mess." He said walking away. He noticed his two sons watching from the top of the stairs as he headed for the door. "And you two go to bed!" Neither of them moved. "I said go!" They darted to their room. He glared back at Barbara and then left.

The thought of leaving him for good had crossed her mind plenty of times, but she knew he would find her, he always did. She grabbed some tissues and wiped her face. "Why God? Why do I stay here?" She cried into her hands. She wiped her face once more and noticed her sons peeking at her from around the corner. She smiled and they came running over. "Hey."

"You okay, Mama?" asked Eddie, Jr.

"I'm okay." She hugged him.

Now, twenty years had past since the last time Eddie Sr. had physically struck her and he was still reminding her, in every way large or small, how sorry he was. He grabbed the left side of his chest one Saturday afternoon at the tender age of 45 as an excruciating pain jolted him from his favorite chair in the living room. The intense pain twisting and turning as he shouted and Barbara came running from the kitchen and quickly dialed 9-1-1.

A near-fatal heart attack, the surgeon claimed after

emergency surgery, is what had brought the iron-fisted husband and father down to his knees forever changing his dominant behavior. But the damage had been done. It had been cemented into the minds of his sons and the heart of his wife regardless of how much he begged for forgiveness after he opened his eyes the next day following the surgery; damage his family was dealing with the remnants of to this day.

Eddie Sr. folded up the newspaper as Barbara opened the car door and got in. "So, what did the doctor say? Everything okay?"

"It's back."

"The cancer?"

"Yeah," she sighed.

He reached over and touched her hand. "Well, we're gonna get through this together. We're gonna beat this once and for all."

She smiled. He started the engine and drove away.

◆ ELEVEN ◆

The fifth-floor one-bedroom apartment was quiet. The scent of sex traveled throughout the darken dwelling. Loud laughter from the bedroom broke the silence of the apartment that was rented and furnished by Anita Cole, the young and curvy assistant of Keith Tate. He put his arm around her as she snuggled her naked body against his muscular frame.

His tall frame was almost the length of her queen-sized bed as they lay post-coital underneath her 100% Egyptian cotton sheets. He let out a breath, enjoying and loving their second night of the week together. From the start Keith had kept their love affair to a three-day-a-week cycle which they had managed to keep successful for the past year and a half.

Anita was no Charlotte and that was what he loved most about it. No analysis. No discussion of feelings. No feeling like a patient which he felt his 20-year marriage had been reduced to. Anita had become what his wife used to be before the children and the patients…a lover and a friend.

"Why can't you just stay the night?" Anita asked tightening her snuggle.

"Now you know the deal. We didn't just start this yesterday." He kissed her softly on the forehead and she smiled. He got out of bed and began getting dressed.

"I know. I just thought tonight would be the exception." Anita said smiling as she stretched her naked, curvy, body across the bed.

Keith put on his pants and tighten his belt. "You know my situation."

"Yeah, I know, but your children are almost grown. On their way to college."

"I know that."

"And?"

"And let's not ruin what we have." He leaned in for a kiss.

"And what is it that we have?"

"Excitement." He kissed her. "I'll see you tomorrow at the office."

"Okay." She smiled.

He put on his suit jacket, grabbed his briefcase and left. She smiled as she fell back onto the bed. She could still smell the scent of their lovemaking as she held the sheet to her nose. A devilish grin appeared on her face at the reminiscent thought of them frolicking across the bed entered her mind. She got up from the bed and headed into the bathroom. She turned the shower knob to her designated position and stuck her hand out testing the water's temperature. She waited a few and stuck her hand under the water again. Just right. She stepped in pulling the curtain. It had been almost two years since she dropped her manila folder of documents in front of Keith and she was beginning to want more. More than what Keith had labeled excitement. She put her hand over her mouth. She pulled back curtain and quickly made her way to the toilet and hurled.

The street lights glimpsed over Keith's body as he passed underneath each one during the forty-five minute drive home from Anita's house. He thought about whether to end the affair with Anita before she got out of hand, but he loved the rendezvous. Something that had become non-existent between him and Charlotte.

He dreaded the arrival at home as the headlights of his black four-door sedan guided around to the rear of his wife's silver Mercedes. He shut off the engine and sat in silence as he looked at the exterior of the five-bedroom, two-and-a-half bath, two-car garage house that he and Charlotte purchased almost 20 years ago. He laid his head back against the head rest and closed his eyes...

A slight breeze gently moved the chimes and the light of the sun accentuated the beauty of the house as the broker stood before them and snapped a picture of a young Keith and Charlotte standing next to the sold sign in front of their new house with Keith touching her belly. They kissed.

"I can't believe it. We did it." Keith said as they turned to face the house.

"I know. Our home. Ours. And we'll be raising our children here." She smiled. "Starting with you." She spoke towards her belly and they laughed.

"I love you."

"I love you too."

They kissed again.

"Here's your camera back, Mr. Tate." The broker said walking up.

"Thank you."

"And the keys to your new home."

"Thank you. Thank you so much, Mr. Walters."

"No problem. Enjoy your new home."

They shook hands and the broker left.

"We're gonna have some wonderful times here." Charlotte smiled.

"Yes. Yes, we are."

Keith opened his eyes looked over at the house. The outside hadn't changed much in 20 years, but he had. They had. He wasn't the same bright eyed bushy-tailed young home owner and father-to-be he had just reminisced about. And nor was Charlotte. He was tired. Tired of the private and long competition with his children over his wife's attention. He had been replaced long ago and he knew it. He felt it. The day their son was born that he was no longer the man in her life.

The toilet swished and swallowed as Charlotte washed and dried her hands using the towel on the back of the bathroom door. Her pink silk nightgown swayed with her hips as she walked to the bed and sat down, positioning herself comfortably under the covers. She grabbed Song of Solomon from the nightstand. It had been a few weeks since she last read the lives of the characters created by Nobel prize winning author Toni Morrison.

"Hey." Keith greeted as he entered the bedroom. He put his bag down and took off his suit jacket and then his shoes.

"How was work?" Charlotte asked without taking her eyes from the book.

"Long and tedious as usual." He walked into the bathroom. He turned on the shower and walked back out. "You know the firm's banquet dinner is next week." He unbuttoned his shirt.

"I know. I didn't forget."

Not once has she looked up from that damn book, Keith thought to himself as he stopped and looked at Charlotte checking to see if she would notice him staring. She didn't. Her eyes never left the book as she turned the page.

"Do I repulse you or something, Charlotte? I mean not once have you looked up from that book to even acknowledge my presence. It's almost like I don't exist to you. Do you even still love me?"

Charlotte sighed, closing the book with her finger between the pages, taking off her glasses. "Of course I love you, Keith. I mean do I have to look at you every second for you to know that?"

"No, but it would be nice to be noticed when I walk into the room sometimes. I'm tired of being third on your list, Charlotte. And I've been there for quite a long time."

"Third? What are you talking about?" She placed the book on the nightstand. "What do you mean by third?" Her cell phone rings. She glances at it. "Hold on, I have to take this."

"Of course you do."

"Hi, Marcy. Is everything okay?" She slides her bookmark inside the book and leaves the room.

Angrily, Keith grabbed a pair of underwear from the dresser drawer and headed back into the bathroom. He stepped into the shower and let the water tower over his body like rain. The warmth of the water reminded him of the days when he and

Charlotte spend passionate moments underneath the Kohler showerhead enjoying the feel of each other's bodies.

He missed that. The woman he fell in love with. The one who paid attention to him. The one that acknowledged him with a smile when he walked into the room. He turned the shower off and stepped out grabbing a towel, drying himself off. He put on his night clothes and walked out of the bathroom, turning off the light.

"Now what were we talking about?" Charlotte asked walking back to the bed.

"Nothing."

"No, nothing. I think we should have a further discussion about what you said early. Are you stressed? Is work stressing you out?"

"Look, I'm not one of your patients, okay. So don't treat me like one."

"I'm not. I can see something must be bothering you and I think we should talk about it. You know, get to the root of what's bothering you."

"Get to the root. Here we go. Drop it, Charlotte. I'm tired and want to go to sleep." Keith turned the light off on his side of the bed and pulled the covers to his head.

Charlotte sighed and put the book on the nightstand and turned out the light. Snuggling under the covers, she wondered where the negativity was coming from in Keith. *Third?* She thought to herself. *What the hell does he mean by that?* She waved off the thought and went to sleep.

♦ TWELVE ♦

March 1993

"Just one more big push okay, Charlotte. I can see the baby's head," said the male doctor from between her legs.

"Just one more push, baby. You can do this," Keith said, holding her hand. He was dressed in hospital garments, along with his parents, and Carol who stood by and watched silently.

"I can't."

"Yes, you can."

"You ready. Charlotte? On the count of three I want you to push, okay?"

"Okay." Charlotte looked at her mother, who looked back at her. Something inside her changed. She wasn't fourteen anymore. She was ready. Ready to show her mother what she had been waiting 12 years to do. "I'm ready."

"On the count of three. One...two...three. Push!"

Charlotte pushed and screamed as she kept her eyes on her mother – a piece of her hoping the glare would attack her like that of a laser gun from a space movie. She released as she heard the tiny screams emanate from her legs.

"It's a boy!" the doctor said. "Mr. Tate would you like to do the honors?" A nurse handed Keith the scissors and he cut the cord. The doctor stood up and handed the baby over to

Charlotte. "Say hello to your son, Mrs. Tate."

Charlotte looked down at her second-first-born son and smiled. "I'm going to name you Tyson." Everything felt right this time looking down at her newborn son. This was a moment she didn't want to end. It was familiar, but different.

"Look at him Keith. He is so precious."

"I know." Keith looked on in amazement.

The nurse walked over. "Let me clean him up for you." Charlotte hesitated as the nurse reached for the baby.

"Let the nurse clean him up," Keith smiled.

Charlotte kept her eyes on the nurse as she took him from her arms and walked with him over to a corner of the room and cleaned him up. Keith touched her hand and she looked at him and smiled, not wanting her feeling of being scared written all over her face. The nurse walked back over with the baby wrapped in a blanket and placed him in Charlotte's arms.

Charlotte touched his hand and his skin was smooth and soft. He smelled fresh and sweet like roses. He tried to grab her finger as much as he could. "It's all about you and me now. Nobody else. You hear me, nobody else." She spoke tears welling in her eyes. "You're the new man in my life now."

"You done already pushed me to the side? I thought I was the man in your life," Keith joked.

You were, she thought to herself. "Wanna hold him?"

"Yeah, let me take him." He took his son from her arms. "Hey, big boy. It's your daddy. I'm gonna teach you how drive, how to shave, how to love. I'm gonna teach you the way your Granddad taught me." He smiled at his dad.

"Make sure you teach him how to study. Oh, wait, I taught you. I guess I'll be teaching him that." Charlotte laughed.

"Very funny. Hey Ma, you want to hold him?" Keith moved to hand Carol the baby.

"Unh-unh. No. She is not allowed to touch my child. Ever." Charlotte said staring at her mother.

"What?! What are you talking about Charlotte? It's your mother for Christ's sake. Here Ma take the baby." He handed her the baby and Carol smiled as she began talking to the baby.

With every fiber of her being, Charlotte wanted to press the issue of her mother not holding, touching, or breathing on her child, but knew she would run the risk of letting a long, regarded, secret out of the box that would otherwise diminish the happy, blessed, occasion.

◆ THIRTEEN ◆

Rain trickled down the side of the blue and white one family house and into the puddle forming in the driveway. Even under the midnight moon, the house stood picture-perfect. Calm and inviting as if it were in the running for the cover of home and garden magazine. But if anyone stood close enough they would hear glass breaking, Barbara screaming and Eddie Sr., shouting.

Barbara crawled her way over the broken glass to the stairs leading up to the bedrooms and rested. The ringing in her ears subsiding. Her face bruised, the right-corner of her mouth bleeding. Eddie Sr. stood just beyond her holding his hand.

"See, what happens when you keep running your motherfuckin' mouth. How many goddamn times do I have to tell you that I want dinner on the table when I get home! But you don't fuckin' listen, do you! Do you!"

"No."

"No. No, you don't. Now, I'm not going to tell you again. I want this cleaned up by the time I get back and my dinner re-cooked and hot, you understand." She didn't answer and he moved towards her, his half-step making noise over the broken glass.

"Yes, I understand." She answered quickly, hoping it wouldn't continue.

He walked away , grabbing his keys heading out the door.

Barbara wiped her face and what was once tears had now begun to turn into anger. She had thought about killing him plenty of times, but knew if she ever went through with it she would never see her children again. She beat her hand against the stairs in frustration. She began picking up the broken glass. Why was she still there? What was keeping her here? She stopped, hearing the floor above creak. She got up and headed upstairs.

8-year-old Bradley and 12-year-old Junior, Eddie Jr., were sitting up in their beds terrified as they heard their parents fighting downstairs in the distance. They jumped as the bedroom door burst opened and their mother stood in the doorway. Her 5-foot-5 silhouette resembled that of actress Nell Carter as she stood there like the boogeyman appearing from the closet. Bradley knew she was coming for him as she always did after a fight. She snatched one of the belts hanging on the wall.

"Get up!" she screamed as she walked over and snatched him out the bed, dragging him across the floor. Bradley screamed as the belt popped hard across his back. "I can't stand your little black ass. You make me sick."

"Mama, stop!" Junior yelled from his bed. "He didn't do anything."

Barbara was breathing heavy as she didn't easy up on the hitting of her thin 8-year-old son. "I can't stand you! I hate you! I hate you! I hate you! I hate you! Get up!"

Beads of sweat dripped down the forehead of Bradley Robinson as he jumped awake his chest heaving rapidly. The night sky flashing every minute or two as the rain showered the City. Now 31, he had long wanted the memories of his childhood appearing every time he closed his eyes to sleep to stop. He looked over at his wife of six years and the mother of his children, Croix, whom even while asleep, was even more beautiful. He wondered how she had put up with him for so long. He wasn't the easiest person to live with it and he owned that. He thought his jolt would have woken her up, but it never did.

He sat on the side of the bed and look at the clock. *2:30 am.* He reached behind the nightstand and grabbed one of the many nip bottles he had stashed around the house. He got up from the bed and twisted the cap on the bottle and sucked down the brown dream chaser as he walked out of the bedroom.

He stopped and opened the door to his daughters' bedroom. Eight-year-old Tia and 5-year-old Ashley were sound asleep. They were his pride and joy. His reason for living. He loved them to death and would do anything to protect them just like any other father would. Even if it was from himself.

He closed the door, quietly, trying not to wake Tia. Unlike her mother she was not a deep sleeper. He wondered, as he often did, if his wife and kids felt the same way about him as he did about himself...a loser, a failure. He knew if he'd ask them they would say the opposite just to be nice or because they didn't want to hurt his feelings, but he knew they did. He turned on the television, flipping the channels to Sports Center and stretched out on the couch, laying there until he fell back off to sleep.

♦ FOURTEEN ♦

Bradley turned off the light as he walked out of the bathroom. He grabbed his sneakers and sat on the foot of the bed and stopped, catching a glimpse of himself in the full view mirror. He walked over and stared at himself in his uniform. It had been years since he had paid attention to himself in his navy blue uniform. *Oh my God,* he thought to himself as he continued to stare. He was 31, but felt 50. He let out a breath and put on his sneakers. The aroma of sizzling bacon and scrambled eggs hit his nose and he smiled.

The stairs creaked with each step he took headed to the kitchen. Croix was scooping the rest of the eggs from the pan onto their plates as he walked in. Her thick black hair neatly pulled into a ponytail. Her burgundy-colored scrubs neatly pressed. She smiled at him and he smiled back wondering why she was still with him after ten years of togetherness.

"Good morning," she said.

"Good morning, Daddy," Ashley and Tia said while chewing their breakfast.

"Good morning." He kissed each one on their forehead and reached for some Tia's bacon and she covered her plate. He walked over and kissed Croix. "Good morning."

She handed him his plate. "Had trouble sleeping again? I woke up to use the bathroom and you were gone."

"A little bit."

"You look tired."

"I'm good."

"Your mother called. She said she was going to stop by."

"Great. Just the person I don't want to see during a beautiful sunny morning." He glanced at the clock on the wall. "Alright, I got to head out." He quickly finished his breakfast and juice. "Let me hurry up before she gets here. I'll see you later." He kissed her and headed for the door.

"Hey, one more thing before you go."

"Yeah, what's up?"

She took an empty nip bottle from the front pocket of her scrubs and placed it on the counter. "I thought you were done."

He sighed. "I am." He cut his eyes in the direction of the girls.

"Well, I found it in the trash in the bathroom."

"It's an old empty one I found in my coat pocket the other day and I threw it away."

Her right eyebrow raised in suspicion.

"What? You don't believe me?"

"I didn't say that. I didn't say anything."

"You didn't have to. Your face said it for you."

"Look, you promised us four months ago."

"After your ultimatum. Look, can we not have this discussion now. I said I was done then and I meant it."

She held up her hands. "Okay. I believe you."

"Thank you." He walked over and kissed the girls on their heads. "I'll see you later."

"Bye, Daddy."

Bradley walked out of the kitchen. It felt like yesterday when she had given him that ultimatum over his love for them or his love of alcohol. It was raining that night four months ago, after their dinner date, that he had chose the love of them, but lately his love affair with alcohol had come a-knocking and once again he answered faithfully. Caving into its alluring, warm presence.

He grabbed his gym bag and headed out the door, startled by his mother Barbara who was just about to press the doorbell.

"Jeez, you scared me."

"Sorry, I didn't mean to," she smiled.

"May I come in?"

"Um, I was actually on my way out to work and the girls are still getting ready for school."

She took a step back as he stepped outside. "Did you get my message?"

"No, I haven't checked my voicemail. Why?"

"Dr. Hollis would like my family and friends to get tested for bone marrow matches."

"The cancer's returned."

"Yeah." She sighed.

"I'll see what I can do. I gotta go."

"Your Dad and I haven't seen you and the girls in a while."

"We've been busy."

"Well, I hope you won't be too busy to attend my retirement party." She handed him the invitation. She felt elated as he took it. "I know our relationship has never been great…"

He sighed. "Can we not talk about that this morning? I'm really not in the mood for it. I'll get in contact with Dr. Hollis and setup an appointment."

"We need to talk Bradley. Seriously. One day, soon."

"About what? About how you don't love me the way you love your beloved Junior. About what…" He quickly glanced back in the house. "…what you used to do to me when I was kid. Nope. No thanks. You spoke enough over the years with your actions."

"Nanna!" the girls shouted as they came running from the house.

"My babies!" She smiled hugging them. "How are my precious girls?"

"Fine," Ashley smiled.

"Hey, Ma," Croix smiled stepping out from the house locking the door behind her. "How are you?"

"I'm hanging in there. And you?"

"I'm good."

"I stopped by to invite you all to my retirement party," Barbara said keeping her eyes on Bradley.

He handed the invitation to Croix.

"You didn't have to come all the way over here to drop this off."

"Well, I'd have a better chance of you all coming if I dropped it off in person," she said glancing at Bradley.

"Alright, I'll see y'all later. I gotta go. I'm already running late." Bradley kissed Croix and left without making eye contact with his mother. He got in the car. The engine started and he drove off.

"Well, we'll be there, Ma. All of us."

"Okay. Thank you," Barbara smiled. "Come give Nanna a kiss good-bye." Tia and Ashley walked over and she hugged and kissed them. It was something she didn't get to do often, but she enjoyed the moments when she could.

Croix started the engine and unlocked the doors to her dark blue SUV. "Go ahead to the car girls." They ran over to car. Ashley racing her older sister to get to her favorite side which was behind her mother. "All right, Ma." They kissed each other on the cheek. "We'll be there."

"Okay."

Barbara waved to the girls, walking over to her car. She got in and breathed a sigh of relief. The fact that Bradley took the invitation and said he was going to get tested made her happy. It had been a while since she had seen them all. They looked good. He looked good. She watched in the rearview mirror as her daughter-in-law backed out of the driveway and headed down the street.

She felt like a stranger. Like a distant relative coming to town for a visit as she started her car and slowly drove away. The friction between her and Bradley was thick and hard like bulletproof glass and she knew she was the creator of it. She hoped this second bout with cancer would be the lead-in to the recovery story of what she had damaged so many years ago.

♦ FIFTEEN ♦

The men's locker room of the neighborhood station of the Boston Police Department was reminiscent of a high school locker room with its evenly lined blue lockers, open shower area and the hint of stale funk from towels that hung on the outside of some of the lockers. Officer Bradley Robinson stood at his locker preparing for his shift. His 6-foot athletic-framed body stood firm in its navy blue uniform. He smelled crisp and clean like a fresh load of laundry. A sharp crease down the front and back of each leg of his pants. He loved to look polished and neat. Something he learned from watching his father get dressed every Sunday for church.

He buckled his gun belt around his waist like that of a cowboy from an old western. Since childhood, being a police officer was something he always dreamt of doing. They were fearless, big men that always seemed to stand with pride against his little 6-year-old frame, but donning the badge and uniform was more than just standing with pride or a power trip. It hid his vulnerability. It was one place he didn't feel rejected and without it, he was naked.

He loved working the day shift. Not as lazy as the overnight or as busy the evening shift, but it still had its moments. He listened at his locker for surrounding noises, movements. Silence. He looked to both sides of him. Empty. He grabbed the black and silver flask from the top shelf of his locker and took a swig.

He closed his eyes as the warm sensation of the Hennessey traveled slowly down his throat and into his chest like a serpent. It was his aid. It calmed him. It was his mistress. The one thing he did in secret.

He snapped the cap and put the flask back in the locker. He stuck a few pieces of peppermint-flavored gum in his mouth and placed the lock on his locker. He walked out and into the squad room where his fellow officers were waiting for their Captain. Bradley walked to his partner and his best friend over the last eight years, Rodney, whom over of his tenure had grown to love the multiple women the badge attracted more than the badge itself.

"What's going on?" Bradley asked.

"Bobby O'Hearn. He's dead."

"What?! Are you serious?" Bradley's heart dropped into the pit of his stomach. Bobby was a close friend.

"Yeah, they found him this morning. Believe it was suicide."

"Damn."

Captain William Wright stood just a few inches shorter than Bradley as he stepped out from his office. Bald, with a skin and voice as dark and deep as Barry White. His inside voice soothed people like a late-night disc jockey, often times making them nod-off in mid-conversation, but this wasn't one of those conversation.

"By now you all have probably heard of the tragic news regarding Officer Bobby O'Hearn. He was a great police officer and a wonderful human being. We work a dangerous job. We all knew that when we signed up. When a police officer dies in the line of duty we are, our hearts are broken, but somewhere in our minds we prepare ourselves for that.

When a police officer takes his own life, it's something we are never prepared for. We cannot let this happen again. So reach out to one another, just not today or this week, but always. Be safe." The Captain walked into his office and shut the door.

"Wow. Poor Bobby," said Bradley as he and Rodney headed out to their police cruiser.

"I know. Did he ever talk to you about what was going on? I know you two were buddies."

"No. Never. He always had a smile on his face," Bradley said as they got in. "Just so sad. Damn, man. Damn."

"I know."

"You ready?" Rodney said his black sunglasses covering his eyes.

"Let's hit it."

"I hope it's qui—" Rodney began.

"Don't say it."

"Don't say what?"

"You know every time you say the Q word it never is."

Rodney backed the cruiser up and drove out of the station's parking lot.

"You thinking about taking the Sergeant's exam?" Bradley asked.

"Thinking about it. You?"

"I don't know. I'll see. It's not on the top of my list."

"Mine either."

"So, what's going on with you and Heather?" Bradley asked. "You haven't said much about her lately."

"There is no me and Heather."

"What happened this time?"

"It just didn't work out."

"It never fails. Every time a woman gets close, you cut 'em off."

"What can I say? I'm not ready to settle down yet. I'm still young. I got time."

"Unh-huh. Forty will be here before you know it, you'll be rushing to settle down and have a family."

"Like I said, I've got time."

They stopped at a red light and Bradley waved and smiled at a little boy crossing the street with his mother. The sight of the boy made him wish he had a son.

"You ever thought about having kids?" Bradley asked Rodney as he watched the boy and the mother cross the street.

"Sometimes. My mother wants me to have some. She wants some more grandbabies." The traffic signal turned green and he drove on. "I don't know. Sometimes I want some. Sometimes I don't. I don't know. If I'm meant to have kids, I'll have them."

"I hear you."

"I mean I'm not rushing it. Kids cost money. They aren't free."

"Don't I know it?" Bradley smiled to himself remembering how much of a tightwad Rodney could be. "It seems like Ashley and Tia are growing like weeds. But they're my babies. I love 'em to death."

"*Unit 1-0-4...*" The female voice emanated from the radio.

"1-0-4..." Bradley responded.

"*Could you head over to 170 Tremont Street, we have a couple of panhandlers arguing outside 7 Eleven.*"

"Acknowledged. 1-0-4 responding," said Bradley

"Here we go," said Rodney.

"Damn, first thing in the morning. Some people just don't quit. I can see it's going to be one of those days."

They pulled up in front of the popular convenience store and saw the disheveled man and woman shouting and slapping each other's hands from their faces.

"This is my spot! You go somewhere else!" the man shouted.

"I'm not going anywhere!"

"This should be fun," said Bradley as he looked from the passenger side out Rodney's window.

"Here we go," said Rodney. He put the gear in park and they got out and walked up. "What seems to be the problem here?"

"Officer! Officer!" the man shouted. "Tell this bitch that this is my spot. She's not supposed to be here."

"Fuck you!" the woman lunged at him, but was grabbed by Bradley.

"Whoa! Whoa! Wait a minute!" Rodney shouted. "First of all, neither one of you is supposed to be here disturbing this business in the first place. Second, there's no need for that type of language."

"Get them out from in front of my store," said the Korean store manager rushing out.

"Sir, are you the one who called?" Bradley asked.

"Yes. Yes, I am," said the manager. "They don't buy. Just harass my customers all day long."

"Okay, sir," said Rodney.

"I hate you!" shouted the woman. "Always stealin' my damn corners!"

"That's what you get for being a slow-hustling bitch!"

"Fuck you!" the woman lunged at him again.

"Hey, hey, hey! Frick and Frack! Beat it! Get outta here! Move it! Let's go!" Rodney shouted. "You go that way and she'll go that way."

They slowly began to walk their separate ways not taking their eyes off one another.

"Keep going," Bradley said, watching the distance between the man and woman become greater and greater.

"And if we get another call about you two again, you both are getting arrested!" Rodney shouted. Bradley and Rodney returned to the police car.

"What a freakin' beautiful day in the neighborhood." Bradley shook his head as they got in.

"Tell me about it."

They got in the police cruiser and drove off.

◆ SIXTEEN ◆

The police cruiser turned into the parking lot and Rodney parked it in the first available space he set his eyes upon and shut off the engine. The day had been long and Bradley couldn't keep his mind off his friend and former colleague.

"You okay?"

"Yeah just thinking about Bobby. I can't believe it. I just can't believe it."

"I know."

"Just saw him last week."

"He was a funny dude."

"Yeah he was." Bradley said getting out. Rodney following suit. They headed into station.

Bradley noticed his father Eddie Sr., at the front desk filling out paperwork and walked over.

"Hey."

"Oh Hey." Eddie Sr., said looking up from paperwork.

"What are you doing here?"

"Bailing your brother out again."

"What he did do this time? He didn't hit Natalie again, did he?"

"Not this time. Driving drunk."

Bradley sighed. "Dad, you know you don't have to keep doing this."

"I know. It's my fault he is the way he is."

"Dad…"

"Well, it is. I wasn't the best role model for you boys. For any boys for that matter. What I used to do to your mother…"

"He is a grown man now and every decision he makes is his choice."

"Yeah, I know that, but I'm also to blame." Eddie Sr. gave the paperwork to the officer at the desk with cash. "You mind coming to the house one day, I need your help cleaning the basement?"

"You finally going to re-do the basement."

"Yeah. I finally convinced your mother to let me do it. So I'm going to need your help to clear it out."

"I'll be there. Just let me know when."

"You didn't ask me." Junior said walking up, still reeking of alcohol. He was older and shorter than Bradley by a couple of inches and his skin, lighter. His voice just as heavy as their father's.

"That's right, I didn't." Eddie Sr. said turning to look at him.

"Well, if it isn't the prodigal son." Junior said lifting his hands.

"Whatever. You know what you need to get your act together."

"Don't." Eddie Sr. said stopping Bradley from moving forward.

"Don't think you're better than me because you wear that badge and uniform," said Eddie Jr.

"Dad, I'll talk to you later." Bradley walked away.

"Okay."

"Bye to you too little brother!" Eddie Jr. shouted.

"Whatever!" Bradley shouted back.

Eddie Sr. and his oldest son left the station.

Bradley walked into the locker room whose atmosphere was like that of a high school locker room after a game as other officers were beginning and ending their shifts. He opened his locker.

"I saw you talking to your Dad. Is everything okay?" Rodney asked

"Yeah, everything's fine. Just my brother acting stupid as usual."

"Wow, 24-years-old…I wonder what was going through his mind," said an fellow officer about their fallen comrade.

"I know," said another.

"Well, not everyone can handle the job. It's sad, but maybe he should have been behind the desk."

"Really Harrison? Really?" Bradley turned around.

"Bradley, come on, he's not worth it," Rodney cautioned.

"Hey, this line of work is not for everybody."

"You need to keep your fuckin' mouth shut! 'Cause you have no idea what the fuck you're talking about! He could handle the job, just not your punk ass! Fuckin' prick!"

"What the fuck is your problem?"

"You! You fuckin' prick! All you and the other guys did was fuckin' clown him, belittle him, make him feel like he wasn't shit when you were over at the five. He told me. So, you and them are as much to blame as whatever else caused him to take his life!"

"Fuck you, Bradley! Alright! Don't you try to put that shit on me, alright! Don't you dare try and put that shit on me!" Harrison shouted, walking towards Bradley. "I am not the cause of your friend blowing his brains out!"

Bradley punched him and Harrison fell to floor as other officers jumped in, prying Bradley off him. Captain Wright walked in hearing the commotion from his office.

"What the hell is going on in here?!" His deep baritone voice rippled through the locker room like an earthquake.

"Fuck you, Harrison! You piece of shit!"

"Bradley!" Rodney said trying to calm him down.

"Robinson and Miller in my office now!" Bradley and Harrison quietly made their way in the direction of his office. "Everyone else, get back to what you were doing!" He walked out. Bradley and Harrison stood ready to defend their respective positions as Captain Wright walked into his office and slammed the door. "I don't know and I don't want to know what the hell got into you two back there, but I will not tolerate that foolish shit in my house on my shift! You got that?"

"Yes sir!" Bradley and Harrison said in unison.

"I know everybody's emotions are on high after hearing the tragic news of Officer O'Hearn, but that is no excuse to act like fools. Let it happen again and I will can both your asses! You understand me?!"

"Yes, sir!"

"Good. Miller dismissed." Captain Wright shook his head disappointedly at Bradley as the other officer left the room. "How you doing? I know you and Bobby were good friends."

"I'm good."

"Good. How's everything at home? How are the girls?"

"They're good. Getting big."

"Good. Glad to hear to it." He said walking behind his desk. "Because that father you arrested a couple of days for beating up his son claimed you broke his nose."

"Well, he hit me first."

"Where? In the chest?" The Captain said getting in his face. "Because I don't remember seeing any marks on your face when you brought him in."

"He missed."

"Well, you didn't. Listen, you fuck up again, you're on your own, you got that. I'm not sticking my neck out for again. I've done it too many times." Captain stared into his eyes. "This is your last warning. Now get out of my office."

Bradley walked out and into the locker room. Rodney wanted to inquire what happened in the Captain's office, but he could see the anger written all over Bradley's face. Bradley grabbed his bag from the locker and slammed the door, walking out.

♦ SEVENTEEN ♦

Bradley turned down the bottle of vodka from his lips as he sat in his car outside of the Boston View Motel listening to the radio. *It's going to be a cool sixty degrees tonight in the City of Boston. A perfect night to sleep with the windows slightly open...* He turned off the radio. He pulled out his cell phone and dialed Croix's number. The phone rang.

"Hello?" She picked up.

"Hey, it's me. I picked up some overtime so I won't be home until the morning."

"Okay."

"I'll see you in the morning. Love you."

"Love you too."

He hung up the phone. He hated lying to her, but it was the only way to keep his love affair a secret. He grabbed the bottle and brown paper bag from the passenger seat and got out the car. He tripped the alarm and headed to the reservation office. Dennis, the gray-haired man behind the desk greeted him with a smile as he did every customer that approached him.

"Hey Dennis."

"Bradley. The usual."

"You know it."

"How are the girls?" Dennis asked as he got the key.

"They're good."

Dennis slid him the key and grabbed his hand as he reached

for it. "Look, I know it's none of my business, but…I'm here."

"I'm good."

"That's what we all say. I've been where you've been."

"You have no idea where I've been old man."

Bradley took the key and left.

It had been a few hours since Bradley's arrival and the room was dark and quiet, smelling of cheap booze, occasionally lit by the flash of headlights from vehicles arriving and departing the parking lot. Bradley looked from behind the curtain like a criminal on watch for the police as he sat at the table. He turned the bottle of cheap liquor to his lips and swallowed hard, wiping the tears from his eyes. "You were a good friend Bobby. A good friend. I'm gonna fuckin' miss you, man." He swallowed again. He picked up the picture of the girls he had on the table, staring at it. "My beautiful angels. My beautiful girls…" He started crying. "I love you so much. Daddy loves you so much. I'm trying the best that I can. I really am." He took another swig. He held his head in his hands.

"I'm just so tired of holding all this pain. Why doesn't anybody want me or love me?" He took another swig. "They're better off without me, God. They are." He said looking up to the ceiling. "I'm tired. I'm just so fuckin' tired. My life…my life just so fucked up!" He throw the bottle against the wall, shattering it. "I should just end it all right now. Why not? Nobody would miss me anyway." He grabbed his department-issued weapon and held it to his temple, placing his finger around the trigger. His cell phone illuminated showing a picture of Croix and the girls smiling. He knew it was the girls calling to say good-night. He just stared at it and then answered it right before the last ring placing the call on speakerphone.

"Hello." He spoke with the gun still to his temple.

"Goodnight, Daddy! We love you!" They spoke.

"Good…night." He cried silently lowering the gun down. "I love you too."

"Alright, into bed." Croix said taking the phone. "Hello?"

"Hello?"

"Is it busy out there tonight?"

"It's alright for now."

"Well, stay safe. And I'll see you in the morning. I love you."

"I love you too. Bye."

"Bye."

He hung up the phone and sobbed.

♦ EIGHTEEN ♦

Lord, please let me get through this family dinner, Charlotte thought to herself as she looked up towards the ceiling while in the kitchen alone waiting for the biscuits to get done. She looked towards the kitchen door as she listened to the distant chatter of her family gathered together in the dining room. It was the fourth Sunday and her turn to host the family for after-church dinner. The one time of the month she somewhat looked forward to. The moment when her sisters and their families were around her table with her husband and family talking about everything under the sun.

The time of month when she could bolster the accomplishments of her 16-year-old daughter Dana and 19-year-old son Tyson, the college freshman, to the rest of the family especially in front of the one person whom managed to still get underneath her skin even at the age of 45…her mother. Carol, now in her late sixties, retired, hair a little grayer, sat opposite the head of the table, her sternness having not dissipated much over the years.

The oven sounded and Charlotte grabbed the oven mitt and removed the biscuits, tossing them into the basket. She backed her way into the dining room from the kitchen and placed the basket on the table and sat down at the head of the table. The quantity of food that covered the middle of the table was reminiscent of a biblical feast. They all bowed their heads and grabbed the hand of the person next to them as Keith said grace.

Keith had been the one thing, besides her figure, that Charlotte was able to hold onto from her past. Forty-seven and a corporate attorney, his once thin tall frame had thickened with age. His skin no longer fragranced by that of his father's Brute, but of his own Kenneth Cole.

Keith finished grace and everyone raised their heads. The chatter resumed as dinnerware and silverware scraped against one another as a scoop there and a scoop there of every dish was put on a plate and then passed from one pair of hands to the next like an assembly line.

"Pastor preached a good service today, didn't he?" Charlotte asked as she passed the collard greens to Keith.

"Yeah, he did. I enjoyed it more than last week's," said Tamara. Now, a 47-year-old materialistic wife to her husband of 19 years Marvin and mother of three teenage children: 17-year-old Shawn, 14-year-old April, 11-year-old Ronnie.

"Congratulations, Marvin, on your promotion. Charlotte was telling me about it the other day," said Keith.

"Thanks. I guess all that hard work and long hours finally got noticed," said Marvin.

"So, you're a marketing director now."

"Yes, which means I have a much bigger office," said Marvin.

"How's my nephew?" Kenya asked.

"He's good. I talked to him the other day. He's thinking about joining the college football team," said Charlotte.

"That's good. Did he choose a major yet?" asked Kenya

"Not yet," said Charlotte looking at Dana who looked bored.

"Oh yeah, I have an announcement to make. Dana has made the honor society." Charlotte said looking at her mother who gave a half-hearted applause in the midst of everyone else's praise.

"Exciting," said Carol unenthusiastically.

"Oh good. Congratulations sweetie," said Kenya.

"It's no big deal," said Dana.

"You don't sound too enthusiastic about it," said her Aunt

74

Kenya.

"Maybe she's afraid she'll be called a nerd like I was," Charlotte smiled.

"Like mother, like daughter," said Keith.

"Yeah well, just don't do everything like your mother," Carol said sternly.

Here we go. It never seems to fail, Charlotte thought to herself as she tapped the table in disgust and sipped her wine.

"Like what? Dating someone like me?" Keith joked.

"That and among other things. You definitely had to grow on me, I'll tell you that," said Carol.

"Dana, I was a fool in high school," said her father.

"Tell me about it." Charlotte laughed.

"Well, all of that changed when I met your mother." Keith touched Charlotte's hand. "She tutored me for an exam I needed to take and that was it."

"Kenya, isn't Erica graduating valedictorian?" Carol said eating dinner

"Yes, Ma," Kenya said plainly.

"Of course she is." Charlotte scoffed, drinking wine.

"Charlotte, you know, Miss Robbie from church."

"Yeah," Charlotte said.

"Her grandson got accepted to Princeton."

"And Dana made the honor society and I'm happy about that."

Kenya noticed the tension building in her sister. "All of your grandkids are doing good Mama. Can we change the subject?"

"I was just saying."

"You always do." Charlotte took another sip of wine. "Excuse me, I think my cell phone's ringing, vibrating."

"You're going to answer it in the middle of dinner," said her mother.

"Well, mother, I don't want one of my patients to commit suicide because I didn't answer my phone." Charlotte got up from the table and walked away.

Charlotte listened to the birds chirp from within the trees just beyond the white fence that marked the end of her property line as she sat on the stairs of her back deck wiping tears from her eyes. She closed her eyes as she heard the sliding door open and then close, hoping it wasn't her mother. She was not in a mood for an argument.

"I don't know why you let her get to you," Kenya said walking towards Charlotte.

"I can't help it, Ken. You know that's a sore spot for me," Charlotte said looking down at her hands as they fidgeted around with the tissue. "Am I a good mother?"

"You're a great mother, Charly." Kenya sat down and started rubbing her sister's back. "A great mom."

"Doesn't she know how that makes me feel when every time I say something about my kids and she always bringing up what your kids or somebody else's kids are doing? As if what my kids do don't mean shit to her. It makes me feel less of a mother every time she does that. And I'm tired of it, Ken. Just tired of it."

"I know. I know. Just don't pay Mama any attention. I don't sometimes. You only got a few more hours and then she'll be going home. Then you don't have see her again until the next Sunday dinner."

"Why does she still treat me like I'm still 14 and pregnant? Like I'm still an embarrassment to her or something. I don't know how many more times I can take these Sunday dinners."

"Hey, if Tamara and I have to suffer through them the other two Sundays, you'll have to as well. Sorry, but that's the way the cookie crumbles, Sis. We suffer, you suffer."

Charlotte smiled.

"Come on, let's go back inside."

* * *

She gets on my damn nerves. I can't stand her. I don't why I even try, Charlotte thought to herself as she stood at the kitchen sink washing dishes. The family was gone and the house was quiet as Dana walked in carrying more bowls and plates from the dining room. "You can sit those right there on the counter, honey. Thanks."

Dana sat the dirty dishes on the counter. She was nervous as she glanced over at her mother.

"Ma, can we talk?"

"Sure. What's up?"

Dana cleared her throat. Nervous. "Ma, I'm…"

"What are y'all doing?" Keith said as he walked in.

"Dana and I were talking."

"Excuse me. Sorry for interrupting." Keith said grabbing a beer from the refrigerator.

"What were you getting ready to say, honey?"

"I'm going to the movies with Tracy and Keisha." Dana breathed a quick sigh of relief.

"And who else?"

"Mike, Eric and Will."

"Alright. Call me when you get there and when you leave and let me know where you're going to be afterwards."

"Charlotte, will you let the girl go. I mean she's 16. Have some trust."

"I do trust her, Keith. Have a good time."

"Thanks, Ma. Bye, Daddy."

"Have fun," Keith said nodding his beer bottle towards her. Dana left.

"You need to lighten up, Charlotte. You need to let her be."

"I just don't want anything to happen to my babies. That's all."

"Nothing is going to happen. They're okay. And they're going to be okay. You've been all over Dana and Tyson since the day they were born. Give them some room to breath." Keith took a swig of his beer. "I wish you were all over me the way you've been over them," Keith mumbled to himself as he took another swig of his beer.

"Huh? Did you say something?" Charlotte said, not taking her attention away from washing the dishes.

"I'll be at the golf course with Steve if you need me." Keith finished his beer. "But you probably won't. You never do." He tossed the empty bottle in the trash and left. He stopped and looked back at Charlotte who was still washing the dishes. He chuckled to himself as he shook his head. *Why bother? I'm not her patient nor her child.* He left.

He grabbed his golf clubs from the closet and headed out the door. He wanted to play a few rounds before the sun and temperature went down. He unlocked the car and put his clubs in the trunk. He got in and drove away.

♦ NINETEEN ♦

Bradley sat in the waiting area of the Oncology department at Boston City Hospital, dressed in his uniform minus the necessary equipment and badge, flipping through a magazine as he waited for his name to be called by his mother's doctor. His relationship with his mother had never been on great terms, but he figured getting tested as a bone marrow match was the least he could do.

He glanced up from the magazine as other people were called in by the nurse. No matter how hard he was with his mother, the return of her cancer was beginning to make him question life without her presence. Would he be happier if the oppressor of his childhood no longer existed? Would it make the childhood, that plagued him, disappeared completely from his memory? He knew they were bad thoughts to have, but he couldn't help but wonder.

He put down the magazine and closed his eyes, taking a deep breath, knowing the real reason why he was sitting there. He loved her, even if he continued to question himself whether she truly loved him.

"Bradley Robinson," said Dr. Hollis as she opened the door. He put the magazine down and walked over.

"Hi, how are you? Good to see you."

"I'm good," Bradley responded shaking her hand.

"It's been awhile."

"Yes, it has."

"I thought you work during the day. Your mother told me you work during the day."

"I do. It's my day off." He said following her down the corridor, around a corner and into her office.

"Oh, I thought with your uniform on you were working." She said closing the door. "Have a seat."

Bradley sat down as did the doctor.

"As you may already know, your mother's cancer has returned. And it seems to be more aggressive this time. So, we're hoping a bone marrow transplant will help fight it."

"Okay."

"Now, I'm not going to lie to you. The extraction of your bone marrow for the test is very painful. Very painful."

"Okay."

"You'll be fine. You seem like a strong young man."

"I am," he smiled.

"Alright, Nurse Mayes is going to take you into the other room and get you ready for the procedure, okay?"

"Okay. Hi." Bradley said to the young nurse as he got up. His eyes couldn't help but to look down at her round ass it bounced with each step she took as he followed her into the other room.

"Just change into the hospital gown and Dr. Hollis will be right in."

"Thank you."

"You're welcome."

The nurse closed the door as Bradley began to undress.

♦ TWENTY ♦

The Common Ground restaurant was filled with its usual afternoon lunching professionals as Kenya and her friend and fellow attorney, Randi, walked in and were guided by the hostess to an empty table. A young male waiter came over and politely took their order and discussed the soup of the day. They passed on the soup and ordered their usual lunches. The waiter walked away.

"So, how's your Mom?" Kenya asked.

"She's doing the best she can," said Randi. "Her speech a little slurred. And she can't move the right side of her body at the moment, but she's hanging in there."

"Have the doctors figured out what caused the stroke?"

"They don't know yet. Could have been anything, but I'm leaning towards maybe her sugar level was too low." said Randi.

"I'm so sorry," said Kenya as she sipped her tea. "Well, you know if you need me for anything, don't hesitate to call."

"Thanks," said Randi.

The waiter returned with Kenya's steak salad and Randi's chicken salad.

"Anything else?" asked the waiter.

"No, thank you," said Kenya.

They watched the young waiter's butt bounce in motion as he walked away.

"Girl, if I was 15 years younger, I would be all over that," said Randi tenderly biting her bottom lip.

"Well, his ass does look cute in those pants. Anyway, how's everything with you and Marcus?"

"Done."

"What happened?"

"Let's just say he wasn't the man I thought he was. Our break is too short for that conversation."

"Hmmm." Kenya sipped her tea. "Is this a wine or an ice cream story?"

"Wine, girl." Randi laughed.

Across the restaurant, through the many patrons, Kenya was taken aback. Was what she was seeing a figment of her imagination? *I don't believe it,* Kenya thought to herself. *I can't believe this fool is up in here with somebody.*

"What? What's wrong? You see somebody?"

"Yeah. Excuse me. I'll be right back."

Kenya wiped whatever food that may have around her mouth and got up from the table. As she walked across the restaurant, reaching closer to her target, becoming more stunned by what she seeing. *This son of a bitch. I can't believe it.* She thought to herself she approached the table.

"Hi Keith," she said cheerfully. "How's it going?"

"Uh, Kenya. Hi," said Keith as he moved his hand from Anita's, surprised. "What are you doing here?"

"Having lunch like I always do every Wednesday. Hi, I'm Keith's sister-in-law, Kenya. I'm the sister of his wife. And you must be..."

"This is--" Keith interjected.

"Let the woman speak, Keith."

"I'm Anita. Keith's secretary." They shook hands.

"Excuse us, Anita. Kenya, can I talk to you for a minute?"

"You can talk to me for the next ten minutes if you want." Keith grabbed her arm, quickly moving her to a quieter section of the restaurant.

"Let go of me, Keith."

"Look, there's nothing going on between Anita and I."

"Really? From the way you two were holding hands, it looks

like she's preparing more than just your briefs."

"She's just a friend."

"Look, don't give me that she-just-a-friend crap. Men have been using that line forever. Are you cheating on my sister?"

"You have the audacity to ask me that?"

"The audacity? You're the one out in the world holding hands with a woman other than your wife and who is more than just a secretary."

"Instead of standing there judging me and my marriage, why don't you concentrate on yours and leave mine alone." Keith walked away.

"I'm not finished yet," she said grabbing his arm.

"Well, I am." He looked down at her hand on his arm and she moved it.

She followed him out as he returned to his table. Staring him down as she made her way back across the restaurant to her table. Keith smiled, resuming his conversation with Anita knowing their evening rendezvous was off and home was his destination after work.

* * *

The elevator reached the tenth floor of the John Hancock Tower and the doors opened. Keith and Anita stepped out and walked through the frosted glass doors of the Benson & Mitchell Corporate Law Offices. The floor was busy with secretaries answering phones and lawyers walking and talking with each other.

"We need to talk. Meet me in my office," Keith whispered to Anita.

Anita knew something was up back at the restaurant when Keith returned to the table after his short, intense, private conversation with Kenya. She headed down the hall and around corner to his office.

"Fred, do you still have the files on the Whitmore-Ellis vs. Fidelity case?" Keith asked, peeking into his colleague's office.

"Yeah."

"Can I take a look at them?"

"Sure, I'll bring them down to you."

"Ok, thanks."

Keith walked to his office and shut the door. Anita kept her eyes on him as he walked behind his desk, waiting to hear what he had to say.

"We need a break, to cool off a bit."

"Okay," she said looking him straight in his eyes.

"A small one. Just long enough to deal with the consequences of what happened at the restaurant. I hope this is not going to be a problem, our little hiatus." He sat down.

"Not at all, boss," Anita smiled.

"Good, because I'm not trying to be Michael Douglas."

"Anything else you need me to do before I quit?"

"Quit?"

"Yeah. At the end of the day I'm leaving."

"Leaving? Why?" he asked, walking from behind his desk. "It's just a break, not the end of the world. You don't have to be this dramatic."

"I'm tired, Keith. I'm tired of being the other woman. I want more. I've been wanting more and if you're not willing to give me more then I need to leave."

"Don't leave...don't quit," he said moving closer and wrapping his arms around her waist. "It'll work out. I promise." He leaned for a kiss as Fred opened door, startling both of them. He quickly separated himself from Anita. "What's up, Fred?"

"Yeah, I got those files you asked...for," Fred said, looking curious.

"Mr. Anderson," Anita said, walking out quickly.

"Anita," Fred responded.

"Thanks, Fred." Keith took the folder. "I'll return them to you by the end of the day."

"Yeah...no problem." Fred closed the door.

Keith hit the folder against his desk. He was pissed and embarrassed by what had just occurred, not to mention what he had experienced at the restaurant. "Damn you, Kenya." He said slamming the folder on his desk, sitting down. He was already dreading the ride home.

* * *

The house was quiet as Charlotte sat in her home office transcribing notes from her iPad to a leather bound journal that she used as a backup, separate one for each patient. She loved the easiness of technology but knew it would take one mishap and all the important patient information would be gone forever.

She stopped writing, exercising her hand not wanting it to cramp up. It was late, much later than she expected as she glanced at the clock. It was way past her bedtime. She rubbed her hands over her face trying to rejuvenate herself. She heard the front door open and close, and keys cling in the dish near the door. She knew it was Keith. *He's home early*, she thought, resuming what she was doing. Keith peeked his head in.

"Hey."

"Hey," Charlotte said looking up. "You're home early."

"Yeah, we decided to take a break tonight. New patient?"

"No, just transcribing one I already have."

"Did you hear from Kenya at all today?" Keith asked.

"No. Why?"

"I ran into her earlier today while at lunch. Just wondering if she had told you," Keith said relieved.

"No."

"Well, I'm gonna head to bed. I'm a little tired."

"Okay."

"Good night."

"Night," Charlotte said putting back on her glasses and resuming her work.

The phone rang and she noticed her mother's name and number appear on the caller ID. *What does she want?* She grabbed the phone from its base and pressed the talk button, slowly putting the phone to her ear.

"Hello?"

"What took you so long to answer the phone?"

"Hi, Ma."

"Are we still on for lunch?"

"Yeah, we are," Charlotte responded monotone. *Please cancel.*

"Well, don't sound so down about it."

"I'm not. I'm looking forward to it." She rolled her eyes.

"Well, I was just checking. I'll let you get back to whatever it is you were doing."

"Alright, I'll talk to you later."

She hung up the phone and sat back in her black leather executive chair wishing she had never started the every other week lunch dates with her mother which had begun a year and a half earlier. It seemed like an excellent way, she thought, for her to begin to mend a long-ago broken relationship with the woman she loved dearly and still held resentment towards, but the progress attempted to be made was always being undercut by the banter during the Sunday dinners. She let out a breath and resumed her work.

♦ TWENTY-ONE ♦

The warm sensation of Jack Daniel's No. 7 coated Bradley's throat as it had for the past four hours since he had arrived at The Anchor. The dark liquor was no longer tasteful, but he didn't care. He never did. His cell phone vibrated on the bar counter and he looked over at it. It was his mother. He sent her to voicemail. He was in no mood to talk with anyone, especially her.

"Yeah, like I saying, Bobby O'Hearn was a great kid. Funny as hell too. I can't even imagine what his mother is going through right now. I was just talking to the kid recently, you know."

"It's sad to lose someone you know like that," said the stocky, tattooed bartender.

"Let me get another one."

The bartender shook his head and walked over. "This is it. This is your last one." The bartender grabbed the bottle from the shelf poured Bradley another drink.

"Hey, as long as I'm paying, you're pouring." Bradley pulled the glass back towards him. He drank down the rest of the Jack Daniel's in his glass and slammed the glass on the counter. He took out his wallet and gave the bartender his credit card. The bartender swiped the card and printed out a receipt. He signed his name and put his card back in his wallet. "Keep the change.

Have a good night." He laughed, pushing his chair out, bumping into a couple of guys walking by, spilling their drinks.

"Come on dude! What the fuck?!" shouted one of the men.

"Sorry. Sorry."

"Watch where the fuck you're going, asshole!"

"Hey guys, take that shit outside!" the bartender shouted.

"I said I was sorry," said Bradley.

"Just fuckin' great! You just ruined my fuckin' brand new shirt, you stupid piece of shit!"

Bradley punched the guy in the face and he fell back. The guy swung at Bradley hitting him in the face. The bartender picked up the phone and dialed 9-1-1 as Bradley and the guys continued to brawl and other patrons tried to separate them.

"9-1-1, where's your emergency?"

"I got a huge fight going on here at the Anchor bar. You need to get the police over here fast!"

"Come on! Come on motherfucker! You ain't got all that mouth now!" Bradley shouted, other patrons holding him back.

"Are there any weapons sir?"

"No weapons. Just get the police here. I want these assholes out of my bar right now."

"Okay, sir. The police are on their way."

"Okay, thank you."

Bradley didn't know the officers that led him out the front door of the bar and into the police cruiser. They were rookies and weren't from his precinct and he was elated. No one to go back and spread around what had just occurred like a disease. He lowered his head as one of the rookies opened the back door and he got in. Now he was feeling like the numerous guys he had put in the same position over the years. Pitiful. Lost without a cause. He tried to ease the pain of the handcuffs by trying to move his wrists, but it didn't work. He had forgotten how tight they were since he hadn't worn any since his days training in the academy. He rested his against the window and closed his eyes as the young officers got in and started the engine. It was only a short ride to their precinct and he knew little to no conversation would make it seem quicker.

Bradley moaned as he moved his head and slowly opened his eyes. The light from the ceiling blinding him. He looked around and noticed the concrete walls on either side of him. He sat up realizing that he was in a cell. He rubbed his temple trying to ease the massive headache that had rapidly kicked in.

"Well, well, well, look who finally decided to wake up." Captain Wright said walking up. "I don't usually take overtime but something told me to take some tonight and I'm glad I did. You've really outdone yourself this time, Officer Robinson. You have truly reached the bottom."

Bradley remained silent, continuing to massage his temple, not wanting to hear the condemning tone of his Captain's voice. "When can I go home?"

"You think you deserve to be let out of there? What the hell were you thinking getting drunk in a bar with your uniform on? And fighting? You really must've lost your damn mind! I mean I couldn't believe my eyes when I saw them bring you in, passed out. Are you really trying to get yourself fired? I mean..." He shook his head disappointed. "You've been going off the handle a lot here lately. Do I have to remind you of the man's nose you broke last week? Or the other guy's jaw three months before that? I'm not sticking my neck for you anymore, Bradley."

"Can I please just go home?" Bradley asked, standing up. Captain Wright scoffed and opened the cell door. Bradley walked out. "Take your ass straight home, you got that."

"Got it."

Captain Wright followed him out and stood by the front desk and watched as Bradley walked out. He looked up to the ceiling shaking his head and sighed like a stressed parent. Over time, he had become a work-father to some of his officers, especially Bradley. The first time he walked into his precinct he knew there was something in him. Bradley reminded him a lot of himself. He walked in the back and over to the rookie that had walked Bradley in. "Officer Jenson. Are you working on your report for the fight at the bar?"

"Yes, sir."

"Omit Bradley Robinson from the report. He's one of us. I'll take care of him. Cancel the report. And release the other two in a few hours."

"Okay. Whatever you say, sir," said the rookie.

"Thanks." Captain Wright walked away.

It was after midnight when Bradley walked into the quiet, dark bedroom to a sleeping Croix. He walked into the bathroom and closed the door. He sat on the side of the tub and turned on the shower. He looked at his scratched-up hand. How was he going to explain this to Croix? He knew she was going to ask about it in the morning during breakfast. Was the Captain right? Had he reached the bottom? He stood up and turned on the faucet and unbuttoned his shirt. He grabbed his toothbrush and the toothpaste and brushed his teeth trying to remove any hint of alcohol touching his lips.

He rinsed out his mouth and turned off the faucet, putting his toothbrush back in its proper place. He took off his shirt, then the rest of his uniform and stepped in the shower, pulling the curtain across. He let the water sprinkle over his body as he stood there still taking in what the Captain had said to him earlier. He grabbed his body sponge from around the water knob and his body wash and lathered twice, hoping the scent of his evening would be gone before Croix rolled over to snuggle against him in bed.

♦ TWENTY-TWO ♦

The next day the shift had ended for Bradley and Rodney as it began – quiet and easy like the rise of the morning sun. No shootings. No stabbings. At least not in their district anyway. Rodney pulled into the first available spot he laid his eyes upon as he turned into the station's parking lot. He put the car gear in park and shut off the engine. The day was quiet compared to most, but it was long.

"Oh my God," Rodney yawned. "Today was long as hell. It seemed like the clock was never going to reach 3:30."

"I know. Tell me about it," Bradley said as they got out of the car. "So what's on the agenda for you tonight? Theresa? Whitney? Sadie? Trina? Maxine?"

"Funny. I'm actually going to chill tonight. My brother and I are supposed to watch the game."

"The Heat and the Thunder?"

"Yeah. You should come over."

"I got plans," Bradley said walking into the station.

"Robinson!" Captain Wright shouted from the doorway of his office.

"What does he want?"

"I have no clue," said Bradley. *This must be about the other night.* Bradley thought to himself walking over and into the Captain's office. The Captain closed the door and walked behind

91

his desk. Bradley went to have a seat.

"No need to sit down. This isn't going to take long."

Bradley trembled inside. Captain Wright had never said anything like that before to him or any of the officers. He had an idea of where the conversation was about to head, but wanted to know for sure.

"I had the officer that arrested you 'correct' his report the other night," said the Captain. Bradley relaxed inside hearing the Captain had saved him once again. "You know Bradley, I've watched you over the years, even before you came to this precinct, go from a wide-eyed rookie to a good police officer. But along with that, I've noticed your anger. And at times, it's reared its ugly head. But now, it's getting out of control. I mean, you're getting into fights at bars, breaking people's noses." He took off his glasses. "You remind me a lot of myself when I was your age. And you are causing too many eyes from the higher-ups to look at my station. So with that being said, you are hereby suspended for 40 days."

Bradley felt his heart drop into his chest as the words "suspension" and "40 days" traveled from the Captain's mouth to his ears.

"Sign this." Bradley signed the paper. "Your 40 days begin as soon as you walk out the door. I'll say it again. You are a good man, Bradley, but you're drowning and this is your lifeline so I suggest you take heed to it."

Bradley stood there silently. How was he going to explain this to Croix?

"This is not punishment, Bradley. It's a stepping stone. That is all."

Bradley turned and walked out of the office, closing the door behind him. He was pissed. Angry with the Captain, with himself. He felt like punching something, but knew it would only make matters worse as he walked quickly to the locker room where Rodney was changing his clothes. He turned the combination wheel of his blue lock three times to the right and stopped at the first number, then spun it left stopping at the second number, and then right again, opening the locker. Rodney knew whatever was said in the office didn't go over well at all.

"You okay? What happened?"

"I'm fine."

"B, what happened?"

"I said…I'm fine." Bradley grabbed his bag and coat and slammed the locker shut.

"B?"

"I said I'm fine!" he shouted, walking away.

♦ TWENTY-THREE ♦

"Daddy's home," Tia whispered to herself jumping out of the bed and rushing over to the window to get a view of him as the headlights of her father's black Audi flashed across the house as he pulled into the driveway. She never slept easy until she saw his face. When she was a toddler she'd fight sleep, tooth and nail, just to see him, especially if he worked late. But as she got older she learned how to pretend sleep for her mother until he arrived home. He was her hero. Her knight in shining armor. Her prince. She loved him more than he knew.

The moon had been shining for the last six hours and Bradley had driven half the night trying to clear his mind of what had happened earlier in the day and he was now at the last place he wanted to be as he shut off the engine, turning out the lights. His cell phone vibrated on the cup holder. It was Rodney calling again. He let the vibration continue resting his head against the driver's seat and took a swig from the bottle of vodka he had pulled from his hiding spot underneath the seat.

The Captain's words was still playing over and over in his mind like damaged record. Suspension. Forty days. Suspension. Forty days. *Stupid! Stupid! Stupid!* He thought as he hit his hand against the steering wheel. "I'm just so fucking stupid." The Captain was right. He had reached the bottom.

"Don't nobody want me. I don't even want me." He cried to

himself. "Look at me. I ain't shit. I'm nothing. I'm a nobody. My own mother don't love me." He spoke to no one wiping the tears, laying his head back against the headrest once again.

He looked over at his non-lit house, not feeling worthy enough to go inside. The thought of telling Croix and the girls that he had been suspended conjured up further tears. How was he to face Croix and tell her he fucked up?

"I'm not a good dad. I'm not a good husband. All I do is just fuck everything up." He said wiping tears. "They don't need me." He sniffed.

He wiped more tears and grabbed the pistol from the passenger seat and held it to his temple. A round in the chamber. He closed his eyes and tilted towards the open sunroof. "I'm doing this for you Tia and Ashley. Daddy loves you." He opened his eyes and stopped, slowly removing his finger from the trigger, lowering the gun. A witness stood in the window, tears streaming down her face.

Tia, unbeknownst to him, had been watching his every move through the sunroof, their eyes meeting distance apart. He placed his index finger over his lips and then motioned for her come downstairs. He turned the key in the ignition and rolled up the windows, closing the sunroof.

He took a deep breath trying to keep his emotions in his check as he got out of the car and made his to the way to the house, wanting to break down with every step. How was he going to explain this? What Tia had seen? He took another deep breath trying to calm himself down. He stuck his key in the door and the knob turned and Tia opened the door, crying. He picked her up and she sobbed uncontrollably. "Daddy's okay. Daddy's okay. I'm okay." He said closing the door. He carried her into the dark living room, turning on light, and sat down.

"Tia, honey, I'm okay." He pulled her from his shoulder and gently held her face in her hands, his eyes watering. "Stop crying, baby." He wiped her tears with his fingers. "Daddy's okay. He's just got a lot on his mind. I'm sorry you had to see that." He rubbed his hand over her hair. "We're gonna keep this between us okay?" he said wiping his wet eyes with his fingers trying to catch the tears before she saw them. "This will be our little secret, okay?" He rubbed her head again. "I love you." He hugged her. "Go upstairs and get in the bed behind Mommy okay. I'll be up in a second." She got off his lap and walked upstairs rubbing her eyes. He listened until she was out of hearing distance and sobbed, knowing the time had come upon him to make an effort towards change.

* * *

The morning sun gradually lit up the bathroom as it peeked out from behind the moving clouds. Bradley let the water from the shower tower onto his bald head and down his tall body. He had been awake for most of the night, drifting off to sleep a couple of hours before the alarm sound. He wanted to hide in the shower all day, but he knew at some point he would have to face his family.

The image of Tia's tearful face haunted him. She had slept through the night her small arms wrapped around him tight. What had he done to her? Psychologically? Emotionally? He thought as he lathered up and rinsed. Had his actions forever changed what she thought of him? He turned off the shower and grabbed the towel from the rack and stepped out.

The steps creaked as Bradley, dressed in a white t-shirt and jeans, headed downstairs towards the kitchen. He had made up in his mind while getting dressed the excuse he was going to use about not going to work. He stopped at the bottom of the stairs and took a deep breath, trying to release any hint of uneasiness. He walked into the kitchen.

"Good morning." He smiled.

"Good morning, Daddy," said the girls.

"Hey," Bradley said to Croix grabbing a glass from the cabinet.

"Hey. Not going to work today?"

"Nah. I decided to use some extra days this week." He poured himself some orange juice.

"I see someone made it into our bed last night," Croix smiled at Tia and she smiled back.

"Yeah, she couldn't sleep last night." Bradley smiled at Tia.

"Alright girls, finish up. We gotta go," Croix said putting the pans in the sink. "Maybe I should drop the girls off at school, take the day off and stay home with you." She whispered to Bradley.

"Maybe some other time. I'm tired. I didn't sleep well last night."

"Well, fine then." She pouted like child.

"You're such a character. Y'all are going to be late." Bradley smiled.

"Alright girls, give Daddy a kiss goodbye."

Bradley walked over, kissed and hugged both of his girls tight. "Love you."

"Love you too, Daddy."

He followed Croix and the girls out of the kitchen to the front door. "I'll pick them up after school."

"Okay." She kissed him. "Bye."

"Bye."

Tia opened the door and Rodney stood on other side just about to press the doorbell. "Rodney!" Tia screamed and jumped in arms, followed by Ashley.

"How are my two favorite little people in the world?"

"Good," they responded as he put them down.

"Hey, Rodney," said Croix.

"Hey." He kissed her on the cheek.

"Come on, girls. Let's go," said Croix.

"Bye, Rodney!" the girls shouted walking to the car.

"Bye!"

Bradley let out a breath having no idea Rodney was coming over. Talking was not part of his plan of lounging around the house wallowing in regret. He stepped aside allowing Rodney to step in.

"I was calling you all night. What the hell happened to you?" Rodney said walking inside.

"I got suspended." Bradley closed the door.

"Suspended?! For what?!"

"I was drunk and got into a fight at bar a couple of days ago and got arrested." Bradley sighed as he walked into the living room and sat on the couch.

"How long is the suspension for?"

"Thirty days."

"Why didn't you tell me?"

"I didn't want to bore you with that bullshit."

"I'm your best friend! You should've told me."

"I really fucked up, Rod. I'm afraid to tell Croix about it because then she'll find out I've been drinking and then she'll take the girls and leave."

"You don't know that."

"Um, hello, remember the ultimatum she gave me last year?"

"Oh yeah, I forgot about that."

"I don't know what I'm gonna do. I'm drowning, dude. I'm drowning. I can't lose them. I just can't." Bradley felt like breaking down, but held his composure.

Rodney pulled out his cell phone and dialed a number.

"Who are you calling?"

Rodney held up his hand as the line rang. "Hello, Auntie?"

♦ TWENTY-FOUR ♦

"I'm not taking any more patients, Rodney. I'm sorry." Charlotte stood in front of the mirror styling her hair talking to her nephew on speakerphone. She had grown tired of her usual ponytail and twisted her hair into a bun. She marveled at herself as she remembered how good the style made her look.

"Please, Auntie Charlotte." Rodney pleaded on the other end. "I think he may be suicidal." Charlotte sighed at the thought of adding someone else to her client list. "He's my best friend, Auntie. You know I wouldn't bother you if it wasn't important to me."

"Yeah, that's true." *What's one more patient?* She thought. "Let me check my calendar." She grabbed her iPad from her bag and looked over her calendar. "Okay, tell him I can see him tomorrow afternoon around one."

"Thank you so much, Auntie. Thank you."

"And tell him don't be late because I have a two o'clock right after that."

"Okay. Thanks again."

"And tell your Mother to call me."

"I will."

She hung up the phone. Her last male patient was Enrique, a young man as sweet as sugar who thought the only way to face his pain was to apply a razor to his wrists; greeting her recently with a hug tight enough to leave a permanent crease in her

99

blouse when they ran into each other on the street.

The stairs creaked with each step as she headed downstairs to the kitchen where Keith was probably getting himself some breakfast. The usual bagel and orange juice.

"Good morning," she said walking in.

"Morning." Keith poured himself of a cup of orange juice. "Did you talk to Rodney?"

"Yeah, I just spoke to him." She grabbed a mug from the cabinet and poured herself some coffee. "He wants me to take his friend on as a patient."

"I thought you said you weren't taking on any new patients and you were going to spend more time with us. You and me."

"I know, but I'm doing this as a favor for him. He is family."

"Yeah, but his friend isn't."

"He really wants me to help him and I agreed to do it. It's my job to be there for other people."

"When are you going to be there for me? For us again?"

"What are you talking about Keith? I am here for you. For us."

"When? When was the last time we did something together? Every time I ask you to do something you're always too busy either helping a patient or doing something for the children."

She looked at her watch. "Alright, I got a few minutes to spare. Tell me what's going on with you, Keith. What is this problem you have with me and my career all of sudden?"

"A few minutes." He scoffs. "I see how important I am. A few minutes." He felt less as a husband walking out of the kitchen.

"Keith? Keith?" Charlotte shouted. He didn't answer as he grabbed his briefcase and headed out the door. *I don't know what's gotten into him lately*, she thought. After 20 years of marriage, she knew something was troubling him. He had never acted like this before, so pissed off with her. She knew he wasn't much of a discusser. He never talked much about his feelings to her or anyone. He, like most of the male population was an inside man. And whatever thoughts and feelings he had inside were beginning to come up and as a trained psychologist she knew a bigger blow-up was near.

♦ TWENTY-FIVE ♦

Bradley checked the time on his watch. *Fifteen minutes. Good I should get there a little early.* Nervousness traveled throughout his 6-foot-1 athletic framed body intensifying with each step. He was doing this for the girls, he kept reminding himself, as he headed in the direction of the office. They were his pride and joy. His reason for living.

He stopped at the crosswalk and waited for the walk signal unlike most human beings. He rolled his eyes at the pedestrians jaywalking as oncoming traffic was approaching the intersection. *And that's how you get hit by a car,* he thought shaking his head. It was one of those moments he wished his uniform donned his broad shoulders and the city enforced the jaywalking laws because citations would have been given. He loved his career. It gave him a sense of pride, honor to protect those who needed it. But over the years it had become his protector, his shield, allowing him at moments to escape, hide the hurtful parts of himself.

The walk signal appeared and he stepped into the crosswalk along with the crowd, passing a woman in her mid-twenties. He smiled and she did too. *If I wasn't married,* he thought to himself as his head followed the direction of his eyes which were fixated upon her ass as it switched up and down. He and Croix allowed themselves to admire other people from time to time, even in each other's presence, knowing their hearts belonged to each other.

He checked the time on his watch again. A few minutes had passed and he still had more than enough time to sit down and catch his breath when he arrived. His long-legged strides slowed in pace as he realized the office was a block away. He tried to imagine how the conversation with Rodney's aunt was going to play out. He stopped and took a deep breath, trying to rid his mind of the preconceived conversation.

He stopped as he reached the street where Dr. Tate's office was located. *Do I really want to do this? I should just call and reschedule.* His palms were sweaty. He closed his eyes and took a deep breath. *Why am I nervous about this? It is Rodney's Aunt. Maybe she'll tell him everything that I'm going to say. She wouldn't do that. She can't do that. Patient/Doctor confidentiality.* He took another deep breath, trying to calm himself. *Remember this is for the girls. For Tia.* He checked his watch again. Five minutes. He resumed walking.

Seventy-five. Seventy-five. He repeated to himself in his head looking at the numbers on the buildings he passed, the first beginning with sixty-nine. He noticed double-digit number shining against the glass doors with a hint of gold and crossed the street. He entered and got on the elevator, pressing the fifth floor.

He unbuttoned the collar of his shirt and tugged his light-blue shirt lightly back and forth trying to relieve the body heat. The elevator slowed as it reached the floor and the doors opened. He stepped out and looked around the quiet reception area. He noticed the three secretaries sitting behind the curved desk and walked over.

"Hi." He smiled, it lighting up the room and not to mention the eyes of Dr. Tate's secretary, Maria. "I have an appointment with Dr. Tate."

"What's your name?"

"Bradley."

"You can have a seat."

"Thank you."

He sat down, grabbing a magazine and flipping through the pages as Dr. Tate stepped out from her office conversing and laughing with a colleague, her plum-colored skirt hugging her curvy hips which Bradley admired from his distance.

"I'll talk to you later, Ann," Dr. Tate laughed. "Bradley." He put down the magazine and walked over. She shook his hand. "Welcome." He walked into the spacious office, looking around, liking its décor. It was the type of office he always wanted if he had chosen a career that required one.

"Nice office."

"Thank you. Have a seat." She closed the door.

Bradley sat down on the white plush sofa noticing the box of tissues on the wicker table before him. Dr. Tate sat down across from him.

"So, how long have you known my nephew Rodney?"

"Since the academy. The police academy."

"How long have you been on the force?"

"Almost eight years now."

"Okay. So, what brought you here?"

"Well, according to my Captain, I have an anger problem, so that's why I'm here."

"Do you have issues with your anger?"

"There have been times when I've gone a little overboard with apprehending someone while on the job, but nothing I couldn't handle."

"Are you married?"

"Yes."

"How long have you been married?"

"Six years, but we've been together for ten."

"Kids?"

"Two beautiful daughters."

"Have they ever been caught in the middle of your issues with anger?"

"Have I ever harmed my wife and kids? No. I usually drink my issues away. Or at least try to."

"How often do you drink? Once a day, twice a day, three times a week."

"Sometimes more than I like to admit."

"Has your drinking ever affected your performance on the job?"

"No, not really."

"Have you ever been suicidal?"

He looked away thinking about Tia. He cleared throat. "At times I have."

"When was the last time you had those thoughts?"

The feeling of shame and embarrassment filled his eyes with tears. He cleared his throat. "A couple of days ago."

"What happened?"

"I was, uh…" He grabbed a couple of tissues from the box. "…outside in my car. I just got suspended from my job and a friend of mine, a cop, had committed suicide… and I was just at the end of my rope with everything: life, my career. And I put the gun to my head and looked up and there was my 8-year-old daughter looking out her bedroom window at me. And I just stopped."

"Then what happened?"

Bradley closed his eyes letting the tears stream. "I put the gun down and motioned for her to come downstairs."

"Where was your wife and your other daughter?"

"Asleep. It was late, real late. Tia, that's her name, doesn't sleep well until I'm in the house."

"So, then what happened?"

"I got out of the car and met her at the front door and just grabbed her and held her. She was in tears, I was in tears, it was just a big mess."

"So, how did you explain to her what she had witnessed?"

"I didn't, really. I told her that I was okay and that everything was going to be okay. I knew right then I needed some help. I've never wanted to hurt my family and I did in the most deplorable way. I'm just stupid."

"No, you're not, Bradley."

"Yes, I am. If I was going to do that I should've just done it in a hotel room alone." He said wiping tears. "Have you ever felt not wanted Dr. Tate? Like you just don't matter?"

"At times. But what human being hasn't?"

"Well, I've felt like that my whole life. Like I just don't

matter."

"But you do matter. I bet you matter to those two little girls back at home."

He smiled.

"See, just the thought of them puts a smile on your face."

"They do."

"Think about them. Let them be your lifeline."

"I know. But sometimes I just feel like such a failure. That I'm not a good father or husband. I don't know...sometimes I feel like a big mistake."

"What makes you say that?" She glanced at the clock. A few minutes remaining.

"I just never felt loved my entire life, you know, by my family, my mother. It's just...I don't know. I always feel like I have something to prove."

"Like what?"

"You know that I'm a good person. That I'm a lovable person."

"So, who are you trying to prove it to?"

He thought a moment. "I don't know."

"Well, I think I'm going stop right there for day."

"Wow, it's been an hour already."

"Yeah, time flies when you have a lot to say."

"Now...Bradley..." She moved her iPad from her lap to the small table beside her. "Where do you want to be by the end of this? Now I ask that because my approach to therapy is a little different than most therapists'. I like to use a three-step phase with most, if not all of my patients made up of three major questions: Who you were? Who you are? And who you want to be? Now, I got a sense of who you are based upon what you mention to me here today, but who do you want to be?"

"Who do I want to be?" He questioned while trying to formulate an answer.

"You don't have answer that today."

"Oh good." He smiled.

"The answer to that question is your first assignment."

"Oh no, not homework." He laughed.

"Yes, the start of many assignments. Do you have your

insurance card?"

"Oh yeah." He pulled his insurance card out from his wallet and handed it to her.

She wrote down the name of the healthcare provider and his client ID number. "Your co-pay is fifteen." He took the money from his wallet and paid her and she handed him back the insurance card. "Okay…" She stood up and as did he. "I'll see you in two weeks."

"Okay."

She walked him to the door. "Bradley, I commend you for coming here. I don't get that many men as patients because most men don't like to talk, but I'm glad you did."

"Yeah me too. See you in two weeks."

"Same time."

"Okay," said Bradley

Dr. Tate watched as he walked down to the elevators and stepped in. "Edith." She said calling the next patient. The female patient got up and into the office and Dr. Tate closed the door.

* * *

Bradley sat in the back, quietly, and listened as people got up to speak. It was his first attendance of an Alcoholics Anonymous meeting and he hoped no one called him out. He continued to listen to the members of the group tell their tales about how their affair with the bottle deepened their sorrow and ravaged their relationships with their wives, husbands and children.

He realized as he continued to listen that he was no different from any of the men or women that sat before him or beside him. The only thing that separated them were their careers. The manager of the group walked to the podium as the last person spoke and ended the session and Bradley walked out just as quietly as he had walked in.

Bradley pulled into the driveway and turned off the car. He smiled as he laid his head back against the driver's seat. He had to admit he felt good leaving Dr. Tate's office. So good in fact that he thought about canceling the sessions. He hadn't felt quite this good in a long time. He thought about the stories he had heard while at the meeting, looking at the house, wondering how much pain and suffering he had put Croix and now Tia through. He hoped Tia hadn't mentioned to her mother what she had witnessed, but if she did, he'd have to deal with it. It had been a few days and Croix hadn't uttered a word to him about it. He knew there was no way she could hear that and not say a word.

He exited the car and tripped the alarm. He walked to the house and opened the door. "Daddy! Daddy! Daddy!" the girls shouted as he walked in. "How are my babies?" he asked hugging them. "How was school?"

"Good," they said in unison.

"Good. Did you do your homework?"

"I did!" said Ashley.

"I just have to do my math."

"Well, go get it done." Tia started up to her room and he pulled her back. "Hey, can Daddy ask you two a question?" He took a second, looking at them, smiling. "Do you love Daddy?"

"Of course, Daddy," said Tia.

He smiled. "And how about you, Ashley?" He tugged her nose and she giggled.

"Yeah."

"Thank you." He hugged both of them. "Thank you. Where's Mommy?"

"In the kitchen!" Tia yelled heading up the stairs to her room. He headed into the kitchen with Ashley right beside him. The scent of Croix's mother's meatloaf recipe tickled his nose as he reached the kitchen door and walked in.

"Hey." She smiled washing the dishes.

"Hey." He walked up behind her and wrapped his arms around her waist. He kissed the back of her neck. "How was your day?"

"It was fine. And yours?"

"It was okay." He said. "Can I ask you a question?"

"Shoot."

"Do you love me?"

"Of course I love you. Why do you ask?"

"No reason in particular. Just asking."

"Everything okay?"

"Everything's fine." He kissed her. He had found it. This. Moments like these with his wife and daughters and the happiness he was feeling inside was his answer to Dr. Tate's question. He wanted more of them and hoped he didn't sabotage them as he usually did.

◆ TWENTY-SIX ◆

Dana sat on the stairs waiting for her mother to come through the door from work. Her palms were sweaty, her body trembling with fear. She was scared. Her cell phone chimed and she picked it up. It was a text from her boyfriend of two years, Will. *"Did she get home yet?"* the message said. *No, she replied. She's on her way in,* Dana texted quickly hearing the click of the front door lock. She put her phone down. Charlotte walked in carrying a multitude of grocery bags, along with her purse and work bag.

"Hey," Charlotte said juggling the bags.

"Hey," Dana said without making eye contact.

"Can you lock the door for me, honey? Thank you."

Dana got up and shut the door, locking it. She grabbed some of the bags from her mother's hands.

"Thank you. It's Friday night. I'm surprised you're not hanging out with Daphne and Will," Charlotte said headed to the kitchen.

"I didn't feel like hanging out with them tonight," said Dana following her mother into the kitchen. "Can we talk?"

"Sure." Charlotte put the groceries on the counter as did Dana. "What's on your mind, sweetheart?"

Dana felt the nerves trembling throughout every inch of her body.

"Dana? What's wrong?"

Dana cleared her throat. "I'm pregnant."

Charlotte stared into daughter's eyes blankly like a cyborg whose system had been shut down.

"Ahhh!" Dana screamed grabbing her face as the sting from her mother's heavy-handed slap rippled throughout her small round face like that of a pond after a thrown rock.

"How dare you do this to me?" Charlotte grabbed her daughter's face. "After all the hard work and everything I've done for you and your brother and this is what you do? You've ruined everything!" Charlotte let her face go as if coming out of a trance noticing the horrid look on her daughter's face. "I'm sorry," she gasped.

Dana ran from the kitchen bolting out of the front door almost knocking down her father who was on his way inside.

"I'm sorry! Baby, I'm sorry!" Charlotte said running from the kitchen after her, stopping as she noticed Keith at the door.

"What the hell is going on?" he asked closing the door.

Charlotte said nothing as she turned and walked back into the kitchen.

"Charlotte…" he said following her.

"She and Will broke up," she lied tending to the groceries.

"Oh, she'll get over it."

"Yeah, that's what I told her."

"Young love. She'll be over him in about two weeks. Watch what I tell you."

I don't think so, Charlotte thought to herself as she put the groceries away.

"I'm going to take a shower."

"Okay," Charlotte said stopping what she was doing waiting for him to leave.

Keith walked out and she let out a breath. *Lord, why now? Why is this happening all over again?* Charlotte thought shaking her head, bracing herself against the counter. *Why Dana? Why my daughter? Why not Kenya's daughter?* She could just hear her mother's condescending, unapologetic, voice in the back of her mind. She took a deep breath calming herself down and put away the rest of the groceries.

* * *

The next morning Charlotte sat at the small dining table that was just off the kitchen, by the bay windows, looking out at the backyard. It was bright, clear and serene, watching the small brown-colored birds fly between the trees in the distance. She had begun the day earlier than usual as she sipped on her cup of Folgers in her #1 Mom mug that was a gift from the kids on Mother's Day eight years ago.

She was hoping Dana would walk in for her usual toast and bacon breakfast that had been sitting on the counter for the last 30 minutes and was now cold. She knew Dana was still in the house and hadn't left for school. She hadn't seen or spoke to her since the night before. She wondered what was going through her 16-year-old daughter's mind. Were they the same fearful, low self-esteem thoughts she had at 14?

She felt terrible, ashamed even, thinking about how she treated her. In no way whatsoever did she ever want to treat her kids the same way her mother had treated her. And now she had become the one person she never wanted to emulate...her mother. The thought of it made her cringe.

She became still, listening intently, as the middle step of the stairs creak in the distance. The door alarm beeped once as the front door opened and then close. It was probably Keith, she thought, sipping on her coffee again.

The middle step creaked again and she knew it was Dana. There was no way her baby girl would pass up her toast and bacon. Her eyes kept glancing at the doorway beaming with nervousness. Keith walked in and her internal flame quickly blew out.

"Good morning," he said grabbing a mug from the cabinet and half-filling it with coffee.

"Good morning."

"Why are you so quiet? What's wrong with you?"

Charlotte sipped her coffee. "Dana's pregnant."

"What?"

"Yeah, she told me last night."

"Well, there goes college." He said sipping his coffee. "Is she going to keep it?"

"I don't know."

"Well, she better not if she knows what's good for her."

"What?" Charlotte put her cup down on the counter. "I can't believe you just said that."

"Charlotte, if she keeps this child it is going to ruin her life. How is she going to attend school, work and take care of a child? She's 16. What does she know about raising a child?"

"We can help her."

"Oh no. I raised my kids. I'm not raising my grandkids too. I'm sorry. I hope she doesn't think she's going to have this baby and expect us to raise it while she's off living her life. I don't think so. Not happening." He sipped his coffee. "I'm telling you if she keeps this baby it's gonna be a mistake."

"Well, what do you suggest we do, Keith? Tie the child up outside."

"I suggest she and Will talk about it and decide what they're going to do before it's too late." He downed the rest of his coffee. "I gotta go to work."

Charlotte looked down at her cup of coffee and felt the tears stream from her eyes and roll down her cheeks as she got from the table and walked over to the kitchen sink. She poured out the rest of her coffee and threw the mug across the room and it shattered against the wall. She screamed and fell to her knees, holding her stomach.

"I miss my baby. I miss my baby," she cried. "Lord, why did you let her take him from me? I didn't do anything wrong. I didn't do anything wrong. I didn't..."

She couldn't move even though she wanted to. She wanted to pick herself up, but couldn't. Broken, her body felt heavy like a boulder. She took a deep breath...and another... and another. She grabbed hold of the counter and picked herself up off the floor. She took another deep breath.

The silence accentuated the ticking of the apple-shaped clock hanging on the wall beside the sink. She knew her makeup was a mess and walked upstairs to the bathroom. The black mascara had streaked each cheek. She pulled out her makeup bag from underneath the counter and began removing the mascara with wipe. "She gets to choose." She stopped, staring at herself in the mirror. "She gets to choose. My daughter...gets to choose."

She lowered her head, crying, realizing even though their situations were the same, Dana had the luxury of a power she wasn't afforded the opportunity to use...the power of choice.

♦ TWENTY-SEVEN ♦

Bradley patiently waited for Dr. Tate's white office door to open and his name to be spoken from her lips as he checked the news feed of his Facebook page. He smiled to himself reading one of Rodney's status update. He looked at the time displayed in the upper right corner of his cell phone and it was ten minutes past their scheduled meeting time. The door opened and Dr. Tate stepped out. "Bradley, just letting you know I'm here. I'm just finishing up with another patient."

"Okay." He smiled. She went back inside, shutting the door. He was beginning to like the sessions. The fact she was Rodney's aunt made him feel comfortable, at home, more ready to discuss what he had kept to himself most of his life.

The office door opened again and Dr. Tate stepped out, saying goodbye to a mother and daughter. She waved Bradley in and he walked inside.

"How are you?" Dr. Tate asked as she shut the door.

"I'm okay." He sat down.

"Okay? What do you mean by 'okay'?"

"Well, I haven't taken a drink since the last time we met. I'm not saying I haven't wanted one, I just haven't taken one."

"Well, that's a good start."

"I guess so."

"So, the last time you were here we were discussing what

brought you here?" Bradley nodded. "So, tell me about your childhood?"

"Well, I grew up right here in Boston with my mom, dad and my older brother."

"How was it? Your childhood?"

"Tough. It was a tough environment."

"Tough? What do you mean by 'tough'?"

He sighed. "My father used to beat my mother."

"So, you grew up an abusive household."

"Yes."

"As a child, how was it growing up in that environment? Witnessing your father hitting your mother?"

"Terrifying. We never knew when he was gonna blow. Any little thing could set him off. If my mother didn't have dinner ready when he wanted. If it wasn't cooked the way he wanted. If she said something and he didn't like the tone of how it was said. I mean anything. Most times I hated to see him come home. My brother and I would be in our room quiet, scared."

"Did you two ever witness it firsthand?"

"Sometimes. Most times we could hear it from our room. Sometimes, we would listen from the stairs and hoped that our presence would get him to stop."

"Would it?"

"No. He would yell at us to go to our room, which we did. And if we didn't he would move towards us, and we would shoot up to our room."

"Did your father ever hit you or your brother?"

"No. Well, once he whipped my brother and I because my brother broke his favorite guitar which he had told us numerous times not to touch. And like a fool, my brother was playing around with it and broke a string. And tried to blame me for it." Bradley smiled thinking about it. "And my father was beyond pissed when he found out. He came bursting into the room. 'Which one of you did this?' and of course my brother pointed at me and me to him. So, my father just whipped both of us so one couldn't gloat about the other getting in trouble. It was pretty funny, now that I look back on it."

"What is your relationship like with your mother?"

He took a deep breath. "Oh, my mother…" He looked off, thinking, trying to find the right words. "Difficult."

"Difficult? Explain."

"Well, I tolerate her when she is in the presence of me and my children. She doesn't love me. Never has."

"Why do you believe she doesn't love you?"

Bradley looked away and then back to her. "She used to beat me. And I mean beat me. After my father would beat her, she would come to our room and beat me. And it was always after my father would leave the house."

"Share, if you will, one time when your mother abused you."

"There were many times, but this one stands out in my mind because of my Michael Jackson Bad poster on the wall above my bed…"

"You can't do that! That's not fair!"

Barbara put the last piece of the broken vase in the trash and watched from the kitchen window as Eddie Jr., 11, and Bradley, now 7, played baseball in the backyard. The feeling of pain ran throughout her face as she touched her bruised cheek. It had been two hours since Eddie Sr. had once again shown her how much love he had for her. She turned on the water and wet the dishrag watching Bradley as he ran around the backyard touching each fictitious base with his foot. She rung the rag tightly with her hands and turned off the water. She walked outside.

"Hi, Mama," said Junior.

She didn't respond, walking over and grabbing the collar of Bradley's white alligator-shirt pulling him into the house. He started screaming, knowing what was in store for him.

"No, Mama!" Junior screamed.

"I'm sorry! I'm sorry!" Bradley shouted.

"Shut up!" She picked him up, carrying him upstairs to his room and threw him inside, kicking the door closed with her foot. She picked up a belt that was lying on the floor and started whipping him. He screamed, falling, as he moved closer to his bed.

"I can't fuckin' stand you! I hate you! I hate you! I hate you!" she shouted as the belt smacked against his thin-framed body and he moved about the bed trying to dodge the hits.

Using the wall as leverage, his hand ripped through his Michael Jackson poster as he fell onto the bed, screaming. He quickly got up and resumed moving about the bed, falling into his dirty-clothes hamper, butt first. He covered his face and head with his hands as the licks continued coming at him with the speed of a freight train. "I can't stand your little ass! I can't stand you!" she screamed as she started crying. "You've brought me nothing but trouble! That's all you do is bring me pain! I hate you!"

"And I just remember being in the hamper just feeling like this was a bit much. That it was just too much. And I knew from that point on that my mother didn't love me."

"Did your father know about it?"

"I don't believe so. If he had, he probably would have killed her."

"How long did the abuse go on for?"

"From about 8 to 12."

"Why do you believe it stopped?"

"Because I grew. By my 13th birthday I was about 5'7" – 5'8", much taller than she was. But the damage had been done by that point. And when I was 14, I tried to kill myself. I was just about to hang myself in the garage when my brother walked in and caught me."

"How were you feeling at that point?"

"I was tired, Dr. Tate. Just tired of everything. Not to mention I had acne real bad and a girl who I really liked told me I was too ugly to date which hurt me to my core because I never thought about or looked at myself in that way. Of being handsome or ugly. Just never thought about it. So, not only did my mother not love me, the world didn't like me, is how I looked at it. And I just kept everything inside and never talked about it. And after a while, it turned into anger. I mean I kept my head in my books and ran track, but every other week, I seemed to be in a fight. I can't tell you how many times my dad had to come up to the school and speak with the principal."

"So, when did the drinking start?"

"At a party. Somebody had some and I tried it for the first time. I forgot all about everything and just had fun. And then I had odd jobs until I went into the police academy at 22 where I met Rodney."

"Why did you join the police force? What was the reason behind making that decision?"

"Well, it was something I wanted to do since I was a kid. I've wanted to help people." He looked away and then back at Dr. Tate. "Plus, it was the only way I could face the world and not feel broken twenty-four hours, seven days a week. Those eight hours I wear that uniform…" He stopped, feeling the emotions rising inside, his eyes watering. "…is the only time I don't feel like a victim." He grabbed some tissues and wiped the tears from his eyes.

Dr. Tate glanced at the clock. It was fifteen minutes past the end of their session. "We'll stop right there. We've gone way over our time today."

"Oh, I'm sorry."

"Don't be. It's okay. You did great today."

"Thank you."

"I'll see you in two weeks."

"Okay."

♦ TWENTY-EIGHT ♦

A couple of hours had passed since Eddie Sr. and Bradley had started cleaning out the basement and they were halfway done. They had managed to separate most of the boxes that were considered junk to one side of the basement and the rest in a pile that Eddie had deemed safe-keeping.

"So where did you want me to put this stuff again?" Bradley asked.

"What is it?"

"Some more of your and Mom's papers."

"Yeah, you can put that over there with the stuff at the bottom of the stairs. Your mother and I will look over it later."

"Okay." He placed the box on top of another in the viewable section. He let out a breath and sat down on an old chest. It had been quite a while since they shared father and son moments like this and he was enjoying it.

"Thanks son for helping."

"No problem."

"I would've asked your brother, but…"

"Hey, why deal with the stress if you don't have to, right?"

"Exactly. Have you spoken with him?"

"No, I haven't. There haven't been any calls to 911 so I guess he and Natalie must be doing okay for now."

"I wonder where I went wrong with that boy."

"Well, you went wrong when you beat up Mom."

"I know," Eddie said lowering his head. "And I've asked God to forgive me for all the wrong I've done to you, Mom and your brother. It's my fault he's the way he is."

"Well, Dad, you can't keep beating yourself about the choices he's making. He is a grown 35-year-old man."

"Yeah, I know. How's everything with you and Croix?"

"We're okay."

"Good. Good."

Bradley smiled to himself and chuckled as he thought about a moment long ago. He chuckled again.

"What's so funny?"

"I was just thinking about when you used to take us fishing."

"Yeah. You were scared of everything. I had to put the worm on the hook because you were scared of the worms. Had to take the fish off the hook because you were too afraid to touch the fish. The only thing you ever did was cast out and reel in."

"It was always weird to me. The fish flopping around."

"And till this day it baffles me how someone who was so scared of a fish grew up to be a cop."

"I know," he laughed. "You remember that time we went fishing and Uncle Leroy sneezed and his teeth flew into the water?"

"Yeah, yeah," Eddie laughed. "And the fool tried to go get them, too."

"Oh, that was so funny. I miss Uncle Leroy."

"Yeah. Good times. Good times."

"Looks like we don't have too much left to get done. We did a lot."

"Yeah, we did. We just got to take the rest of that stuff to the trash and that other stuff upstairs."

"We did pretty good," Bradley said looking around at what they got done and noticed a yellow box over in the corner. "We missed one." He walked over and picked up the box.

"That's probably your mother's box."

Bradley blew the dust off the top, sat it on a counter and opened it. "Oh man, my track team trophies. All of them," he said elated. "Wow. And my letterman's jacket. You two kept this. I thought you had gotten rid of this stuff."

"Your mother kept it."

For the first time in a long time, Bradley felt a shift towards his mother. A shift from disdainfulness and discontent to a feeling of warmth. The feeling was moving so rapidly throughout his body, he felt his eyes welling. Maybe he had been wrong about her all these years. Maybe she really did love him.

"I wonder if it still fits," he said, pulling the jacket from the box, barely getting his arm through the sleeve. "Well, I guess that answers that." He folded the jacket back up and put it back in the box along with the trophies. "I'll look at the rest of the stuff when I get home," he said closing the box.

"Wanna start taking this pile out to the trash?"

"Yeah. And I can put this box in the trunk while we're at it."

Barbara wiped the sweat from her forehead as she was still in the backyard tending to her garden as she had been when Bradley arrived a few hours earlier. She looked over and noticed them coming up from the basement carrying boxes. "Y'all almost done?" she asked holding her hand above her eyes trying to block the glare of the sun.

"Almost," said Eddie.

Barbara's face dropped and her eyes widened when she noticed the yellow box Bradley was carrying in his hands. Quickly, she got up, took off of her garden gloves and hurried over. "Stop right there. Where did you get that box?"

"I found it in the basement tucked in the corner. It has my old track trophies and my letterman's jacket in it. I'm gonna take it home and show the girls."

"No, you're not. That box belongs to me." She reached for it and he moved. "Excuse me?"

"Excuse me. The box may be yours, but the contents belong to me. Now, I'll return the box to you when I'm done."

"I'll be damned if you think you're leaving here with that box. It's mine and I want it. Now give it here!" She reached for it again and he pushed her back.

"Dad, get your wife."

"Barbara, what the hell is wrong with you? It's just the boy's trophies. Now, if he wants to take the box home, let him take the box home. It's time to let the shit go."

Silence.

"Come on, son, let's take this stuff to the trash."

Barbara wanted to scream, but couldn't. She wanted to move, but didn't as she watched the one thing she had kept to herself for years walk away in the hands of her son. A truth, that once revealed, would bring more pain to her than the cancer ever would. A truth that only a few people knew, that would destroy her entire family.

♦ TWENTY-NINE ♦

Charlotte stood in the line outside of the window to the Birth Records department at City Hall anxious about what she was hoping to find. She tried not to run a preconceived scenario in her mind about what she thought was going to happen at the window, but she couldn't hold the thoughts.

She moved a step forward with line as a customer left from the window. She looked around at the different lines of people standing in front of the various windows of City departments. Some were paying their taxes, others filling out forms. *Oh my God, I'm almost the next one up*, Charlotte thought to herself as she moved a step forward with the line. She knew she was taking a chance doing this. She had no information about him. None. No name. Just a date of birth.

She stepped up to the slim-faced woman behind the counter.

"Can I help you?" the woman asked, popping her gum.

"Yes, I'm looking to see if I could get a copy of a birth certificate. It's for my son." Charlotte smiled.

"What is the child's name?"

"Um, that's the thing. I don't know the child's name."

"Wait a minute. You don't know the name of your child?" The woman looked at Charlotte as if she had two heads.

"Ma'am, my child was taken from me years ago... Look, it's a long story that I don't feel like getting into right now, but I do know his date of birth."

"Look, Miss…"

"Watson."

"…Miss Watson. We're going to need more than just the child's date of birth. We're going to need his name in order to find the birth certificate. Now, I have a line so could you please…"

"Is there any way you could look it up with the name John Doe or John Smith. I mean how many nameless children could there have been born on August 5, 1980 at Boston City Hospital? I mean really…"

"Look, I'm sorry that your child was taken from you, but I told you what I need. So, could you please… thank you." The woman popped her gum.

"Could you please just look for me?"

"My God, would you come on already!" a man shouted from the line.

"Could you? I really want to find my son. Look, here's my card, if you find anything." Charlotte put her card on the counter. "I would greatly appreciate it."

Charlotte walked away as the next person in line stepped up to the window. *What've I got to lose*, she thought to herself as she headed to the exit. She knew this was her one-and-only shot in filling the void created so long ago and that it would be by the grace of God if the woman behind the counter found any information at all.

* * *

Charlotte rang the doorbell and knocked on Kenya's door. *Please be home.* She banged on Kenya's front door again and pressed the doorbell repeatedly. She felt like a piece of glass that was going to shatter at any moment. *Kenya, please be home.* The door opened and there Kenya stood dressed in sweats, her hair in a ponytail.

"Thank God!" Charlotte hurried in as if being chased.

"I was just about to call you. We need to talk," Kenya said closing the door.

"I need a drink. A big one."

"Why? What's wrong?"

Kenya asked following her youngest sister into her living room. Charlotte tossed her purse onto the couch and raided the mini-bar.

"Charly, what's wrong? What happened?"

Charlotte grabbed a glass, poured herself some of her brother-in-law's favorite scotch, and tossed it back. The warmness of it soothed her. She poured herself some more.

"Charlotte, what's wrong?"

"I hate that woman," Charlotte said as she walked over to the couch and sat down.

"Who?"

"Our mother."

Kenya sighed. "What did she do this time?"

"It's nothing. Never mind." Charlotte took down the second glass of scotch. "Dana's pregnant."

"What?"

"Yeah." Charlotte put down the glass. "I slapped her when she told me."

"You did what?"

"Yeah. Now she's not speaking to me."

"I bet."

"I don't know what to do."

"Well, what can you do except support her in whatever decision she makes."

"I will. I just wasn't expecting that from her. I thought she was smarter than that."

"Like you were."

Charlotte looked at her.

"We all make mistakes at some point. It just so happens you both have similar ones," said Kenya.

"Yeah, but this is different."

"How? Because you were 14 and she's 16."

"Because she gets to…" Charlotte stopped.

"Gets to what?" Kenya asked.

"Nothing. Never mind."

"Look, just let the dust settle and then y'all talk about it," said Kenya.

"Kenya, whatever you do, don't tell Tamara, please. Don't tell her Dana's pregnant because she'll tell Ma and I am not in the mood to deal with Ma's bullshit."

"Oh so, my niece is pregnant," Tamara said walking in from the kitchen with a glass of wine for her and Kenya. "I heard everything from the kitchen," she said, handing Kenya a glass and then sitting down. "You should think more highly of me."

"Just don't tell Ma."

"I won't."

"What was it that you were going to talk to me about, Ken?"

"We can talk about that some other time," said Kenya.

"I'm going to get me a glass of wine." Charlotte got up and walked in the kitchen.

Tamara waited until she was out of hearing distance. "Why didn't you tell her about Keith?"

"I was when she first walked in, but you hear how she was about Dana being pregnant. I didn't want to add more to the fire."

Kenya smiled as Charlotte returned and sat down.

"So, what's going on with you two?" Charlotte asked.

"Nothing," said Kenya.

"Same here," said Tamara.

"Did y'all watch the Real Housewives of Atlanta last night?"

"Giiirrrl, let me tell you...." said Tamara sitting up and putting her glass down.

♦ THIRTY ♦

The smoke blew from her mouth and nostrils and quickly evaporated like smoke from the exhaust of a car. She pulled the cigarette from her lips looking at the moving images of the men and women of Grey's Anatomy, her mind somewhere else. On that yellow box.

Barbara picked up the glass of red wine from the table and drank down what was left. She had been waiting for the phone to ring since Bradley left, but it hadn't. Maybe he hadn't looked further in the box yet. Or maybe he just decided to leave it in his basement. The anticipation of whether her youngest son would discover the contents of that box was killing her. What could she say that would make what she did seem right? She took a drag of her cigarette as she leaned forward. The front door unlocked and Eddie Sr. walked in carrying brand-new power tools.

"Hey," he said shutting the door with his foot.

"Hey." She put out her cigarette.

He knew she was worrying about something that was the only time the cigarette smoke filled the air. "What's got your stomach in a knot?"

"It's nothing."

"Well, you're putting out butts again in the ashtray, so something must be bothering you."

"I said it's nothing."

He put the tools down and sat down next to her on the couch and began rubbing her back. "Honey, we're gonna get through this together. Just like we did the last time. If you want, we'll attack it more aggressively this time. Whatever you want."

"What I wanted was for you to stop beating me 30 years ago! That's what I wanted!" She got up, grabbed her empty glass and headed for the kitchen.

He sighed. "And I will apologize every single day for the rest of my life." He got up and followed her into the kitchen. "Barbara, I've been a changed man for the last 20 years."

"I tried so much to get you to stop. But oh no, you wouldn't, you couldn't. You had so much control." She spoke to herself with her back to him, pouring another glass of wine. "I tried everything to get you to stop. Everything!" She slammed the bottle on the counter, breaking it, cutting her hand. "Dammit!"

"Honey!" He grabbed a towel and wrapped it around her hand.

"Thank you."

"Yeah…no problem."

Perplexed, he knew this was more than just about the abuse he had thrust upon her so long ago. He knew she was scared.

* * *

"Hey Louisa," said a much younger Barbara as she walked into the section of the maternity ward where the babies slept. She walked up to the sink and washed her hands.

"Hey Barb…what happened to your face?" Louisa asked with her heavy Spanish accent.

"Stupid me, I walked into a door. It's nothing. I'm okay." She shook the excess water from her hands and grabbed a paper towel from the dispenser on the wall, drying her hands.

"Either you got a lotta doors in your house or you going blind."

"I'm good, Louisa. You don't have to worry about me. I'm fine." She grabbed a couple of gloves from the middle box hanging on the wall and put them on. "How is your daughter?"

"Eating me out of house and home. I don't know what I'm gonna do with that girl I tell you. How's your little boy?"

"Eddie Jr. is good. He's 4 now," she said walking into the baby room. "Come here, little man," she said picking a baby up from its bassinet.

"You're gonna wear yourself out with them."

"I can't help it. They are so cute." Barbara sighed, sitting down holding the baby in her arms. She touched his tiny little fingers.

"You want another baby?"

"Yeah, but the doctor said I'm not going to able to have any more."

"Why?"

"Because of my home life."

"Because of this," said Louisa grabbing Barbara's face.

"No, no, no, that's not it. I have a medical condition," Barbara lied.

"Yeah, uh-huh. Keep telling yourself that. If my husband ever did that to me, I would cut his balls off."

"I'm okay. We're okay," Barbara said, touching the baby's tiny hand. "It'll get better. I know it will."

After suffering four miscarriages and gone through two abortions, Barbara desperately wanted another baby, hoping the sweetness of an innocent child would permanently relieve her of her plight. "I don't make girls. I only make boys." Eddie would shout at her once they learned the sex of the baby she was carrying, resulting in yet another yelling, screaming, hitting bout. She looked down at the baby and smiled, praying that one day, God would answer her silent cry.

◆ THIRTY-ONE ◆

Bradley pulled into the driveway behind Croix's SUV still elated by the fact that his mother, whom he despised, had kept a box of some his greatest moments of his life. He smiled as he turned off the engine and rested his head against the headrest. He looked up at the window of his daughters' bedroom, no Tia standing in view. She hadn't been sleeping well since that night and he was worried about her.

But that feeling of happiness crept back in, diminishing all depressing thoughts he was about to have regarding his witnessed suicide attempt. He smiled as he looked over at the yellow box sitting in the passenger seat. Was he wrong about his mother all these years? Did she really love him after all? He knew his mother keeping all of his high moments in a box was not going to completely repave their heavily damaged road, but to him it felt like a start. Maybe the time had finally come for him to begin that long, hard road to forgiveness.

He got out of the car, grabbing the box. He wondered what was so important in the box that had his mother so shook up when he was leaving. *Whatever. Not my problem.* He unlocked the front door and went inside.

"Daddy! Daddy! Daddy!" the girls shouted, running towards him.

"Here are Daddy's babies!" He put the box down, hugging

both of them. "How was school today?"

"Fine!" They smiled.

"Good. Come on into the dining room I have something to show you two." He stood up. "Croix!"

"Yeah!" she shouted from upstairs.

"Can you come down here a minute? I have something to show you."

"Okay! I'm in the bathroom! I'll be down in a minute!"

"Okay!" He picked up the box and walked with the girls into the dining room. Ashley got on her knees in a chair beside him.

"What's in the box?" Tia asked.

"Well, that's what I'm going to show you." He opened the box. "Look at these." He pulled out the three trophies and Ashley's face lit up. "Wow," she said, "You won all those?"

"Yep. Running track in high school."

"Can I hold one?" Tia asked.

"Yeah."

"Can I, too?"

"Gawd, Ashley. Why do you have to do everything I do?"

"Tia..."

"Sorry, Daddy."

"Here, Ashley."

"Oh, what do we have here—a little show and tell?" Croix said walking up.

"Yeah. I was helping my dad clean out the basement and found this old box of my mother's and it had all of my high school stuff in it. My trophies, local newspaper clippings, report cards, and...check this out." He pulled the jacket from the box. "She even kept my letterman's jacket." He attempted to put it on.

"I know you're not going to try and put that thing on." Croix laughed.

The sleeves went halfway up his wrists. Croix and the girls roared into laughter as he formed different poses. "I was fly."

"You have seriously lost your mind."

He laughed. "I know. Let me take this thing off before I mess it up."

"You better." Croix laughed.

"What else is in the box, Daddy?" Tia asked, peeking inside.

"Um, I don't know." He looked inside. "Looks like just a folder." He pulled it from the box as the doorbell rang.

"I got it," Croix said and walked over to the door.

"Watson. Hmm. It must belong to Ma," Bradley said, reading the name on the tab that was faded.

"Bradley," Croix said as he looked over and noticed his bruised and battered sister-in-law Natalie standing before him with his 7-year-old niece Dominique and 9-year-old nephew Bailey.

"Natalie." He dropped the folder and rushed over. "What happened?"

"I'll take the girls upstairs," Croix said. "Hey, who wants to watch Kung-Fu Panda 2 and eat ice cream?"

"I do!" Ashley shouted.

"Me too!" Tia shouted.

"Bailey and Dominique go upstairs with your cousins so I can talk with Uncle Bradley, okay?" said Natalie to her children.

"Alright, the first one upstairs gets extra ice cream!" Croix shouted. The kids dashed upstairs almost knocking each other over. Croix touched her sister-in-law's shoulder and she smiled, ready to break down.

"Come on." Bradley wrapped his arm around her shoulder and walked her into the dining room. "Tell me what happened," he said sitting her down.

"He came home drunk as usual and started yelling and screaming about shoes being out the wrong way…just started going off. I don't know how much more I can take of this, Bradley. I don't," she cried.

"I know, Nat. I know." He hugged her. "You and the kids will stay here tonight."

"Thank you."

"No need to thank me. It's what I'm here for."

* * *

The clock above the kitchen door read 10:00 p.m. as

Bradley sat at the table looking over the information about the Sergeant's exam. The sessions with Dr. Tate seemed to be working, even though he still hadn't told Croix the truth behind his "vacation" use. He had not wanted a drink in a while and he was beginning to feel better than he had in a long time. He smiled as he listened to Croix and Natalie laugh in the living room. It was like music to his ears hearing Croix laugh. It had been quite a while since he heard it and for a split second he felt a little jealous that it wasn't him making her emanate such a loud, happy sound.

"Ahhhh! Daddy! Daddy! Daddy!" Tia's screams echoed throughout the house like a bullhorn as Bradley jumped up from the kitchen table and rushed up stairs. Croix and Natalie following. "Daddy's here. I'm here, baby," he said rushing into the room and over to her bedside. He switched on the Disney princess lamp. "I'm here. I'm here. Everything's okay."

She grabbed him tightly. "I don't want you to go, Daddy. I don't want you to die."

"I've told you before Daddy's not going anywhere okay. Daddy is not going to die. I promise." He wiped the tears from her face, then hugged her.

"What's wrong baby? You had another nightmare," Croix said standing in the doorway.

"Yeah."

"You wanna sleep in Mommy and Daddy's bed tonight?"

"Yeah."

"Can I come, too?" Ashley moaned, half asleep.

"Yeah, you can come, too," said Bradley. He rubbed Tia's face and smiled. Her nightmares of witnessing his self-attempted demise were happening more than he expected and he knew it was only a matter of time before Croix would learn what happened. In that moment, he knew he needed to tell her everything even if it meant losing her forever.

♦ THIRTY-TWO ♦

A row of short and long yellow school buses lined the sidewalk outside of the James J. Chittick Elementary School as Croix pulled up and placed the vehicle in park. She hated even being a few minutes late getting the girls to school. She got out, walked around to the other side and opened the door for the girls to get out. They gave her a hug and kiss.

"Have a good day, okay."

"Okay. Bye Mommy!" The girls walked away and got in line filing in school. Croix waved to Tia's teacher, Mrs. Stine.

"Oh, Mrs. Robinson! Oh, Mrs. Robinson!" Mrs. Stine said running over to her.

"Hi, Mrs. Stine."

"Hi. I wanted to talk to you about Tia. She's been sleeping a lot in class."

"She has?"

"Yes. I wanted to bring it to your attention. Is everything okay at home?"

"Everything is fine. I know she has been having bad dreams recently. Tia! Tia, honey, come here!" Croix shouted and she came running. "Mrs. Stine has been telling me that you've been sleeping in class. Is everything okay, honey?"

Tia remained silent looking in opposite direction of her mother and teacher.

"Is it about your Dad?"

Tia started crying. "It's private."

"She's been having bad dreams about her Dad. He's a police officer," said Croix to the teacher who nodded her head understanding. "Can you whisper it in my ear honey?" Tia whispered in her mother's ear and Croix's face changed into a look that was as indescribable as the words that were coming from her daughter's mouth.

"Everything okay, Mrs. Robinson?" asked Mrs. Stine.

"Fine." Croix smiled, worried. "Stop crying honey, okay?" she said, wiping Tia's face. "Everything's going to be okay. I'll talk with your Dad, okay?"

She kissed her on the forehead. "I love you."

"I love you, too."

"She'll be fine," Croix said standing up, "once she meets up with her friends. Thank you, Mrs. Stine, for calling that to my attention."

"No problem. If you need anything…"

"I'm good. Thank you. I just need to talk with my husband. Have a good day."

"You too, Mrs. Robinson." Mrs. Stine smiled, not knowing what to make of the concerned energy she was getting from Croix.

Croix got in the car and sped off, her mind thinking a million and one thoughts. She pulled over wanting to collect herself and process what her daughter had told her. If what Tia had told her was true, how could she stay with a man, a husband, a father who was suicidal?

Croix laid her head against the steering wheel and cried. This was worse than the alcohol. It was worse than the first and only time Bradley had struck her. This was about the welfare of her children.

How he could keep this from her? Why would he keep the way he was feeling from her? Croix hugged the steering wheel as the tears continued flowing from her eyes like a raging river. She leaned back from the steering wheel and wiped her eyes. The time had passed for her to call in sick from work, but she'd handle Bradley when she got home.

* * *

The second hand of the analog clock on the fireplace mantle ticked as the time read 10:00 a.m. Since the suspension, Bradley had grown to love the quiet mornings after the girls and Croix left for school and work. He still kept Croix in the dark about the suspension, telling her that he was using vacation time. Nor had he yet explained to her the reason behind Tia's nightly screaming episodes.

Bradley walked out of the bathroom and sat on the foot of the bed to put on his sneakers. He was running late for his appointment with Dr. Tate and was moving swiftly. DING-DONG! The doorbell rang. *Who could that be?* he thought to himself as he headed downstairs. DING-DONG!

"Hold on! I'm coming!" he shouted.

DING-DONG!

"I said I'm com—," he said as he swung open the door to his awaiting mother.

"We need to talk," said Barbara.

"I can't right now. I'm late for an appointment," Bradley said stepping back in, grabbing his keys. "Can't we do this some other time? I really have to go." He stepped out closing the door behind him, locking it.

"What I have to say is really important, Bradley. Please."

"Well, can it wait until later?" he asked, making his way to his car.

Barbara sighed. Bradley was just as stubborn as his father. "It's about the box."

"What about it? You want it back? Fine, if you want the damn box back, I'll give it to you right now," Bradley snapped, making his way back towards the house.

"No," Barbara said. "I don't want the box back."

"Then what is this about?"

"Never mind. Go where you have to be. We can talk about it some other time."

Bradley turned and headed to his car. "We'll talk later."

"Okay, sure." Barbara huffed.

She knew it was only a matter of time before he reached the bottom of the box and when he did, she'd have more explaining to do than Lucille Ball.

♦ THIRTY-THREE ♦

Dishes and silverware clanged as waiters carried them to and from the kitchen while the chatter of patrons filled the Silver Slipper restaurant. Charlotte stared out the window sitting across from her mother, comparing her teenage pregnancy against her very own daughter's.

"Hey!" Carol shouted as she clapped her hands getting Charlotte's attention. "Get your head out of the clouds. The food is here."

"Oh sorry," said Charlotte as the waiter placed their lunches on the table.

"Enjoy."

The waiter left.

"Now you're supposed to be here with me. What's got your mind this afternoon?"

"It's nothing."

"It's got to be something if you've been staring out that window as long as you have. Do I bore you?"

"No. Just thinking."

"About what?"

"Look, Mama, I'm not going divulge the inner workings of my mind to you. So, just eat your food," Charlotte said beginning to eat.

"You might want to take the bass out of your voice, young

lady, when you're speaking with me. I may be up in age, but I am still your mother."

"Please don't remind me."

"Excuse me?"

"Nothing. Can we just eat?"

Carol sipped her water washing down some of the grilled chicken salad her daughter was paying for. "So, why didn't you tell me Dana was pregnant? I had to find out from one of your sisters."

"Tamara." *She still can't keep her fuckin' mouth shut,* Charlotte thought to herself as she chewed her food. "I didn't feel it was my place to tell you. I thought Dana should tell you."

"You could've told me yourself."

"Look, Mama, does it really make a difference who told you? Now you know."

"I see the apple didn't fall far from the tree."

Charlotte dropped her fork and just looked out the window. *Lord, give me peace.* She wanted to grab her mother around the neck and choke her until she saw heaven. "Really, Ma?"

"What? Is she keeping it?" asked Carol.

"I don't know. She hasn't made that decision yet."

"What about the father?"

"What about him?"

"Is he a decent young man?"

"Yes, Will is. They'll be graduating together and going to the same college."

"Well, if Dana keeps this child she can forget about college. She won't be able to go to college, take care of a baby and work. Him either."

Wow, I can't believe I'm hearing this again. "Mama, it's her life. If she wants to keep this baby, it's her decision."

"Look, I'm just saying."

"I know what you're saying. I heard it 31 years ago." Charlotte motioned for the waiter and he came over. "Can I have the check please?"

"Certainly." The waiter left.

"Was it something I said?" Carol asked plainly.

Charlotte didn't say anything as her leg began to shake underneath the table. She was ready to scream and let out 30 years of mixed feelings, but didn't want to embarrass her mother or herself in public. The waiter returned with the check, and Charlotte scribbled her signature.

"Mama, I gotta go."

"But we just got our food."

"I know, but I have patients waiting. I'll call you later."

"Okay, whatever."

Charlotte got up and left the table. Carol knew it would be another week before she heard from her again. The waiter returned. "Do you want me to bag that up for you?"

"Would you, hun? Thank you."

Carol handed him the plate and watched as Charlotte crossed the street and got into her vehicle. She loved her daughter with all her heart, and after all of these years, she still saw herself in her—the disappointing teenager she had once been herself.

* * *

The phones ringing and the chatter of workers at the Department of Children and Families filled the atmosphere on the fifth floor of John W. McCormack Building as a younger Carol took off her big-rimmed glasses and put them down on the desk. The day was growing longer it seemed and it was only noon. She grabbed her coffee mug. Seeing it was empty, she got up and headed to the break room.

"Hey, Alan," she spoke making her way to the break room. He was one of the few men that worked in the office. She walked into the break room where two of her fellow workers, Maureen and Shirley, were eating their lunch. "Hey, you two."

"Hey, Carol," said Maureen. "How are the girls?"

"They're good. Kenya will be graduating this year."

"Oh that's great," said Shirley. "Heading off to college, I hope."

"Of course. I'm making sure of that," Carol said, refilling her coffee mug.

"Anything new with you two?"

"Same old, same old," said Maureen.

"Me too," responded Shirley.

"Did you hear about those two kids who died in that fire last night in South Boston?" Maureen asked biting into her sandwich.

"Yeah. I heard about it on the news this morning. So sad," said Carol.

"They were Louise's cousin's kids."

"Oh no," said Shirley shocked.

"So sad," said Carol. "I'll see ya'll later."

"Okay," Maureen and Shirley said in unison.

Carol left the break room and walked over to the other side of the room where Louise worked. She was her work-friend—the only person who she spoke to outside of the office. Louise was on the phone as Carol walked up. She motioned one minute with her finger.

"Okay. Okay. Alright, I'll talk to you later. Bye-bye." Louise hung up the phone. "Hey."

"The girls just told me, I'm so sorry for your family's loss." Carol hugged her.

"Thanks."

"You know if you need me for anything, let me know."

"Okay. Thank you."

Carol walked back to her desk and sat down. The office phone rang.

"Department of Children and Families, this is Mrs. Carol Watson speaking."

"Mrs. Watson?" said the female voice on the other line.

"Yes."

"Hi, this is the nurse from the hospital. The one that helped deliver your grand--"

"I know who you are." Carol said coldly. "Is he safe?"

"Yes, your gran—"

"Is he safe?"

"Yes. Your gran—"

"Don't," Carol whispered sternly.

"Well, if you or your daughter ever want to see—"

"We don't. Thank you."

"He'll be living in a house on Salem Avenue, number 465...," the female said quickly into the phone as Carol hung up. She stood up checking her surroundings for listening ears and noticed everyone was busy and sat back down, nervous, a part of her questioning whether she had made the right decision.

◆ THIRTY-FOUR ◆

Charlotte walked through the main entrance of Boston City Hospital with a nervous energy. It had been years since she had last stepped foot inside the hospital. Recent construction had made the ambulatory care center more inviting with whiter walls and an expanded area. She rubbed her palms together wanting to relieve them of perspiration as she walked up to the information desk and the two security officers behind it. The guards had changed, but the position of the desk hadn't. She felt exactly as she did when she was 14...scared.

"Hi," she spoke with a smile.

"Hi," said one of the guards.

"Do you know where the medical records department is?"

"Yeah. Take the elevator down to the basement."

"Thank you." Charlotte walked to the elevators and pushed the down. *Wow, these haven't changed*, she thought to herself as the one of the four set of elevator doors opened and she stepped inside. Another woman rushed over to get on. "This one's going down."

"Oh," said the woman stepping back. The doors closed and then opened a few seconds later. Charlotte stepped out and followed the arrow on the sign for medical records department. She walked the short corridor and then through the glass doors into the department to the woman behind the desk.

"Can I help you?" asked the older woman unenthusiastically, looking up from her eyeglasses perched on the edge of her nose.

"Hi. Do you all still have any records from August of 1980? I'm looking for my son's medical records."

"Oh, I'm sorry, most of those records were destroyed in a flood back in '86," said the woman. "We have everything from September '86 on. I'm sorry."

"Do you still have birth records?"

"All birth records are at City Hall. I'm sorry."

"Thank you." And with that, Charlotte left.

Charlotte unlocked the door and walked inside the house feeling defeated. She knew going to the hospital and finding anything on her son was a stretch, but it was truly her last shot. She put her purse and work bag down and took off her shoes, her feet feeling instant comfort.

She walked into the living room and saw Dana watching television. It was first time since Dana had revealed her pregnancy that they both were in the same room for longer than a few seconds. Dana noticed her and shut off the television, getting up to leave.

"Wait, wait, wait, Dana. We need to talk," Charlotte said stopping her. "So, sit back down."

Dana sighed and sat back on the couch. Charlotte stuck her cell phone in her pocket and sat next to her.

"Incoming call from Charlotte, incoming call from Charlotte..." The automated voice spoke through the audio system of Keith's car as he headed home. He pushed the answer button on the steering wheel. "Hello? Hello...Charlotte...Charlotte," he spoke, but got no response. He was about to push the button to hang-up, but stopped as heard Charlotte talking to someone in the background. He listened...

"I apologize for responding the way that I did. I'm sorry. Forgive me. I just wasn't ready to hear those words coming from you at this age," said Charlotte.

Dana kept her vision in the direction of the blank TV.

"Dana, did you hear me? I said I was sorry. Dana? Say something."

"I'm scared," Dana said, tears streaming from her eyes.

"I know, baby. I know. Come here." Charlotte held Dana in her arms. "It's gonna be okay. I promise." Dana laid her head against mother's chest, the warmth of her arms comforting her. Charlotte stroked Dana's head. "I know you're scared and it's okay to be. But know that I will be right here through everything, okay?"

"Okay."

"I've been where you are. I was just about a couple of years younger than you when I told your grandmother that I was pregnant. I was scared just like you are right now." Charlotte smiled to herself as she thought back to that day. "She liked to beat me to death."

"Did you keep it?"

"I gave birth to him, but I wasn't able to keep him."

"Why?"

"Because of circumstances beyond my control." Charlotte felt the emotions inside of her welling up. "But you get to choose what happens to you and the baby. Something I wasn't allowed to have."

"What's his name?"

"I don't know."

"How come you and Dad never talk about him?"

"Because your father doesn't know about him."

Keith pulled into the driveway and put the car gear in park, shutting off the engine. He couldn't believe what he had just heard through his car audio system. Was what he just heard from his wife of more than 20 years true? He got out of the car and headed for the house. He opened the door and walked inside...

"Hey," said Charlotte noticing him.

He didn't say anything. He just shut the door. He dropped his bag and walked further inside.

"The next time you want to have a private conversation and

reveal family secrets, you might want to check your cell phone and make sure it's not pocket dialing your husband."

"Oh my God, Keith…" said Charlotte getting up from the couch.

"I heard every word."

"I am so sorry. I didn't want you to find out like this." She wiped the tears as they started to fall.

"Well, how did you want me to find out, Charlotte? On my fuckin' deathbed!"

"I am…so…sorry."

"Damn right you are. I ought to fuckin' knock you into next year."

"Please forgive me."

"Forgive you?! You want forgiveness?! You don't deserve no damn forgiveness! None! How the hell could you not tell me about a son that we had 30 fuckin' years ago? Huh?! And you got the nerve to stand in my face and ask for forgiveness?!"

"I wanted to tell you then, but my mother wouldn't let me. She told me if I told anybody she would kill me."

"Okay. But what about all of the years after that, huh? You still had 20 years of marriage to tell me about him, Charlotte!"

"I know, I know. And I'm sorry. I am so sorry." Charlotte moved to touch him.

"Don't touch me! Don't you fuckin' touch me!"

Charlotte moved her hand back, scared. The tears fell from her eyes like a raging river, each one making the smallest of puddles on the floor by her feet.

"I need to get out of here. I can't even fuckin' look at you right now. I can't." Keith walked over and grabbed his keys from his coat pocket and headed for the door.

"Keith…"

"Shut up! Shut the fuck up!" He stopped and took a quick breath, composing himself. He looked at her, wishing the anger of his stare could strike her down. "I want you out of this house!" He walked out and the door slammed behind him.

Charlotte collapsed to her knees. The world as she knew it had now been forever changed and there was nothing she could do about it. This was something that no high-priced education could get her out of. Dana walked over from the couch, got on the floor and hugged her and Charlotte cried in her arms.

◆ THIRTY-FIVE ◆

Keith pressed his foot against the gas pedal of his Mercedes, wanting it to feel the way he did. Confused, betrayed and enraged. He blew through a red light almost causing an accident. He'd been driving for hours turning down streets like a criminal trying to elude the police. He pulled into the darkened parking lot of the closed golf course he frequented every Sunday with his colleague Stephen, turning off the headlights and shutting down the engine.

He didn't know how to feel with a million thoughts flowing in and out of his mind. He was numb, disturbed even, as he tried to wrap his mind around the words that came from Charlotte's mouth. *Thirty years...I have a son that's thir...* He banged his fist against the steering wheel. How could he not have known? How could she not have told him about the pregnancy? He banged his fist against the steering wheel. "How could she have kept this from me?! How?!" he shouted, banging his fist against the steering wheel once more.

His cell phone rang and he looked down at it in the cup holder. It was Tyson. He was in no mood to speak with anyone including his now second-born son. He let the call go to voicemail.

"How could I have missed it? Was I that dumb in high school that I didn't notice her gaining weight?" he pondered as he pushed his seat back and looked up at the night sky through the open sunroof trying to comprehend how his wife gave birth to a child he knew nothing about.

* * *

Hours had passed since Keith had left Charlotte on the floor in a puddle of her own unforgivable deceit and she sat alone on the stairs leading up to the bedrooms. After hours of sitting with her mother, Dana had left to visit her boyfriend Will.

Charlotte held her third glass of bourbon in her hands between her legs looking lost, swirling it around. She wanted to call him but knew he wouldn't answer his phone. She wiped tears from her eyes, the situation playing repeatedly over and over in her mind. She wondered how she could be so stupid and not check her phone before she put it in her pocket.

She took a sip of her drink, calming her nerves. She knew how her patients felt, the loneliness, the betrayal, the disappointment She was at the end of her rope with no one around to throw her an extension. She had wanted to tell him so many times over the years, but the words never materialized. She had been afraid of this...this moment. The moment when she would be all alone sitting in her own pity. The moment when the man she loved her whole life would no longer love her.

The front door lock shifted, the knob turned and the door opened, with Keith walking in. She lifted her head like a young girl waiting to be greeted with punishment for making a bad decision. The tension was raw and deep as they stared at one another. She wiped the tears streaming from her eyes in hopes it would get him to say something to her...it didn't.

Keith stood before her with no words to speak. Looking at her was difficult. He was disgusted, ashamed and confused. He walked towards her and up the stairs without further eye contact. He walked past her not wanting any part of him to touch her. He walked into their son's room and slammed the door shut.

She closed her eyes as they began to burn from the endless flowing of tears. She threw the glass of bourbon and it shattered

150

against the front door. She felt defeated. Not only couldn't she find anything about her son, but she had lost the one thing that her mother couldn't get rid of and now he, too, was gone.

♦ THIRTY-SIX ♦

Bradley pulled into the driveway after a day of running errands and playing a game of basketball with Rodney and friends. He anticipated the sound of his girls running towards him, greeting him in a few minutes as he exited the car. The alarm chirped and the doors locked as he headed for the house.

He unlocked the door and walked in. It was quiet. Unusually quiet for Croix's car to be parked outside. "Ashley! Croix! Tia!" he called out locking the door. "Ashley! Tia! Croix!" he called again, this time his cop instinct kicking in as he reached around to his right hip for his service weapon, but realized he wasn't dressed in his uniform. "Ashley! Tia! Croix!"

"I'm in here," Croix spoke from the living room sitting on the couch.

He breathed a sigh of relief. "Why didn't you answer when I called out?"

She didn't respond.

He noticed the packed bags on the floor beside her. "Where are the girls?"

"They're at my sister's," she said, holding her hands in a prayer-style trying to sort out her emotions. "I can't do this anymore, Bradley."

"Can't do what anymore? What happened?"

"I know why Tia has been having nightmares." She held up

her hand. "Don't...talk." She got up from the couch and started pacing back and forth, beyond pissed. "All day I've been wracking my brain trying to understand why you put not only yourself but our daughter's life in jeopardy and I can't. I can't. I just can't. You have truly lost your damn mind."

"I'm—"

"Shut up, Bradley! Just shut up! You don't deserve to say anything to me right now! You probably scarred our daughter for life!"

"I know that and I'm sorry. I'm so sorry. I had no idea she was looking out of her window."

"And I don't even want to think about..." She stopped as the thought entered her mind. "Not only have you scarred our daughter, you swore her to secrecy about it. You weren't even going to tell me. I could fuckin' kill you right now." She picked up the liquor bottle and threw it at him. It shattered against the wall as he ducked. "So, we don't mean nothing to you, huh?"

"You and the girls mean everything to me." He walked over to her and tried to touch her.

"Don't touch me! Don't you fuckin' touch me! I am done! I'm done with you!" She picked up the bags and headed for the door.

"Croix, please!"

She walked outside and headed for her car.

"Croix please! Don't leave! Just please—" He grabbed her arm.

"Let me go!" She snatched her arm away. "Whatever it is, whatever this shit that you keep holding onto, you need to let it go because it's hurting us and I can't take it anymore. The drinking, the lying about working overtime, and now this. You're losing it, Bradley. And you expect me and the kids to stay here with you? You need help. Serious help."

"I have been getting help. I've been seeing a therapist," Bradley spoke wiping away tears. "Just please don't leave me. Not now. Don't let go of us."

"Right now, Bradley, there is no us. And there may be no us ever again," she said, putting the bags in the car. "I'll be at my sister's until I can clear my head."

"Croix, please don't take them away from me. You and the girls are all I have. Please...Croix...please...I'm lost without you."

"You're lost with me." Croix opened the door and got inside.

"Croix, please open the door! Please! Please!" She started the engine and peeled off. "Croix!"

He wanted to jump in his car and chase after her, but he couldn't move. He was frozen. Stuck in the experience of the moment that was occurring right before his eyes. Neighbors looked on from various directions as he stood on his front lawn looking at Croix's SUV drive farther away in the distance. His chest heaved and his body shook as he sat down on the grass crying. Everyone he loved was gone. What was left? Who was left to love him now?

He was alone. This was worse than any suspension Captain Wright could have given him. His cell phone vibrated in his pocket and he took it out, answering it without even looking.

"Croix?"

"Mr. Robinson?" the female voice asked on the other end.

"Yeah" He cleared his throat, bringing strength back to his voice, trying to mask his emotions.

"Hi, this is Dr. Hollis, your mother's oncologist."

"Hi."

"I was wondering if you could come to my office I wanted to discuss the results of your bone marrow test."

"Now is not a good time, Doctor."

"Can you stop by tomorrow around noon? It won't take long."

"I can't. I'll be at work."

"I promise it won't take long. It's very important."

"I'll see what I can do."

"Okay."

He hung up. *What the hell does she want?* he thought getting up from the lawn, heading into the house, shutting the door. His body called for a drink more than ever before. He sat down at the dining room table, a million thoughts rushing through his mind. He picked up the glass centerpiece from the table and threw it across the room, shattering it. Everything that was deemed breakable and not nailed down became a target as he began destroying the house like a human tornado.

He stopped his swing in mid-air noticing a family picture of him, Croix and the girls. He knelt down and picked up the picture. He smiled, tears falling down his face. Realizing that moment was forever gone, he sat back against the wall feeling cracked and chipped as the picture frame he held in his hands.

♦ THIRTY-SEVEN ♦

The elevator doors opened and Bradley stepped out. He walked up to Maria, Dr. Tate's secretary, checked in then sat down between two women in the waiting area. He hadn't slept a wink since Croix walked out and his mind was on instant replay. Each second, each minute of the events playing over and over, giving him a headache.

He pulled out his cell phone and tried to distract himself by checking his Facebook news feed. It wasn't working. He turned his phone off and put it back in his pocket. He sat back, leaning his head against the wall, closing his eyes trying to calm his anxiety level which was rising with every thought. He wanted to hit something to release the stress that was building, but he was glad there wasn't anything close enough for him to cause a scene.

Charlotte sat behind her desk with her head in her lap. Her world was falling apart. Keith didn't utter a word or even look in her direction when he got himself a cup of coffee this morning. She grabbed a couple of tissues from the box on her desk and wiped her eyes. She was in it. Deep, in the abyss of the wound that she had created during the first day of school in the hallway when she didn't say a word, to the boy she'd eventually marry, about the child she had borne. A wound so deep, it would take more than her three-phase therapy curriculum to heal.

She sat up and glanced at the clock. She was five minutes late for another session with Bradley. She knew she looked like a mess, grabbing the mirror from the desk drawer, refreshing her makeup. She took a deep breath…and then another trying to get her head in the right space to listen. She got up and headed for the door. She couldn't let the people who came to express their pain know that she, too, was in pain.

She smiled and opened the door. "Bradley." He opened his eyes and got up from the chair. "How are you?" she asked as he walked into the office.

"I'm okay." He sat down on the couch.

"Are you sure?" She sat down across from him. "You look like have a lot on your mind."

He sighed, feeling the emotion building within. "She left me!" He burst into tears.

Dr. Tate closed her eyes for a quick moment feeling Bradley's pain as she, too, felt like breaking down and confessing her own pain. She let her emotions pass and regrouped. "Who, Bradley? Who left you?"

"My wife. She took the girls and moved out." He broke down. "And I don't know what to do, Dr. Tate. How do I get them back?"

Dr. Tate grabbed a couple of tissue for herself and held the box to him. "Bradley." He looked up and grabbed a couple of tissues. "Take the box."

He took the box placing it next to him on the couch. "Tell me, Dr. Tate, how do I get them back?" He wiped his eyes.

"You can start by telling me what happened."

"I explained before how I stupidly tried to take my own life and my daughter witnessing it from her bedroom window."

"Yes."

"Ok. I came home yesterday from running errands and playing basketball and it was unusually quiet when I walked in and her car, my wife's, was parked outside. So, my first thought was something terrible must have happened because the girls usually come running to greet me as I walk in."

"And they didn't?"

"No, they didn't. So, I walk in and Croix is sitting on the couch with bags packed beside her. She said the girls were at her sister's house and that she couldn't do it anymore. And that's when she said, and I knew, Tia had told her." He cried. "I'm just so fucking stupid," he said wiping his eyes.

"You are not stupid, Bradley." Dr. Tate leaned forward.

"Yes, I am. What grown man decides to try and kill himself in front of his home, in front of his kid? And then swears the kid to secrecy? Me. I'm a coward."

"Listen to me, Bradley, you are not a coward. Do you know how much strength, energy it takes for a man to ask anyone for help? I commend you. You're here. You're still here. And that should mean something. I mean, you came here today. Most men would have used their wife leaving as an excuse not to come, but you didn't. And you should be very proud of yourself." She paused.

"Look at it like this, this moment is a result of the actions that were done yesterday and yesterday's moment was a result of the actions or steps taken before that." She stopped and leaned back realizing what she just spoke hit home. "Sometimes the best way to deal with the pain is to just let it be. Let it be whatever it is meant to be. Don't...," she sighed, "...try and control it. Trying to control how we are meant to feel hurts just as much as the thing that created the pain in first place." She wiped her eyes. "So, I have to just sit in it."

"Dr. Tate? Are you okay?" Bradley asked perplexed by where the conversation was headed.

"Yes, I'm fine." She cleared her throat, sitting up. "Would you mind seeing another therapist?"

"Excuse me?" Bradley answered surprised.

"I'm sorry, I didn't mean to say it like that. Please forgive me. Would you mind if I referred you to a colleague of mine?"

"But I feel comfortable talking to you."

"I know. And I'm sorry. I just have a lot of personal issues going on at the moment which will take up a lot of my time."

"Come on, Dr. Tate. Really? I just spilled my heart out to you and you're just gonna drop me? Just like that? No. I don't think so. I'm not starting over. I'm not starting from the beginning again. For me, it's either now or never. So, I guess we'll have to work around your personal problems because I'm not seeing anyone else. I'm sorry."

"Okay. I'm sorry, Bradley. I just have a lot on my mind right now." She sighed. "I can't believe I just said that." Silence begins to form between them. "Can I ask you something?"

"Certainly," he said.

"If you learned—discovered—a big, huge, enormous secret about your wife, what would you do?"

"I don't know. It depends on what the secret is."

"What if the secret was 30 years old?"

"It depends on what the secret is."

She sat back, letting out a breath. "I've shamed, embarrassed and lied to my husband. I know I shouldn't be saying this, but I don't care. When I was teenager, I became pregnant and had a child. A baby boy." She smiled. "My mother made me hide the pregnancy and the birth from everyone. My friends, extended family and the baby's father, who's now my husband and has been for the last 20 or so years." She wiped the tears as they fell. "So, that's the secret my husband discovered about me."

Bradley sat back, confused. "If you and your husband have been together since you were teenagers, how wouldn't he know you had a child together? What happened to the baby? If you don't mind me asking."

"It's fine," she said, still wiping her eyes. "My mother had him taken away."

"He's alive."

"Yes..." The tears resumed. "...he is alive. And I have no clue where he is."

"And you kept all this from your husband until recently?"

"Yes," she said wiping tears again. "So, if you discovered a huge, enormous secret about your wife, what would you do?"

"Wow. I would..." Bradley sat up. "...probably respond the same way my wife did when she learned about mine."

♦ THIRTY-EIGHT ♦

Charlotte sipped on the red wine as she sat in the living room waiting for Keith to get home. She wondered if she had gone too far by telling Bradley about her private life. She hoped he didn't tell Rodney. She didn't want any of it getting back to her sister-in-law, who she couldn't stand. Keys jingled near the front door as it opened and Keith walked in. She looked at him making eye contact. She wanted him to utter a syllable or a sound in her direction but he didn't. He just walked away.

"Keith! Keith!" Charlotte pleaded.

"What, Charlotte?! What?" he said, walking back.

"Talk to me, please."

"About what? What is there left for me to say to you?! What?!"

"Don't talk, just listen, then."

"What else is there for me to listen to from you?"

"Don't you want to know what happened?"

"No, not really. There is nothing that you need to say that will make everything alright."

"Can you please just listen to what I have to say?"

He sighed. "Fine." He put his briefcase down and walked farther into the living room. She moved on the couch hoping he would sit next to her, but he sat across from her. She sipped her wine trying to shake off the rejection.

"I'm waiting...," he said, sitting back.

She put down the wine and cleared her throat. "Ok, do you remember that summer when we were in high school and I didn't talk to anyone the whole summer?"

"Yeah."

"Well, that was the summer I gave birth. August 5, 1980, I gave birth to a handsome baby boy." She smiled.

Keith moved his eyes around, thinking. "Wait a minute, so that means you got pregnant the first time..."

"Yes."

"How could you keep something like this from me all of these years?"

"I know. I'm sorry." She wiped the tears from her eyes. "My mother made me."

"Your mother? What does she have to do with it?"

"She made me keep it a secret. The pregnancy, the birth, everything."

"How?"

"As I started gaining weight near the end of the school year, she made me wear bigger clothes to hide my stomach. And when school let out for the summer, she made me stay in the house. That's why she had told you I never wanted to see you again. She made that up to keep all of my friends and you away."

"You could've told me when we got back to school, Charlotte."

"I know. I wanted to, but I was too afraid that my mother was going to find out that I told you. You know how my mother was."

"Is."

"She would've killed me."

"Where is my son? Excuse me, our son?"

"I don't know."

"You don't know? What the hell do you mean you don't know?" he asked leaning forward.

"I don't. When I gave birth, my mother gave the baby away."

"What do you mean she gave the baby away?"

"Yeah, she gave him away. Told the nurse he was a mistake.

That we didn't want him," Charlotte said, finishing off the wine and refilling the glass. She wiped her eyes.

"Alright, let me get this straight…" He got up and began pacing the floor. "…your mother, my mother-in-law, deemed my child, my child, a mistake and gave him away?!"

"Yes. And there was nothing I could do."

Keith knocked a vase off the mantle.

"I tried to go back and get him after school started, but he was gone," said Charlotte.

Keith looked out the window taking everything that he had, and was hearing, in. "What's his name?"

"He doesn't have one."

Keith scoffed.

"My mother didn't allow me to name him."

"This just keeps getting better and better by the minute. So, you're telling me my son could be anyone. He could be the young man that delivers our mail; the homeless man out on the street; or the manager at the local grocery store."

"Yes."

"Who else knows about this?"

"You, me and my mother are the only ones who know the truth. My mother told my sisters the baby was dead."

Silence filled the room as Keith continued to process everything. "This is killing me right now, Charlotte. This is killing me."

"I know. I know," Charlotte said, getting up and walking over to him. "I am so sorry. There were so many times I wanted to tell you and every time I thought about it, this moment popped into my head." She touched him. "The thought of losing you scared me more than the thought of telling you. Please forgive me, Keith." She wrapped her arms around his waist. "Please."

He was cold, dead inside and not even the embrace of his pleading wife could warm him. He just stood there, staring out the window, not even wanting her hands touching him, but he didn't have the energy to move them away. He turned his head. "Don't mistake this moment or my silence for forgiveness because it's not." He walked away.

◆ THIRTY-NINE ◆

Chatter and the clanging dishes filled the atmosphere of Charlotte's dining room once again as everyone was gathered around the table for Sunday dinner. Keith and Charlotte weren't a part of the chatter; they remained quiet, recovering from the events of the day before.

Keith had again slept in their son Tyson's room, leaving Charlotte to sleep alone in their queen sized bed. He couldn't help but wonder what else Charlotte had forgotten to mention over the course of their togetherness. Did she ever cheat on him? Did she have any more children? Were Dana and Tyson really his children? Those questions and more gnawed at him throughout the night.

What did his son look like? Did he look like him or Charlotte? Or both of them? Was he tall like him or short? Did he play sports in high school like he did? He pondered for hours on end. Now, he sat at the dining room table trying his best to keep his composure, keeping his eyes fixated on the plate of food he was dabbling in. The mere presence of Carol caused an irritation in him that he hoped didn't rear its ugly head.

"Why are you two so quiet?" asked Tamara.

"Yeah, Keith, why you so quiet?" Kenya said sarcastically.

"I've got a lot on my mind."

"I bet you do," she said giving him a look that reassured him that she hadn't forgotten about the incident at the restaurant.

"Dana, what 'cha gonna do about that baby, honey?" Carol asked.

"Will and I talked it over with his parents and Mom…and we're gonna keep it." She smiled.

"Raising a child at your age is not all smiles and games. What 'cha gonna do about school?" asked her grandmother.

"Don't worry about it, Ma. We already talked about it. Her, Will and I got it figured out," assured Charlotte. "Along with Will's mother."

"Well, I think it's a bad idea." Carol scoffed. "A 16-year-old girl don't know nothing about raising no baby."

"And neither does a 14-year-old girl, but that didn't stop you from taking my son away, did it?" Keith snapped.

"Excuse me?" Carol said, shocked by Keith's response. She looked at Charlotte.

"Keith, you need to cool your heels when you're talking to my mother," Kenya snapped.

"Kenya, this doesn't concern you."

"When you're disrespecting and cursing at my mother…you damn right it does."

"I know everything, Ma. Charlotte told me everything. Where is my son?"

"Tyson should be away at school," said Carol calmly.

"Ma, don't act like you don't know what I'm talking about. Where is my son?"

"I don't know what you're talking about. Talk to your wife."

"Why? I told him everything I know," said Charlotte.

"Well then, leave it alone."

"No, I am not going to leave it alone." Keith banged his fist on the table. "I can't. The fact that I'm even letting you sit at my table is killing me."

"Alright, that's it, Keith!" Kenya stood up. "Say one more disrespectful thing to my mother and I swear I will leap across this table and beat your ass!"

"Why don't you mind your damn business for once, Kenya? Damn, you're just as nosy as Tamara."

"Kiss my ass, okay? At least I'm not fucking my secretary!"

The room went silent as Charlotte gave Keith a look that would have killed him if it could. "Kenya, you knew about this?"

"I was going to tell when you came over to the house that day, but…"

Charlotte slapped him. "You son of a bitch! That's why you've been working those late nights three-times-a-week. How long have you been screwin' her?!"

"That's not relevant right now," tried Keith.

"What the fuck you mean it's not relevant? The shit is very gotdamn relevant! How long, Keith!" She slapped him again. "How long?!"

"I know you don't think me sleeping with my secretary trumps me finding out I have a 30-year-old son!"

"Yes, the hell it does!"

"When was the last time we had sex, Charlotte? Huh?! When was the last time? What, two, maybe, three years ago! When was the last time we did something together? If you're not doing something for the kids or trying to please your fuckin' mother, you're always helping or taking on new patients! I love my kids, but I'm tired of competing with them and your patients for your gotdamn attention, Charlotte! I am! I'm done! I've been doing it for far too long."

"Well, if you're done, get the fuck out!"

"I'm not going anywhere. I want to know where my son is."

"What is this son you keep referring to, Keith?" asked Tamara.

"Ask your mother and Charlotte, they know. This entire family is just one big black pot of goddamn secrets."

The room went quiet as Kenya and Tamara looked back and forth between their mother and sister.

"Ma? Charlotte?" Kenya said. "Is there something you want to tell us?"

Charlotte sighed, knowing it was time for her sisters and everyone else to know the truth. "Remember when I was pregnant when I was 14."

"Yeah, the baby died," said Kenya.

"Well, that's not true."

"Marvin, can you take me home? I'm ready to go home,"

said Carol.

"Marvin, keep your ass right there. Don't you move," said Charlotte. "Everybody needs to hear this. I've been holding onto this for far too long." She took a deep breath. "The baby I had when I was 14 did not die. He's alive."

The room went silent again. Kenya sat back down in disbelief. "What? Wait a minute, I can't right now, I just can't. I can't believe what I'm hearing. The baby you had all that time ago is alive...?"

"Yes."

"Well, why did you and Mama say that the baby was dead when you came home from the hospital?"

"Because Mama gave the baby away," Charlotte said, looking her mother straight in the eyes.

"What!" shouted Tamara.

"Yeah, Mama had the doctor and the nurse take the baby from me. And she told me not to tell anybody. Not even Keith."

"Excuse me." Kenya got up from the table and hurried out of the room.

"If I didn't do what I did, you wouldn't have the life you have now. You wouldn't have the career or the lifestyle you have right now. You would've ended up like those other girls. On welfare, slumming around those damn projects if weren't for what I did," said Carol.

"You have been treating me like shit. Like I don't matter. Like my family doesn't matter," shouted Charlotte. "You embarrass me every chance you get. Reminding me how much I shamed you and our family. How big of a disgrace I was. I've been living in hell for the last 30 years because of you! You!"

"Don't you dare blame me for you not telling your husband! You had numerous opportunities after that to tell your husband the damn truth!"

"You had no idea what it felt like to have your child taken away from you! None!"

Carol grabbed her glass and threw it, just missing Charlotte's head, taking everybody aback. "Don't you dare stand there and tell me I don't know what's like it, okay. You don't know my story, little girl. You don't. I am still your mother and

I'll be damned if I stand here and take this shit from you any longer." The high emotion made her tremble as grabbed her purse and walked out.

"Mama," said Tamara as she watched her mother walk out.

"Let her go. Just let her go," said Charlotte.

"What the hell is going on in here?" Kenya said rushing back in after trying to calm herself down in the bathroom. "Where's Ma?"

"She left," said Charlotte.

"No, I don't think so. She's not just going to walk away without explaining herself," Kenya said fired up.

"Ken, stop. Don't. Just…let her go. The truth is finally out now. Just let her be."

Carol's body was still trembling as she took a seat on the back deck in the quietness of the sunny day. She was embarrassed, ashamed and hurt as she took a piece of butterscotch candy from her purse trying to curb the craving of a pall mall. It had been over 20 years since she last lit and held a cigarette between her lips, but her body was definitely yearning for one. She closed her eyes and began praying. "Lord, please forgive me for all that I have done. I did what I thought was right. And I ask that you please forgive me. I am so sorry." She just lowered her head and cried.

◆ FORTY ◆

Richmond, Virginia • May 1954

"Carol, put the dry linen in my room and I'll fold 'em later," her mother Mae-Ann shouted as she sat on the back porch snapping peas with her sister Ellen.

"What are you feeding that 'chile?" asked Aunt Ellen. "She seems like she's gaining weight by the minute."

"I'm telling you, she's eating me out of house and home. Harold! Maxine! Wash up for dinner!" shouted Mae-Ann. Harold, 10, and Maxine, 8, continued to run around not paying her any mind. "Carol, tell your brother and sister to get washed up for dinner!"

"Harold! Maxine! Get washed up for dinner now!" Carol shouted as she took the rest of the linen down from the line and headed for the house. Her hurting feet made her pace to the house slower than usual. The weight she had gained over the last five months made her teenage body ache in places it hadn't before. Her brother and sister darted past her, almost knocking her down, making their way into the house.

"Y'all two stop running before y'all hurt yourselves or I'll whoop your asses!" shouted Mae-Ann. At 5-foot-9 with a strong backhand, she was a woman of her word and not to be messed around with. She was tough. She didn't take mess from nobody, not even her husband, and especially not her children.

Carol made her way into her mother's bedroom and dumped the linens onto the bed. She left the basket at the foot of the bed. She touched her stomach as an unfamiliar pain travelled through. She straightened up and started out of the room. Another sharp pain. She made it to the bathroom and quickly shut the door. She lifted her shirt and looked at her protruding belly, which she had managed to hide successfully with clothes too big for her size. She had tried everything she could think of to get rid of it. Falling down stairs, hitting herself, everything, and yet it continued to grow.

She touched her stomach. It blended perfectly with the areas of thickness her weight gain had caused. However, she knew sooner or later she would have to explain its largeness, but hoped the time would never come. Another pain came, harder, much harder than the previous two. So much so that she had to take a seat on the toilet. Something was wrong. Maxine burst into the bathroom, startling Carol. She quickly pulled her shirt down. "Get out of here!"

"What's wrong with you?" Maxine asked with a curious look on her face.

"Nothing! Get out of here!"

"Mama! Auntie Ellen! There's something wrong with Carol!" Maxine shouted running away. Carol got up and made towards the bathroom door as her mother and aunt arrived.

"What's wrong, baby?" asked her mother.

"My stomach is hurting."

"Ellen, call 911."

Ellen dialed 9-1-1 and Mae-Ann walked Carol over to the couch, but she refused to sit down, knowing if she did, it would reveal her shame. "I'll stand," she said.

"The ambulance is on its way," Ellen relayed to the group from the kitchen doorway.

The pain began to subside as Carol paced around the room. She relaxed a little, relieved she wouldn't draw any further suspicion from her aunt and her mother.

"The pain is going away." She breathed easy, praying in the back of her mind. "See, the pain is gone now."

"I don't care. You're still going to the hospital," said Mae-Ann.

The station-wagon ambulance pulled up with its flashing lights and wailing siren. Ellen opened the door and the two paramedics walked in. "Where's the patient?" one of them asked.

"She's right there," said Ellen.

"I had a pain in my stomach, but it's gone." Carol smiled.

"You're going to the hospital," said her mother.

Another pain shot through Carol's stomach which she tried to play off, even though her face was saying otherwise.

"See, it's not gone," insisted her mother. "Can you take her out, please? We'll follow you in my car. Thank you."

"Come on, young lady," said the paramedic as he helped Carol outside.

"Maxine and Harold, put your sneakers back on and let's go."

Carol got into the ambulance with one of the paramedics as the other shut the door and walked around to the driver's side. They drove off, with Mae-Ann, Ellen and the kids not far behind.

At the hospital, Carol sat on the bed waiting for the doctor to come in. She was trembling with nervousness, knowing her secret was going to be revealed when the doctor walked into the room. She was glad her mother and family waited just beyond the door in the hall. The doctor walked in and closed the door. Carol began rubbing her legs, terrified.

"Hi, I'm Doctor Novak." He pulled over a stool and sat down beside her and smiled. "I hear you've been having stomach pains."

Carol nodded in agreement.

"Okay. Lie down and let me take a look at you." He put on a pair of gloves, lifted her shirt and gently touched her stomach. "Do you feel any pain?"

Carol shook her head "no."

"How about here?" he asked, touching another area of her stomach.

"No."

"Okay, you can sit up." Carol sat up as the doctor took off

the gloves, throwing them away. "Either that's the biggest tumor I've seen or you're pregnant."

Carol broke down. The shame, the guilt, the deceit was finally over. The doctor handed her some tissues. "Here." She took them and held them in her hand, letting the raging river of tears fall where they may. "Your mother doesn't know, does she?"

"No."

"Well, we're gonna have to tell her, you know that."

"Please don't tell her. Please," Carol cried.

"We have to. If something happens to you or the baby while you're at home, she's going to find out."

"Can you tell her?"

"Sure." The doctor waited a few minutes giving Carol time to gather her composure. He opened the door. "Mrs. Watson…"

Tears streamed down Carol's young cheeks, glancing occasionally at her mother from the backseat. She knew her ass was headed for a trouble that God himself wouldn't be able to save her from. Mae-Ann was quietly steaming on the ride home from the hospital. She was only this quiet when she was beyond pissed. She still couldn't believe them, the words that flowed from in-between the doctor's lips. She stood there staring at her oldest daughter, the anger inside moving up her spine to the top of her head like water in a kettle reaching its boiling point.

"Is she okay to go home?" Mae-Ann had asked the doctor.

"Yeah, she can go home. But if it happens again, just bring her back in."

"Will…do," said Mae-Anne, looking back at Carol.

When Mae-Anne pulled into the driveway of the house, everyone quietly got out and walked inside. She began striking Carol as soon as she walked in. The keys stinging Carol's back with each hit. Ellen and the kids sat on the couch quietly as Carol screamed with each strike, her mother brought forth now with the bottom of the broom across her back. Carol held her stomach as they made their way towards her room, the broom coming down harder and harder. Carol fell stomach first onto her bed as the beating continued.

CRACK! Carol let out a horrendous scream, one that made her Aunt Ellen jump from the couch and head back there. "That's it."

Carol just knew her back had just been broken, hearing the breaking of the broom. Her mother raised the broken broom to strike again, but Ellen jumped in.

"Mae, stop!" Ellen shouted, grabbing her arm. "That's it! Enough! You tryin' to kill this 'chile? Not to mention the baby?"

"I don't give a damn about her or that damn baby!"

"Now, Mae, you don't mean that!"

"Like hell I do!" Mae-Anne stepped back and slammed the broken broom down. "You better be glad your Aunt was here to save yo' black ass!" she shouted, trying to catch her breath. "You have forever shamed this family! And you are no longer a daughter of mine!"

"Mae, just go outside! And cool off! I got her."

"You better!" Mae-Anne walked away. Ellen closed the door.

Pain filled Carol's young body as the tears kept flowing and she moved around on the bed trying to sit up. "Stop cryin', baby. Stop cryin'," Ellen said rubbing her face. "It's okay. Everything's gonna be alright." She held her. "We told you about going out here and being fast. Hangin' around with these fast girls, didn't we?" She slapped her hip. "I'm very disappointed in you. Very disappointed, but you'll soon learn your lesson." She kissed her on the top of her head and got up. Carol's crying had slowed. Ellen opened the door. "Be glad you weren't my daughter, 'cause I would've hung yo' black ass from that tree out back."

Ellen closed the door leaving Carol in her own pool of tears.

◆ FORTY-ONE ◆

"Croix, please call me." Bradley sighed, hanging up the phone. He stood outside the police cruiser waiting for Rodney to return with his medium regular coffee from the donut shop. He was worn. He hadn't slept a wink since Croix walked out the door and it was written all over his face. He was ragged. Like he hadn't showered in days even though he had.

He thought about calling Croix again as he had been every minute of every hour it seemed since she left. *Never mind,* he thought, putting the phone back in his pocket. He knew he'd get the same thing he had been: her voicemail. Rodney came out of the donut shop with two coffees in his hands.

"Here. You look like shit." Bradley took the coffee and didn't say anything. "You're welcome."

"Thanks," Bradley responded as he walked over to the passenger side. The chatter over the radio broke the silence as Rodney opened the driver's side door and they got in. Since the two had met on the first day of the academy, this was the worst Rodney had ever seen his partner. He started the car and they drove off. He looked over at him, knowing Bradley wasn't in any mood to talk further about Croix or Tia, but he knew the longer Bradley kept quiet the further down he was going.

"Did she say how long she and the girls would be gone?"

"No." Bradley sipped on his coffee and stared out the

173

window hoping for no more questions.

"What are you gonna do?" asked Rodney.

"I don't know, man. Continue seeing your aunt, I guess. That's all I can do right now. There's nothing more I can do. I mean she's not answering my calls or my texts."

"Can you blame her?" Rodney slowed down and stopped at a red light. "B, how many times have I told you if you need to talk, call me?"

"Yeah, I know. I just need to deal with it on my own."

"And you thought blowing your brains out was the only way to deal with it?" The traffic light turned green and Rodney drove on. "You're staying with me tonight. I need to keep an eye on you."

"I'm good." Bradley sipped his coffee. "I don't need a babysitter. I can get through this. I have to – for my girls. Trust me, I won't do anything like that ever again. That's why I haven't taken a drink since that night." He sipped again. "Besides, I don't need to hear you and the broad of the week hanging from the ceiling and shit, or whatever it is you do." He laughed sipping his coffee. The joy of laughter followed by the warmth and richness of the coffee made him feel good. If only for a moment.

"Whatever." Bradley smiled as he turned into the driveway of the Ambulatory Care Center of the Boston Medical Center and pulled over.

"Give me about 15 minutes," Bradley said, putting his coffee in the cup holder and getting out.

"Okay." Rodney pushed the button on the radio. "104 to base…"

Go ahead 104… The female voiced over the radio.

"Requesting a code 10."

Code 10 granted, sir. Enjoy.

Bradley turned down his radio as he entered the hospital and quickly made his way onto a closing elevator and pressed the fifth floor. The elevator doors closed and it moved swiftly, buzzing as it passed each floor, slowly stopping as it reached the fifth floor. The doors opened and he stepped out. He passed a small gathering of doctors and interns as he walked the long corridor towards his mother's doctor's office. *She couldn't tell me I wasn't a match over the phone. She really wanted me to come down here for this.* He walked past the waiting area and up to one of the three secretaries checking patients in.

"Hi, my name is Bradley Robinson. I'm here to see Dr. Irene Hollis."

"Oh yeah. She's expecting you. I'll let you in." The woman got up from her desk and walked over to the door, scanning her ID, and Bradley walked in.

"Thank you."

"You're welcome."

"Hi," Dr. Hollis said, walking in his direction. "I was just about to check to see if you were here yet. Have you been waiting long?"

"I just got here."

"How are you? How is everything?" she asked, walking back towards her office.

"Everything is good."

"Good. We can talk right in here," she said, letting him go in first. She shut the door as he sat down. "Okay. As you know, your mother's cancer has returned and it is more aggressive than it was before. We're hoping a bone marrow transplant will help fight it."

"Okay."

"I'm sorry to say that you are not a match, but we do have her on the transplant list and we are testing other family members and friends to see if they match up."

"Okay. Is that all?"

"Well, that's not my main reason for calling you here. Well, it's part of the reason. The reason I called you here is..." She let out a breath trying to think of an appropriate approach to what she was about to say. "How well do you know your parents?"

"Excuse me?" Bradley said surprised by the question. "Doctor, if there's something you need to say just come out and say it."

Bradley got back in the police cruiser and slammed the door, his mind racing with a million and one thought about what his mother's doctor just told him. Is it true? Is what she said absolutely the truth? Was everything he had ever known about his life a complete lie?

"Is everything okay?" Rodney asked.

"Just drive."

Rodney started the engine and they left. Every person, every building, every tree, every bird, even the clouds felt strange, looked different to Bradley as he stared out of the passenger side window. His anger level rising with every second. He banged his fist repeatedly against the dashboard, scaring Rodney, who quickly pulled the car over.

"Yo, B, what the hell is going on?"

"Nothing. I'm cool. Just drive."

"Really? What's really going on? Is it your mother? I know you told me the cancer is back…is it worse than they thought?"

Bradley sighed, knowing Rodney wasn't going to let up on the questioning. "I'm not a bone marrow match for my mother."

"Aw man. I'm sorry. What are they going to do?"

"They are going to keep her on the list and keeping searching. Now, can you drive please?"

Radio static. *Unit-104, the female voice emanated from the radio.*

"1-0-4…," Bradley responded.

Yeah, could you guys head over to 111 Harold St? There is a report of family trouble. Kid said his dad is beating his mom.

"1-0-4 responding," Bradley responded.

"Isn't that your brother's house?"

"Yeah." Bradley sighed, knowing what he was getting himself into.

Rodney turned on the sirens and floored the gas pedal. Bradley stared out of the window as Rodney made quick turns and sped through streets, his mind still on what Dr. Hollis had told him back in her office.

* * *

Rodney hit the switch turning off the sirens as they approached the front of Eddie Jr.'s house. He opened the door and bolted up the stairs to the front door. He heard his sister-in-law Natalie screaming and niece and nephew crying. He banged on the door. "Bailey! Dominique! Open the door!" He banged on the door repeatedly. "Bailey! Bai—"

His nephew opened the door, crying. Eddie Jr. pushed his bloody, bruised wife onto the couch and raised his hand to assault her again and Bradley grabbed him.

"Unit-104 to base, we're going to need medical assistance here at 111 Harold," Rodney spoke into his radio as he rushed over to assist Natalie, crying and battered on the couch.

Bradley pushed his brother and he swung at him, missing. Bradley gave him a quick jab to the stomach and the face and he fell to the floor. Bradley turned him on his stomach and handcuffed him, then picked him up and sat him in a chair.

"So, you takin' me to jail now, Officer Dolittle?" Junior smirked.

"Shut up, you fuckin' punk. You're just like Dad! Just like him!"

"You think you better than me because you wear that stupid little uniform! You ain't better than me! You ain't shit! Mama's bitch!"

"I said, shut up!" Bradley punched him.

"Yeah, that's right. Go ahead, beat my ass like Mama used to beat yours."

"Shut up! Shut up! Shut up!" Bradley said, punching him repeatedly.

"Bradley!" Rodney ran over and pulled Bradley off his brother. "What the fuck is your problem? Are you trying to get yourself fired?"

Bradley didn't say a word as he tried to catch his breath, keeping his eyes on his brother.

"See, you're no better than me, little brother."

"I am not your brother!"

Bradley looked at Rodney who was staring back at him in

disbelief, and walked outside, passing the Paramedics as they entered.

"I don't need no damn doctor! I'm fine!" Junior shouted as the paramedic moved his head as she tried to clean his face.

Bradley walked out to the sidewalk. He paced back and forth, boiling with rage. He kicked the cruiser, denting the door. He walked a little ways down the street and sat down on the curb. The anger making his body tremble. He put his arms across his knees, resting his head against his hands. Croix and the girls were the last things on his mind. He was done. He'd had enough. He wanted out, of everything. His life...his family...his career. He wanted more than a drink. The thought of ending it for good at this moment seemed like the appropriate decision.

What did he have to lose? His girls? At the rate he was going with Croix, he felt like he was already losing them. He let out a breath and looked up to the partially clouded sky as if waiting for a sign from Jesus himself. He closed his eyes, they filled with tears. He watched from a distance as Rodney escorted his handcuffed brother from the house to the police cruiser. If what Dr. Hollis had told him had been true and everything about his life was a lie...he wanted answers...and he wanted them now.

♦ FORTY-TWO ♦

The balanced bass and treble of the music could be heard from the backyard of Eddie Sr.'s and Barbara's modest one-family house as Bradley pulled up. The street was full of cars belonging to Barbara's co-workers and friends. She was all smiles and laughter as she walked around the backyard conversing with those who came to celebrate her retirement.

Bradley got out of the car and slammed the door. Still dressed in his uniform, he had left the station without saying anything to Rodney. He made his way to the backyard walking fast in a huff. He made a beeline to his mother, not even acknowledging his cousin who spoke to him as he walked by.

"Hey, you made it," Barbara smiled.

"I need to talk to you right now," Bradley said sternly.

"Right now?"

"Right now." He started towards the house walking past his father, who was working the grill, without speaking.

"I'll be right back," Barbara said, following Bradley.

"What's wrong with him?" asked Eddie Sr., noticing Barbara walking by.

"Who knows." She walked up the deck stairs and into the house and was greeted by her nephew, Jermaine, her sister's son.

"Hey Auntie, where did you want the ice?"

"In that blue cooler near the table where the food is."

"Okay." Jermaine stepped out closing the sliding door behind him.

Barbara walked into the living room where Bradley was looking out the window, anxious. She searched for a hint of calm but it was nowhere to be found. She knew her day of reckoning had arrived.

"What is so damn important that you're pulling me away from my own retirement party?"

"I visited Dr. Hollis's office," he said, turning around.

"The bone marrow test. Yeah, I know, you told me you went weeks ago."

"Well, I got the results today."

"You did. Are you a match?"

"No, I am not a match because we are not related."

"Excuse me? What are you talking about?" Barbara felt her heart drop. She knew exactly what he was talking about. "Of course, we're related. You're my son."

"According to the blood they drew for the bone marrow test, we are not! So, I suggest you start talking, right now! Was I adopted? Am I orphan? Am I a foster child? What!"

"Can we not talk about this right now? Can we talk about this some other time?"

"There is no better time than the present moment, Barbara."

She sighed. "You were adopted. I'm sorry. I didn't want you to find out like this."

Bradley scoffed. "And you weren't ever going to tell me?" he shouted moving around. "My whole life has been a lie! For 30 motherfuckin' years, my entire life has been a lie!"

"No, it hasn't. You are my son. I love you," Barbara said with tears in her eyes.

"You do, huh! Really?! So you beating the shit out of me every time Dad beat your ass was love? Huh?" he shouted getting closer to her, then moving away.

"I'm sorry. I am so sorry."

She gasped as he grabbed her face. "I used to say that every time you beat me, but it didn't mean shit to you. Why do you think you saying it now would mean anything to me?!" He pushed her away and she fell back on the couch. "You are a lying piece of shit! And I don't ever want to see or hear from you ever again! You are no better than Dad...Edward...was!" He walked out.

"Bradley! Bradley!" she shouted as she got up from the couch, chasing after him.

He stormed out of the house and down the stairs.

"There you two are," said Eddie, Sr. as he came to the doorway. "I was beginning to worry..." His speech slowed noticing the unfamiliar look on his son's face.

"Bradley! Bradley!" she shouted as she rushed down the stairs.

"What's wrong, son?" asked Eddie.

"I am not your son!" Bradley shouted, drawing everyone's attention. He walked away.

"What?! What the hell is going on?"

"Ask her!" He looked up at her. He turned to leave and noticed Croix and the girls looking along with everyone else. "Sorry." He walked out to his car.

"Bradley! Bradley!" shouted Eddie, but Bradley kept on walking. "What the hell happened in there?"

Barbara wiped her eyes. "Everything's fine. We just had a little disagreement, that's all." She smiled. "Carry on. Back to the party."

Everyone slowly began to socialize again as Barbara made her way over to Croix and the girls. "Hey, how's Grandma's babies?" She hugged them. "Hi, Croix."

"Hey, Ma." Croix knew, hugging her, that whatever went on inside the house had shaken Bradley to his core.

Bradley got into the car and slammed the door. He beat his hand against the steering wheel in a fit of rage. He turned on the engine and sped off.

"Good seeing you, too." Barbara waved good-bye to the last few guests leaving the retirement party. Eddie turned the music off.

"I had a great time. Didn't you?" she said walking over to

him.

"Yeah. So, what the hell happened between you and Bradley?"

She sighed. "I don't want to talk about it, Eddie," she said, grabbing pans of left-over food and going up the stairs.

"Barbara…," he said, not too far behind with a couple of pans himself.

"We can talk about it some other time."

"No, we're gonna talk about it now," Eddie said, following her into the house and putting the pans on the counter.

Barbara marched back outside and down the stairs, he still behind her.

"Whenever the hell went on in here must not have been too great because he had a look in his eyes I never seen before."

Barbara didn't say anything, making a small collection of things to carry back in the house. She headed back inside.

"Barbara, the boy looked me in the eyes and said in front of everyone he's not my son! I demand to know what the hell is going on!"

Barbara sighed, dropping her head. "Drop it, Ed."

"I'm not going to drop it, Barbara."

"Ed…just…leave it alone, okay?" she said, wiping her eyes.

"No, I'm not going to leave it alone."

She closed her eyes causing more tears to stream. *Just tell him.* She sighed. "Fine then, Eddie. I'll tell you." She picked up a knife from the sink and turned around, facing him.

Eddie became nervous. "Barbara, what's the knife for?"

"Because you're not going to like what I have to say."

"Well, what is it that you have to say that requires you to hold a knife?" he asked uneasy.

She sighed, already feeling the pain. "Do you remember the day I gave birth to Bradley?"

"Yeah."

"Well, that whole day is a complete lie…"

♦ FORTY-THREE ♦

Bradley drank down the rest of the beer that was in the bottle and asked for another as he sat at the bar of Louie's Tavern. It had been a couple of hours since he arrived and he was well on his way to drinking until he forgot what his mind had been constantly playing over and over. The bartender popped the cap and gave him another bottle. "Thanks."

He had driven around for hours after leaving his parents' house trying digest everything he had been told by from the mouth of the woman whom he had known to be his mother. He wondered how much more he could take. The suspension, Croix taking the girls and leaving and now this. Just when he thought he was putting himself back together with therapy, pieces were still continuing to break.

He pulled into an empty space outside of Louie's Tavern and walked in, taking a seat at the bar. Now, hours later and ten or so beers in, his mind had begun to ease the stress it was causing itself. He finished a beer and asked for another. The bartender popped the cap off another and gave it to him.

"Excuse me, is anyone sitting here?" asked the female voice.

"No, there is..." Bradley started turning. "Oh, Dr. Tate."

"Bradley, how are you?" she asked, sitting down.

He shrugged his shoulders. "What are you doing here?"

"I just felt like having a drink or two."

"What are you having, miss?" asked the bartender.

"A glass of chardonnay. Thank you." She placed her purse in her lap. "So, what's on your mind that's got you here, Bradley? I thought we had stopped this."

He took a swig of beer. "Life...or at least the one I'm living."

"Tell me what happened. What's going on?" The bartender sat the glass of wine in front of her. "Thanks."

"I just found out I was adopted." He took a swig of beer. "I found out about it when I got my bone marrow tested for my mother, I mean Barbara."

"Bone marrow test?"

"Yeah, my mother—Barbara—has cancer. Or should I say it has returned."

"Have you spoken with your mother about it? About what you had found out?"

Bradley scoffed. "Oh yeah I did." He took another swig. "And it didn't go too well. I just feel like my whole life has been a lie, Dr. Tate. Just one big lie, you know? And the sad thing is, she wasn't even going to tell me. I found out from her doctor that we're not related. She didn't have the balls to tell me herself. What type of shit is that?"

"Maybe she didn't know how to tell you."

"'Hey, Bradley, your father and I have something to tell you...you were adopted.' I mean how hard is that, really, Dr. Tate, to say to your son that he was adopted?" He finished off his beer. "My whole life, Dr. Tate, they kept this from me and they expect me to be happy about it. I don't think so. Let me get another, man."

Seeing that he was three sheets to the wind, she motioned the bartender to cut him off.

"This is your last one, buddy," said the bartender. Bradley waved him off. He popped another cap and sat the bottle in front of Bradley.

"So, how's your life going, Dr. Tate? How's everything with your husband?"

"We're barely speaking right now," she said giving a quick smile, sipping her wine.

"That's good. You're not my mother, are you?"

"Um, no. I don't think so." She laughed.

"Just checking."

"How's everything with your wife, Croix is it?"

"Yeah. I've been calling her, but she's still not answering my calls or text messages. My whole world is just a fuckin' mess."

"Well, find the message."

"Huh?"

"In all mess, there is a message and it's up to us to find out what it is."

"Then what's mine? That nobody wants me?" He scoffed and finished his beer.

"I don't believe so. Somebody wants you."

"Who? You?" he said looking at her. "Have you ever crossed that line, Dr. Tate? That line when you and a patient have gone beyond the limitations of your profession."

"Nope." She finished her wine. "And I'm not going to start now. Let me take you home," she said, getting up and giving the bartender her credit card. "Put it all on my card." He slid it through the card reader, gave it back to her and she signed the receipt.

"I'm okay. I drove. I don't need a ride. I have my car," Bradley said, stumbling back as he got up.

"Whoa, whoa, whoa!" Charlotte said catching him. "Ok, that's it. I'm driving you home. Come on." She wrapped his arm around her shoulder and walked him out.

"Does this count as a session?"

"Just come on."

"Hey. Hey. What's your address?" Charlotte asked a passed out Bradley, keeping her eyes on the road. She nudged him trying to wake him up. "Bradley?" There was no use. He was out completely. She sighed. Where could she take him? *Forget it, I'll just take him home.* She knew she was way over the boundary of doctor-patient privilege, but what else could she do? She couldn't risk someone else getting hurt because of him driving drunk. Keith was going to be pissed, but she wouldn't have done this for any other patient. Bradley was a good guy at heart, she sensed that when he first walked into her office, and knew he wouldn't do anything stupid.

She turned on the radio and the mellow sounds of jazz emanated from the speakers. She glanced over at Bradley, his head against the window snoring, wondering how her son's life was. Was it as complicated and complex as Bradley's? Or was he living the life of a Cosby Show episode? *How do I let him go?* She was tired of wondering about him and wished there was a way she could find some closure with it. Bradley made a faint sound moving slightly and right then she knew where her closure would come from.

* * *

Rodney drove the night streets, frantic, looking for Bradley. He picked up his phone and dialed Bradley's number as he had for the past two hours, his call going to voicemail once again. "Bradley, where the fuck are you?"

His cell phone rang. It was Croix. Even though, she had separated herself from Bradley, the look she noticed in her husband's eyes while at his parents' house, concerned her as much as Rodney witnessing him beat his fist again the dashboard. He put her on speakerphone.

"Did you find him yet?" she spoke.

"No, not yet."

"Did you try the Carver?"

"They're closed."

"Where can he be?"

"I don't know. I don't have a clue."

"I'm worried about him, Rod. Whatever happened in that house with his mother had him very angry. I've never seen him that angry before, ever."

"Yeah, I know. He was pretty pissed when we left the hospital earlier, too."

"I hope he didn't…"

"Don't say it. Let's not go there. He's fine. We'll find him. Just call me if you find him, or I'll call you if I do."

"Okay."
"Bye."
"Bye."

* * *

Charlotte pulled into the driveway and dialed Keith's cell. "Please answer the phone."

"What?" he answered, his tone not welcoming.

"Hey, can you come outside? I need your help with something."

Keith hung up without saying another word. A few minutes later the front door opened and he stepped outside.

"Could you come here, please?" she asked waving him over, stepping out of the car.

He walked over as Charlotte opened the passenger-side door, catching Bradley as he almost fell out.

"Who is he?"

"One of my patients."

"What? And you brought him here? Unbelievable."

"Well, I had nowhere else to take him! Help me get him in the house."

Keith grabbed Bradley's arm and lifted him out of the car, wrapping his arm around his shoulders. Charlotte closed and locked the car. Keith made his way into the house with Bradley and bee-lined right to the couch, laying him down. "He's heavy."

"You're just getting old," Charlotte said putting her purse down.

"Funny. So, where did you find him?"

"I went to get a drink and he was there in the bar. He's Rodney's friend."

"Oh, that's him."

"Yeah."

"And you couldn't take him some other place? Like Rodney's house."

"I don't know where Rodney lives," said Charlotte.

"Well, you could've asked, Mother Teresa."

"Oh shut up."

"If anything goes missing, I'm calling the cops," Keith said walking upstairs.

"He is a cop."

"Good. Then the 9-1-1 call will be short and sweet."

Keith shut the door to their son's room as Charlotte watched Bradley sleep for a few moments longer. She shut off the light and headed upstairs.

✦ FORTY-FOUR ✦

Charlotte tossed and turned trying to get herself to sleep. She stopped moving and huffed as she looked up at the ceiling. The digital clock on her nightstand read 1:30 a.m. She was usually in a deep sleep by this time. She pulled back the covers and got out of bed, putting on her house shoes and her robe and headed downstairs. Quietly, she made it down to the first floor and peeked into the living room. Bradley was still fast asleep. She walked into her office and turned on the light. She sat behind the desk and let out a breath.

She knew her sleeplessness wasn't because of Bradley sleeping in the next room. The time had come for her to let go and she knew it. She felt it deep within her soul, it was time to release the hope, the dream of one day ever finding her son. For a second, she thought about calling her mother to see if there was any further information she could get out of her, but quickly realized it wasn't worth it. No more arguing. No more living in the past. She glanced at the family picture of her, Keith and kids on her desk and picked it up. She smiled remembering the day like it was yesterday.

"Keith, you're gonna miss the picture!" a younger Charlotte said with 2-year-old Dana and 5-year-old Tyson sitting between her legs.

"No, I'm not," Keith said, positioning the Polaroid camera

and setting the timer. "There," he said rushing back over, sitting down beside Charlotte, grabbing Dana and placing her between his legs. The camera beeped, beeped, beeped... "Say cheese!" They smiled as the camera flashed, freezing the beautiful moment in the backyard that Charlotte now held in her hands. She thought about how her long-lost son would fit into her family now if she found him. Would Dana and Tyson accept him as a brother? Would her mother ever accept him as her grandchild?

She put the picture down and leaned back in the chair, pondering what her life might have been like if her mother had allowed her to keep him. Would she have graduated from high school? Or gone to college? Would she have the career she has now or live where she lives now? The thoughts made her stomach feel uneasy.

She took a deep breath trying to clear her mind. She grabbed a yellow pad from the drawer and a pen from the cup on her desk. *No pondering. No more questions. No more ifs, ands or buts, about it. Just let it go.* She took another deep breath and began writing:

Dear Son,

I can't believe it's been over 30 years since the day you were born. It still seems like yesterday to me. I thought about you almost every day over all of these years. I can still feel the touch of your tiny hands when you were a baby. You were so soft and delicate and precious. The cutest of all the babies born that day. I was only allowed to hold you for five minutes, but that was best, sweetest five minutes of my entire life. A moment I'll never forget.

I hope you're doing well. You're probably married now with children of your own. Your brother Tyson is doing great in Georgia at Clark Atlanta University. He joined the football team, which your father is happy about. Your sister Dana is doing great in school. She's in the honor society, just like your mother was. She is pregnant and she has decided to keep the baby. I'm proud of her. I refuse to be the way my mother (your grandmother) was with me, to her. Refuse. I will be better.

Your father knows about you. Finally. He didn't find out in the greatest of ways. He overheard me talking with your sister through my cell phone. And it was ugly when he got home. Actually, it's been ugly for quite some time since the truth about you came out to everyone else in the family. I haven't spoken to your grandmother since the last Sunday dinner. I think she deserves the silent treatment from the family for a while. Well, at least from your Aunt Kenya and I. Your Aunt Tamara can only go two days max without speaking to her. She's too much of a gossip queen to go any longer. But we are dealing with it in our own way. Your father and I are working it out.

You know, I prayed every day for that day when I would get to see and touch your handsome brown face. Something keeps telling me to hang on to the hope that day will come to pass, but I can't any longer. I've been holding on for far too long and the time has come for me to finally let go. I began writing these letters so you wouldn't miss a day of my life, even though I've been missing every day of yours. I never kept a journal because these letters to you over these past 30 years have been my journal. And this here shall be my last entry. These letters have been where I've expressed my tears, my smiles and my fears and I have to say that I enjoyed writing every single one of them. I will never, ever forget you. I will forever love and miss you with all my heart.

Your Mother,
Charlotte Marissa Watson-Tate

She put down the pen and covered her face with her hands, bursting into tears as she relived every second, minute, hour of their short, sweet history. She was letting go. Letting go of what was, what might have been and what wasn't ever going to be.

* * *

Bradley slowly opened his eyes and saw nothing but the color tan. He moaned, moving further, and looked around. The place was beautiful, clean, but wasn't his. "What the hell...?" He sat up, but was quickly and painfully greeted with a migraine that out-throbbed previous ones.

"You're awake," said Charlotte, walking in.

"Dr. Tate..." Bradley rubbing his temple. "...where am I?"

"You're at my house. Here's some tea to help you with the hangover."

"Thank you," he said, taking the cup and a sip. He put it down on the coffee table. "How did I end up here?"

"You were too intoxicated to drive and I didn't know your address so I brought you here." She sat down across from him.

"How long was I out?"

"All night."

"I am so sorry if I caused you or your husband any trouble with my stupidity. Let me get out of your hair," he said, trying to get up.

"No, sit and have your tea. You weren't any trouble to us last night. Besides, my husband was the one who brought you in from the car."

Bradley took another sip of the hot tea and looked around admiring her home. "You have a lovely home, Dr. Tate."

"Thank you. Is your hangover starting to wear off?"

"Slowly. Very slowly. Where is your husband?"

"Left for work already. He wanted to say hello, but you were still out."

"Is that you two over there?" Bradley asked, noticing the portrait above the fireplace.

"Yeah, that was us the day we got married. One of the happiest days of my life."

"One of...?" Bradley sipped some more tea.

"Yeah, the other days were when my kids were born. All three of them." She smiled. "I want to help you, Bradley."

"Help me to what?"

"Find your birth parents."

"I told you about that."

"Yeah, last night while at the bar. You don't remember?"

Bradley remained silent sipping more tea, not remembering too much from the night before. "I appreciate the gesture, Dr. Tate, but I don't know if I even want to go that far right now. I'm still trying to process everything. I just got back to work recently. My wife still isn't speaking to me. I just have a lot of mess to clean up and make right before I even think about that right now."

"I understand."

"Why you were so willing to help me do that anyway?" He sipped some more tea.

"I thought helping you would help me find some closure regarding my son."

"Hmmm. Well, if I decide to do that, I'll let you know."

"Okay."

"How's the hangover?"

"It's easing off," he said, drinking the last of the tea. "Where's my car, Dr. Tate?"

"Still parked at the bar. I'll take you back to get it."

"Okay," he said, standing up. "Thank you, Dr. Tate, for everything. Especially for last night."

"You're not leaving me as a patient, are you?" She smiled.

"You're not gonna pawn me off to another therapist, are you?"

"Who—me?" She laughed. "I would never do that," she said grabbing her purse and keys as they left.

♦ FORTY-FIVE ♦

The sun was beaming down on Barbara's back as if it was in judgment of her as she tended to her garden, reminiscing about the conversation she and Eddie had in the kitchen. She stopped to wipe the sweat from her forehead and resumed working. She was trying to keep her mind from reliving the conversation in the kitchen with her husband on the day of her retirement party, but she couldn't. It kept going right back to it like a moth to a flame.

"Barbara, what's the knife for?" Eddie asked, uneasy.

"Because you're not going to like what I have to say."

"Well, what is it that you have to say that you need a knife?" Eddie asked, standing opposite her in the kitchen.

She sighed knowing there was no other choice, but to reveal the absolute truth. "Do you remember the day I gave birth to Bradley?"

"Yeah."

"Well, that whole day is a complete lie. I actually didn't give birth to him…"

A much younger Eddie paced the floor back and forth with his arms crossed waiting for the doctor to come out. Even though this wasn't his first time, it sure did feel like it was. Heart racing, nervousness, the sweating. He sat down for a quick second, his leg shaking. He quickly got back up and resumed pacing.

Barbara screamed as she sat on the bed in the delivery room, her fellow nurses and doctor standing around. They knew of her plight at home and would do anything to help her. The doctor looked at her watch and pointed to Barbara and she screamed. A nurse poured water from a bottle on Barbara's head slowly and she shook her head wanting it to drip down her like sweat. She adjusted the pregnancy suit that she had been wearing for the last five months of the pregnancy.

"And the baby is would be out...right...about...now," the doctor said, looking at her watch. "Corrine." The nurse took the newborn from the bassinet and handed him over to her. Barbara looked down at him and graced his nose with a slight touch and smiled.

"Corrine. You can let him in now," said the doctor.

"Wait." Barbara laid back and closed her eyes as she thought about the day her father died and let a few tears fall. "Okay, you can let him in now."

Eddie slowly walked in and smiled at the new son his wife had just bore. He walked over and touched her hand, kissing her on the forehead in a way she hadn't felt in quite some time. He was tender like he was when they met for the first time on the campus of Boston University almost a decade prior. He took the baby from her arms and smiled at him.

"What's his name?"

"Bradley."

"Bradley."

"Thank you all." Barbara smiled at her colleagues. "Thank you all so much."

"No problem. You know we'd do anything for you," said the doctor.

"That's right," said Corrine. "Anything."

"Let's give them some privacy," said the doctor. And they left.

Barbara looked at Eddie holding their new child and smiled, hoping this bundle of joy would keep him off her back long enough for him to see the error of his ways.

"I'm sorry," Barbara cried, looking at Eddie as they stood in the kitchen. She screamed as Eddie, in a fit of rage, knocked everything from the kitchen counter onto the floor.

"I just wanted the abuse to stop, Eddie," she cried. "I just wanted the abuse to stop. And it seemed the only time it did was when I was pregnant. And since I couldn't have any more children because of you, it was the next best thing I could do."

"You could have left!" Eddie shouted.

"I tried, remember? I tried so…many times, but you were crazy!" She cried. "I can't believe I've stayed with you this long."

"Whose son is he, Barbara? Whose child is he?!"

"I don't know."

Barbara wiped the sweat again from her forehead as the sun continued its glare. Communication with Eddie now had been reduced to nothing at all. She'd enter a room, he'd leave. He couldn't stand the sight of her, his hands clenching into a fist every time he laid eyes on her. He wanted so badly to strike her, but he'd learned in the years since his heart attack, it was easier to just walk away.

Barbara stopped her ground work hearing the back screen door open and close. She heard him walking down the stairs in the distance. She was too ashamed to turn around and look at him, even for a second. She wanted to continue to make her plea of how sorry she was, but knew it wouldn't make a difference. She didn't even want to be in the company of her own presence, so she knew he wouldn't. She continued to garden hearing the car door close and the engine of his black Volvo roar to a start as he backed out of the driveway and sped off.

She threw down the garden shovel and took off her gloves and held her face in her hands weeping. If he could, she wanted God to take her right then. But would he? Or was he ashamed of her, too? She screamed to the sky above, wanting some redemption or salvation. "Why me, God? Why me?" she shouted.

She began pulling the flowers from the dirt, destroying the garden she had worked so hard to maintain over the years. It had now become meaningless. Worthless. No longer important, just like her. She had nothing else to live for. She was dying, her family completely destroyed. Life as she knew it was over.

♦ FORTY-SIX ♦

Bradley pulled into the driveway and was surprised to see Croix sitting on the front steps. He was so happy to see her he couldn't get out of his seatbelt and the car fast enough. She stood as he walked over to her and hugged her tight. The warm softness of her embrace allowed him to break down. She felt like home.

"Come on." She walked him inside as he continued to weep. They walked into the living room and sat down. She rubbed his head, looking at him, wiped his tears with her fingers.

"What are you doing here?" he asked.

"I was worried about you. Rodney and I were looking for you all night. What happened? Where were you?"

"After I left my pare—the house—I went to a bar. And then a friend of my mine let me crash at their house."

"What happened at your parent's house?"

He took a deep breath. "They're not my parents."

"What? What are you talking about?"

"The day you left here, I got a call from my mother's cancer doctor saying that she wanted to see me, to give me the results of the bone marrow test for my mother."

"Are you a match?"

"No. Then she tells me that my mother is not my biological mother. Someone else is."

"Oh my God."

"So, I'm sitting there looking at her like it must be a joke. This can't be serious. And that's when, after work, I confronted my mother about it and she told me I was adopted." He scoffs. "My whole life has been a complete lie. I mean, she didn't have enough courage to tell me. I find out from her doctor. What type of bullshit is that?" He stood up and started walking around. "And all I keep thinking about is all those times she used beat me. Just took all her frustration out on me! She never cared about me because she knew I wasn't her son!" he shouted, knocking pictures off the mantle. Croix got up and wrapped her arms around his waist, hugging him from behind. "God knows I am just so tired of hurting," he cried.

"I know, I know."

"What did I do, you know? What did I do to have a life where no one wants me? You're gone. The girls are gone. My mother, whoever the hell she is, didn't want me. I mean what the hell did I do to deserve such a life? Huh? What?"

"I'm here, Bradley. I'm right here. I'm not going anywhere." Croix said, hugging him tighter.

DING-DONG! The doorbell sounded.

"I got it. It's probably Rodney. I told him I'd call him once I found you," said Croix walking over to the door. She opened the door and it was Eddie Sr.

"Hi, Croix. Is he here?"

"Yeah. Come on in," she said, stepping back to let him in.

Hearing the sound of his father's voice, Bradley refused to turn around. "I have nothing to say to you and there's nothing I need to hear from you."

"Son, listen—"

"I am not your son!" Bradley shouted, turning around.

"I know. I know, son—Bradley—but just hear me out...please."

"Bradley, just let him talk," Croix interjected.

Bradley stood there quietly, staring at the man he used to call dad.

"Your mother told me what happened, and I am so sorry you had to find out like that. I am," he said slowly, making his way towards Bradley. "But I want you to know that you will always be my son. I don't care how you came into my life, but you have always been the best part of my life. And that's the truth." Bradley hugged him, crying. "You will always be my son and don't you ever forget it. I love you."

"Croix, did you find him—" Rodney said, rushing in the house, noticing Bradley and his father.

"Let's go outside," they walked outside.

Bradley and Eddie released from their embrace. "You'll always be my son, okay? I don't care what happened or what she did to get you, you will always be mine."

"Okay." Bradley hugged him, crying.

"How about me, you and your brother go fishing next weekend, okay?"

"Sounds great."

"We can stop at the store and get those cookies you liked to eat when you were a kid. What was the name of them again?"

"Lorna Doones." Bradley smiled wiping his eyes.

"Yeah...Lorna Doones." Eddie smiled. "I'm gonna let you finish what you were doing with Croix. I'll call you later."

"Ok."

"I love you, son."

"Love you, Dad."

Eddie left and Croix and Rodney walked in. They rushed over, helping Bradley to the couch as he broke down.

♦ FORTY-SEVEN ♦

Bradley flipped through the pages of O Magazine as he waited for Dr. Tate to call his name. It had been about a week since he last seen her at her house and he was still processing everything, but on a much lighter note. His cell phone vibrated in his pocket and he took it out to see who it was. Barbara Robinson, it displayed, and he quickly sent the call to voicemail.

She had been calling him since their conversation, but he refused to answer. There was nothing she could ever say that would get him to communicate with her ever again. The thought of changing his number crossed his mind, but he didn't want to go through the hassle of changing it on all of his important documentation or with the girls' school.

He thought about calling her back and bombarding her with the questions that nagged him. Who was he? Where did he come from? Who were his parents? Was the adoption open or closed? Did he have any biological brothers or sisters? He looked down at the floor as the thoughts swirled in his mind. Dr. Tate opened her office door.

"Bradley."

He put the magazine down and headed into her office.

"How are you?" she asked closing the door.

"Okay." He sat down on the couch.

"You sure?" she asked sitting down across from him.

"Well, I'm doing better than the last time you saw me. Still processing things, though."

"Okay. Have you had a drink?"

"Not since I left your house, no."

"That's good."

"I don't think liquor can cure this."

"And why not?"

"Well, like you said the last time, sometimes you just have to sit in the pain. Just face it head on. I've been running away from it for far too long. And I'm tired of running from everything. I mean look where running has got me...no offense."

"None taken."

"It has stripped me of my wife, my kids, the family I thought I knew...even my own identity. So, right now, I've got nothing else to lose, except the running."

"Interesting, interesting. Speaking of your wife and children, have you spoken with them since you discovered the truth about your family?"

"Yeah. Croix was at my parents' house when the whole fiasco happened with my mother—Barbara—and I. She didn't hear it, but she was there. I told her about it later. She was at the house waiting for me the next day after I'd left yours."

"What did she say?"

"She said she was here for me and loved me."

"Has she and your daughters return home yet?"

"No, not yet. She said she didn't feel quite ready for them to come back home with all of this going on. Little afraid that I might, you know...," he said clearing his throat. "...try to...harm myself again. I told her that will never happen again, but she's not ready, so I just have to accept that. It's probably for the best."

"Have you spoken to your parents?"

"My Dad. He had come by the house, too, the same day as Croix."

"How did that conversation go?"

"Good. He told me that I was still his son no matter what. And that he loved me."

"How did it you make you feel? Hearing that," Dr. Tate asked, shifting in her seat.

"It made me feel...happy...in a sense...I don't know. It reassured me that even though I am not biologically his son, he still cares about me."

"You felt loved."

"Yeah. Yeah, I did."

"Have you spoken to your mother?"

"No. I have no reason to."

"Why not? Don't you want to hear her story?"

"I couldn't care less about her story. She's never cared about me and I don't care about her. Her story doesn't concern me right now."

"Don't you have questions that you would like to have answered?"

"Yeah, I do, but not right now. I just can't stand to look at her right now. Right now I'm focusing on getting my relationship with my wife and kids back on track and then, maybe, I'll talk to her, but right now I can't. I just can't."

"So, your mother's cancer returning is not a concern for you?"

"It is, but I'm not going to use that to let her off the hook. I'm not. I need my distance."

"Okay."

"How is everything going with you and your husband regarding...you know?" Bradley asked breaking the silence that was forming between them.

"It is what it is. We're working on it."

* * *

The sound of the chirping birds made Charlotte enjoy the moment even more as she sat on the back deck catching up on the Song of Solomon. She had decided to skip her usual lunch date with Kenya and Tamara to partake in a quiet afternoon alone, wanting to ease her mind of everything that had happened. Keith had begun to exchange morning pleasantries with her in the kitchen, but that was about how far it went. She knew he was processing everything and eased up on the pressure for him to talk to her.

She still hadn't spoken to her mother or her sisters since the dinner and didn't feel it was necessary to call them. Especially her mother. Kenya or Tamara hadn't called her with any emergency news so she knew her mother was still alive.

She put her finger in between the pages, holding her space in the book as she thought back to that day and something her mother had said. *I wonder what she meant about me not knowing her story,* she thought. She had never seen her mother become that angry, ever. Not even on the day she had announced she was pregnant. "Hmph." The phone rang and she answered.

"Hello?"

"You are home," said Kenya. "See, I told you she was home."

"Yeah, I'm home."

"Tamara thought you weren't home. Well, can you let us in? We've been ringing the doorbell for like twenty minutes now."

"Just come around back. I'm sitting on the deck."

"Oh, ok."

Charlotte hung up the phone and placed it on the table beside her. She finished reading the paragraph she was on, placed her bookmark inside and put the book on the table.

"Hey," she said, putting her hand against her forehead blocking the sun from her eyes to get a better look at her sisters as they walked up the stairs.

"Hey," said Tamara.

"We thought we'd check on you to see how you were doing. We haven't heard from you since…" said Kenya.

"I'm good."

"You sure?" Kenya asked, rubbing her back. Tamara sat down as well.

"Yeah, I'm good. I'm just glad it's finally out. That everybody knows."

"How's Keith doing?" asked Tamara.

"He's fine. We're working it out."

"Have you talked to or heard from Ma?" asked Kenya.

"Nope. I have nothing to say to her right now. Have any of you? Tamara? I know you always talk to her."

"Not since then," said Tamara. "She's called me but I haven't answered the phone. I just can't right now."

"Why didn't you say anything all these years?" Kenya asked.

"I don't know. It just never seemed like the right time. Every time I decided to tell Keith, fear would creep in and I'd back out."

"Do you know where the boy is?" asked Tamara.

"No clue."

"Do you want me to find him? What's his name? You know I can find anybody working at the D.A.'s office," said Kenya.

"I don't know his name. He doesn't have one."

"Huh? What?" said Tamara, confused by what just came from her sister's mouth.

"He doesn't have a name? How'd you have a baby and you didn't name him? That doesn't make any sense," said Kenya.

"Mama didn't let me name him. She had the doctor and nurses take him out before I could."

Kenya let out a breath, upset. "Oh my God, I can't believe her! Get your shoes, we're going over there right now!"

"Where?" asked Charlotte.

"Mama's."

"Nope, I'm not going over there. And neither are you. Just leave it alone. It's out now, everybody knows, so…just leave it alone."

"So, are you going to look for him?" asked Tamara.

"No."

"Why? Don't you want to know who he is?" asked Tamara.

"I used to, but not anymore. It's been 30 years and I've let it go." Charlotte let out a breath. "Besides, I can't find him if I don't have a name."

"Well, if you change your mind, you know I'm here for you," said Kenya.

"Yeah, me too," added Tamara.

"Thanks, but I've moved on from it," said Charlotte looking out across the horizon. "And I'm done talking about it."

NINE MONTHS LATER

♦ FORTY-EIGHT ♦

"Aaaaaaaaaaahhhhhhhhhhhhhh!" Dana screamed as she lay back against the bed, beat and exhausted. Her boyfriend Will stood in the corner, scared, looking like he was about to hurl at any moment. Charlotte dabbed Dana's forehead with a wet towel trying to cool her off. She knew exactly what her daughter was going through, but unlike her mother, she was enjoying the experience.

"You're doing good, baby," said Charlotte. "Will, get your butt over here and hold her hand. She can't do this by herself."

"Yes, Mrs. Tate," he said, rushing over to the other side of Dana, grabbing her hand.

"The baby is almost out. I can see the top of the head," said the doctor from between Dana's legs. "I'm gonna need you to push."

"I can't! I can't!" Dana shouted.

"You have to," said the doctor.

"I can't! I can't!"

"You can do this baby. Will and I are right here with you, okay?"

"The baby is almost here, Dana. I just need one big push. You think you can do that for me?" asked the doctor.

Dana nodded.

"On the count of three, okay? One…two…three!"

208

"Aaaaahhhhhhh!" Dana pushed and pushed and pushed until the sound of innocent, sweet wails emanated from between her legs. She fell back against the bed, exhausted.

"It's a girl!" the doctor shouted. "Mrs. Tate, would you like to cut the cord?"

"Will?" Charlotte asked.

"Okay." Will walked nervously over to the doctor, and then vomited at first sight of the after birth.

"Lord have mercy. I'll do it," laughed Charlotte as she walked over and cut the cord.

"Say hello to your daughter, Dana," said the doctor, walking the baby over and placing her in Dana's arms.

"Hi, Erica Dominique Tate-Harris," Dana said, holding her new bundle of joy.

Charlotte wiped the tears from her eyes admiring her grandchild. "She is so beautiful. Let me go tell everybody else." Charlotte walked out of the delivery room, down the hall into the waiting room where Keith, her mother, sisters and Will's family were waiting for word.

"What's going on? Is the baby here yet?" Keith asked.

"It's a girl! She had a girl!"

Everybody shouted, hugging each other.

"What's the name?" asked Will's mother.

"Erica," said Charlotte.

"Oh, here's the doctor," said Keith.

The doctor walked in. "Mother and baby are doing just fine. We'll be moving them up to a room shortly."

"Thank you, doctor," said Charlotte. "Can you believe it? We're grandparents." She said, turning around to Keith, wrapping her arms around him.

"I know. Tell me about it."

"She will be changing diapers."

"Yes she will."

"And doing midnight feedings."

"That too."

The doctor walked back in. "They are ready for visitors."

"Thank you, doctor," Charlotte said as everyone headed out.

The family had surrounded Dana's hospital bed as Charlotte stood in the doorway, silently, watching her daughter who like her had become what she once was…a teenage mother. She wiped her eyes and smiled.

"Where's my grandbaby?" she said walking over to Dana. "She's precious, isn't she?"

"Yes, she is," said Will's mother.

"Grandma, you want to hold her?"

"Sure. Let me get a good look at my great-grandbaby," Carol said lifting the baby from Dana's hands.

Dana grabbed her mother's hand and smiled.

"You are so cute. Yes, you are, you little thing you," said Carol. "What's her name again?"

"Erica Dominique Tate-Harris."

"Erica…I'm your great-grandmother."

Charlotte couldn't help but wonder if she would have been living the same experience her very own daughter was right now if she had been allowed to keep her son as she looked on at her mother holding her grandchild. She had let go of the animosity she held against her mother, but watching her caused a stir inside of her, a feeling she couldn't quite describe.

"Okay, is anybody else hungry? Because I'm starving," she said cutting off that indescribable feeling, not wanting it to disrupt the happiness that was flowing through the room.

"I am," said Will's mother.

"I think the café is on the second floor."

"Okay."

"Honey, you want anything from the cafeteria?" Charlotte asked Dana.

"No, I'm good."

"Will?" Charlotte asked.

"I'm good, Mrs. Tate."

"Okay. Come on, Lydia, let's go have a conversation as grandmothers now."

"Grandmothers? No, honey, it's…Mother, the sequel."

"We'll be back," Charlotte laughed as they left the room.

◆ FORTY-NINE ◆

Bradley turned out the bathroom light, walking out of the bathroom. He grabbed his sneakers and went to sit on the foot of the bed and stopped, catching himself in the mirror. He no longer looked or felt fifty. He felt his age. He smiled and put on his sneakers. He felt like his hard work and the sessions with Dr. Tate were paying off.

The aroma of sizzling bacon and scrambled eggs hit his nose, and the distant chatter of the girls in the kitchen was music to his ears. He had worked hard to have Croix and the girls return home. And now that they were home, he was determined not to mess it up. He got up from the bed and headed downstairs. The stairs creaked with each step he took.

Slowly, he walked up to the kitchen doorway and stood there watching Croix as she scooped the rest of the eggs from the pan onto a plate for him and her as the girls joked, eating their breakfast. He didn't want to miss a minute of them as he had so many times before. His eyes welled up.

"Oh, hey." Croix said noticing him.

"Hey," he said removing the wetness from his eyes with his fingers, walking further into the kitchen.

"Good morning, Daddy," said Tia.

He kissed her on the forehead and hugged her, doing the same with Ashley. "Good morning." He walked over to Croix and kissed her. "Good morning."

"Good morning to you, too."

He grabbed a piece of bacon off the plate.

"So, what's on your agenda today?"

"Going to a meeting."

"How long are you going to continue to keep seeing her? Dr. Tate."

He took a deep breath. "You know, I don't know. It's been nine months and I feel that we've made a lot of progress." He grabbed another piece of bacon. "Plus, I like seeing her. She's pretty cool."

"Well, I'm here for you, you know that right?"

"Do I sense a hint of jealousy?" He smiled.

"Um, no, but if you need me to go to a session with you I will."

"Thanks, babe." He poked his lips out for a kiss and she gave him one.

"Alright, come on girls, let's go. We don't want to be late."

The girls finished their breakfast and got up from the table. "Bye, Daddy."

"Bye. Have fun at school."

"I'll call you later."

"Okay."

They kissed and he watched as she followed the girls out of the kitchen.

* * *

Bradley pulled into a parking space of the George Robert White Community Center, a Boys & Girls Club named in honor of the 20th century philanthropist. He was feeling a bit nervous as he got out and walked inside. He had been coming every second and fourth Tuesday for the last seven months and this day he knew was big. He walked over to the food table and grabbed a pastry

"Hey, Bradley," said a group member.

"Kevin, how are you? How's everything?"

"Good. You gonna speak today? You've been coming for

months now," said Kevin

"Yeah, I am. I'm ready."

"Good afternoon," said the thin man with salt-and-pepper hair walking in. He was the group moderator.

Bradley sat down.

"How's everyone?"

"Good," the group responded.

"Who wants to go first?"

"I'll start," said Bradley, raising his hand.

"The floor is yours." The moderator stepped to the side and sat down as Bradley got up and walked to the front of the room.

"Hi, everyone. I'm a little nervous, but here it goes…my name is Bradley Robinson and I'm an alcoholic."

"Hi, Bradley," spoke the group.

He cleared his throat, letting what he had just said sink in. "My love affair with alcohol began slowly…when I was just 19 years old. I took my first drink at a party and, at first, those were the only times I would drink, at parties. But after I joined the police force, had my daughter, got married, had another child, things started gettin' heavy, at least to me. I would drink all the time. A little right before the start of my shift in the locker room and plenty at the end of shift. I mean it had reached the point where I was hiding nips in the car, around the house, even in my locker at work.

"I had tried to stop, especially after my wife had given me an ultimatum, but I couldn't…or wouldn't. After my shift was over, I would call her and tell her I was working overtime so I could go to the motel and drink. It was my way of hiding my broken promise from her and our daughters." He lowered his head for minute feeling ashamed. "I always felt like…like I just had all of this pressure, you know…to be the perfect husband, the perfect father, the perfect officer, the perfect…son. Like I had something to prove because I never felt good enough for anyone. Not my mother, not even myself. And alcohol was how I dodged dealing with that. It was my escape for years. And the more I drank, the more I ran."

He wiped the tears from his eyes.

"Alcoholism ruins you. It attaches itself to your pain and

refuses to let go, like a leech. It almost cost me everything: my wife...my kids...my career. But now I can say that I am seven months sober..." The group clapped. "...because I stopped running. I have to admit that it has been a struggle, no lie. It has been a struggle, but I'm taking it one second, one minute, one hour, one day at a time. And that's about all I can do. Thank you, thank you for listening." He left the podium and sat back down feeling better than he did when he walked in.

"Who wants to go next?" asked the moderator.

A woman raised her hand and walked up to the podium. "Hi, my name is Valerie..."

"Hi, Valerie," said the group.

"...and I'm an alcoholic."

♦ FIFTY ♦

Bradley flipped through the pages of Time Magazine as he waited for Dr. Tate to call his name. It had been another two weeks since their last session and he was feeling better than ever. He knew speaking at the AA meeting was the source of the new found peaceful energy he was feeling as he smiled at a woman who walked by. Dr. Tate opened the door and stepped out.

"Bradley."

He put the magazine down and got up.

"How you been?" Dr. Tate asked Bradley as he walked in. She closed the door.

"I've been going great since the last time we talked," he said sitting down.

"That's great. Still going to the AA meetings?"

"Yeah, I just came from one. I finally spoke."

"You did? Awesome." She sat down.

"Yeah." He smiled feeling proud. "I was nervous at first, but I made it through."

"Good. Congratulations."

"Thank you."

"So, how's family life?"

"Good. Croix's good, the kids are good. Work is great."

"Good to hear."

"Have spoken to your parents? Your mother? You haven't

mentioned her in a while."

"I speak with my Dad often, but not my mother."

"It's been quite a long time since you last spoke with her. How come?"

He sighed. "I don't know. I'd rather just leave it all alone and just let it be what it is."

"How is she doing health wise?"

"Not too good, my father said. That's probably why I've been refusing to see her. Afraid of what she looks like now." He looked down, feeling somewhat ashamed and horrible that he hasn't seen her.

"Why don't you go see her? What harm can it do? I'm sure you can handle seeing your mother in the state she's in. I mean you have before, right? You had mentioned before that this was her second bout."

"Yeah..."

"So, why not take the time and find the closure you want? I mean look at all the progress you've made since coming here, why stop now?"

"I know. Maybe you're right. I should go see her. Just let it go once and for all."

"You should. Do you want to go on with the rest of your life with questions still unanswered?"

"No."

"So, go see your mother, Bradley. Go see her. Don't go the rest of your life with your glass half empty. Talk to her."

Bradley sat there silently, thinking.

The hour had passed and the session ended as they stepped out from her office into the hallway.

"Trust me. Talk to her. It'll be worth it."

"Okay."

"See you in two weeks. Take care."

"You too."

She watched as the elevator doors opened and Bradley stepped in...and her mother stepped out. She let out a breath. *What the hell does she want?* Charlotte thought about darting back into her office, closing the door, hoping that her mother wouldn't see her, but their eyes had met as soon as Carol stepped out of the elevator.

"We need to talk," said her mother.

"I'm busy. I have patients to see. I can't talk to you right now."

"Cancel them."

"I can't do that. I'm sorry. Besides, what are you doing here anyway? What do you want?"

"Grab your purse. We're going for a ride."

"I'm not in the mood to go anywhere with you right now."

"I don't care what mood you're in…you're going."

"Sorry, Ma, but I am not a little girl anymore. I am not going anywhere with you and you need to leave."

"Look, you want to know about your son or not?" Carol said sternly.

Right then, Charlotte knew if she didn't take this ride whatever information her mother was going to give about her son would never come around again.

"Maria, reschedule the rest of my patients until tomorrow, thank you."

"No problem, Dr. Tate."

Charlotte walked into her office, grabbed her purse and keys and headed back out shutting the door behind her. She motioned in the direction of the elevator and her mother followed.

* * *

Neither Charlotte nor her mother said much of anything to one another as they traveled to a destination unknown to Charlotte. She wondered where her mother was taking her, as they turned down the streets of a quiet residential neighborhood, not familiar to Charlotte. Carol turned down yet another street where the houses looked almost identical. She placed the car gear in park and shut off the engine.

"He used to live in that house right over there." Carol pointed in the direction of the blue and white modest one-family house diagonally across from them. "I used to come by after work some days and watch him play outside with an older boy. There were so many times I wanted to walk up to him and just say hello."

"Why didn't you?" Charlotte asked, tears streaming down her cheeks.

"I was afraid."

"You knew where my son was all these years and you never said a word?" Charlotte said, wanting to wrap her hands around her mother's throat.

"I know. And I am so sorry, baby. Please forgive me, please." Carol cried.

"You knew where my son was and you never said a fuckin' word?"

"I know, I know."

"Do you have any idea the fuckin' hell you put me through?!"

"I know. And I'm sorry."

"Sorry. You're sorry. I can't believe this shit! Not only did you take my child from me, you fuckin' belittled me! You told me I was worthless! That I was an embarrassment! And you were just as bad, even worse!" Charlotte looked out the window and closed her eyes trying to calm herself.

"I always wanted you and your sisters to be better than I was." Carol wiped her eyes. "Finish school, get married, then have babies. And when you told me you were pregnant at 14, I just didn't know how to deal with it. The same way my mother didn't know how to deal with mine."

Charlotte looked at her mother.

"Yes, I, too, became pregnant as a teenager."

"How old were you?"

"Fifteen. And I had tried everything I could to get rid of it. Falling down stairs, hitting myself. I tried everything so my mother wouldn't find out. I hid it, very well actually, for a good five months until I started having pains and I had to go to the hospital...and that's when my mother found out." Carol shook her head, thinking back. "She beat me so bad when I got home I didn't know whether she was trying to kill me, the baby or both of us."

"So what happened to the baby?"

"It died. Stillborn. I'm sorry for what I did. I just didn't want to you to end up like some of your friends who had babies at their age. I wanted you and your sisters to have better than what I had, even if that meant doing what I did."

"So, where is my son?" Charlotte asked, looking at her mother.

"I don't know. One day I came by and they had moved. They lived here until he was about five."

"Who took him?"

"I don't know. I just remember the nurse from the hospital calling me one day at work, not too long after you had him and told me that he was with a family. And gave me this address."

Charlotte looked back towards the window. "Well, it doesn't matter now anyway. I decided I'm not going to look for him."

"Why?" asked Carol.

"I've let it go," Charlotte said, wiping tears from her cheeks. "What changed your mind all of sudden, Ma? Why did you bring me here?"

"That precious great-grandbaby of mine," Carol smiled.

"It's funny how babies can have that effect on people." Charlotte kept her attention on the house. "Can you take me back to my office, please?"

Carol started the engine and drove off.

◆ FIFTY-ONE ◆

It was early afternoon and the city had been relatively quiet thus far as Bradley looked out the car window as he and Rodney sat in the police cruiser at a red light. He smiled at a little girl who was waiting to cross with her mother. She reminded him of Ashley with her bright smile.

"This is how everyday should be. Nice and qui—" Rodney began as the traffic light turned green and they start rolling.

"Nope. Don't you say it." Bradley cut him off.

"What?"

"You know every single time you mention that word, it's never quiet. Dammit!"

"See, so worried about me saying it. So, I like my steak medium-well please," said Rodney.

"I'm not buying a steak my friend."

"Are we backing out on the agreed bet?"

"Fine, I'll get you the damn steak." Bradley smiled.

"With a side of mashed potatoes and rice."

"Yeah, whatever."

Silence began to fill the car. "How's your mom?" Rodney asked.

"She doesn't have long, my father told me. He said she keeps asking for me."

"You haven't visited or spoken to her?"

"No."

"Why not? She's your mother."

"No, she is not my mother." Bradley's cell phone vibrated in the pocket of his uniform and he pulled out. "Speaking of the devil, here's my father calling me now. Hello?"

"Hey, son," said his father. "You still at work?"

"Yeah, why? What's up?"

"Listen, I know you look at us differently now since your mother's—Barbara's—truth has come to light, but she really wants to talk to you. Can you please stop by when you get off?"

Bradley took a deep breath. "We haven't taken our ten yet, have we?" he asked Rodney covering his phone with his hand.

"No."

"Alright, I'll take a break and stop by."

"Thanks, son."

Bradley hung up the phone.

"Unit-104 requesting a Code-10." Rodney spoke into the radio knowing where they were headed.

Code-10 granted, said the female voice.

Bradley got out and headed inside.

Unit-421… the female voice emanated from Bradley's radio

"421…"

Can you guys head over to… Bradley turned down the radio as he walked down the corridor towards his mother's hospital room. He hadn't seen or spoken to her since she had revealed the truth to him about who he wasn't and he was getting nervous as he stepped closer to her room. He walked up, lightly tapping on the door.

"Hey," said Eddie, getting up.

"Hey," said Bradley. "Junior. Natalie."

"Hey," they responded.

Bradley slowly made his way over his mother. He couldn't believe how frail and sickly the disease had made her. It was worse than what he had imagined.

"You made it finally," she spoke softly.

"Yeah, I did," he said, sitting in the chair next to her bed.

"Come on, ya'll. Let's give them some privacy," Eddie said to Junior and Natalie. They walked out of the room.

"I'm sorry. I'm sorry for taking my frustration out on you when you were a child. I'm sorry for not telling you the truth sooner than when I did."

"You don't have to apologize. I forgive you."

"I was selfish and I apologize for that. I got you for my own selfish reason and I caused so much pain and I'm sorry."

He started rubbing her hand, knowing what she was saying was genuine.

"You are a good man, Bradley. A good man. And you deserve to know the truth and find them. Your family."

"I don't care about that right now," Bradley said, his eyes tearing up. "They didn't want me."

"Your mother did, but she was...*(coughing)*... too young to keep you. Her mother wouldn't let her."

"Shhhh...just rest," he said, continuing to gently rub her hair. "I'm sorry for being such a big asshole to you. I'm sorry."

Shots fired...shots fired..., the female voice lowly emanated from the radio.

Bradley's cell phone began to vibrate in his pocket, he knew it was Rodney. "I have to go."

"I know." She smiled.

He stood up and kissed her on the forehead. "I know you did the best you could with what you had."

"Watson was her last name. Your mother's last name was Watson. Look in that yellow box, everything you need is in there."

"Okay."

"Go to work." She slapped his arm.

He hugged her. "I love you," he whispered.

"Forgive me."

"You've already been forgiven." He kissed on the forehead.

He walked out. "I'll see y'all later. Got shots fired," he said to the rest of the family, running down the hall.

Bradley bolted from the main entrance of the hospital and jumped in the cruiser and they sped off, knowing it was the last time he was ever going to see the woman he had called "mother."

◆ FIFTY-TWO ◆

It was after midnight and the moon was shining full and bright in the cloudless night sky as Charlotte sat in the kitchen drinking tea, the information weighing heavy on her mind. *I can't believe her,* she thought sipping her tea as Keith walked in.

"Can't sleep?" he asked, grabbing a glass from the cabinet.

"No."

"Me neither," he said making himself a cup of tea. He sat down with her at the table. "I still can't believe we're grandparents."

"I know."

"Who's picking Dana and the baby up from the hospital?"

"Will's father."

"Okay," Keith said sipping his tea. "What's bothering you? You've been quiet since you came home from work. Tough day?"

"I guess you can say that." She sipped her tea. "My mother came to visit today."

"Oh yeah, what happened?"

"She took me on a little field trip."

"A field trip?"

"Yeah. She took me to the house where our son spent his childhood growing up. Well, some of it anyway."

"What?"

Charlotte raised her eyebrows, sipping tea.

"You mean to tell me she knew where he was all this time and never said anything? Unbelievable."

"Yup. Our grandchild is what had changed her mind and decide to tell me."

"Un-freaking-believable. She's a piece of work, I tell you."

"I know. Tell me about it." Charlotte sipped her tea.

"So, what are you going to do? Are you going to look for him?"

"I don't know. I don't know what I'm gonna do. I'm not sure I even want to travel down that road."

"Well, whatever you decide I'm here."

"Thank you."

It was the next morning and Charlotte sat in the quietness of her office contemplating whether to go through with what she and Keith had discussed the night before. *What do I have to lose? Get closure once and for all.*

"Maria…," she said pressing the button on the phone.

"Yes, Dr. Tate…" Maria responded.

"Who else do I have on the schedule for the day?"

"You have Mrs. Penniman at two o'clock and Ms. Jackson at three."

"Okay, thank you."

The clock read noon. *I should be back by two.* She grabbed her purse and her keys and walked out of the office, shutting the door behind her. "Maria, hold my calls. I may be running a little late coming back from lunch. So just tell Mrs. Penniman to hold tight."

"Okay, Dr. Tate."

Charlotte pressed the elevator button and the doors open as someone stepped out and she in. She pressed the ground floor and the doors closed.

* * *

Charlotte sat in her car in the same spot that she and her mother had been in and stared at the house. She watched the thin framed woman tend to the flower garden in front of the house. She got out of the car and walked over to the woman hoping she would be of some assistance.

"Excuse me, Miss…," Charlotte said walking up.

The woman, in her mid-sixties with her salt-and-pepper hair covered by a big sun hat, turned around.

"…hi." Charlotte continued.

"What can I do for you?" the woman asked.

"I have a question about your house."

"What about it?" The woman stood up. "You're not one of the scammers, trying to take my home, or get my personal information, are you?"

"No, Ma'am."

"You sure?" the woman asked, squinting her eyes.

"Yes, Ma'am. I am a licensed psychologist, not a scammer."

"Well, I ain't crazy. Just getting old. So, what is it you want to know about my house?"

"Who used to own it?"

"Well, ain't nobody been livin' in it since '85 but me and my husband. I don't know who owned the house before we did. Sorry, I can't help you with that. Maybe you can try the registry of deeds. Maybe that can help you."

"Thank you, Ma'am," Charlotte said, walking away.

"Have a nice day."

"You too," said Charlotte.

The woman watched Charlotte as she walked back to her car and got in. Charlotte looked at her watch. It had only been 45 minutes since she had left the office. *I should have more than enough time to check out the registry of deeds,* she thought. *Nah, I better not chance it. I'll have to find parking and everything. I'll go another day.* She started the engine, snapped on her seatbelt and drove off. The woman watched Charlotte turn the corner and then resumed her work.

♦ FIFTY-THREE ♦

It had been a couple of days since Bradley got the word, at the end of his shift, from his father that his mother had passed and he was still having trouble sleeping. His mind raced with a million thoughts as he sat at the dining room table staring at the yellow box he had taken from his parents' basement. It held his track trophies and varsity athlete's jacket that he was sure of, but what was at the bottom of it held his curiosity.

He opened the box and removed his trophies and jacket, revealing a manila folder with the name "Watson", which had faded over the years, written across it. He took out the folder and opened it. It was his medical records from the day he was born. He looked at it, still curious as to why the woman he knew as his mother would keep all of this from him.

"You coming to bed?" asked Croix who was half-asleep.

"I can't sleep. Got too much on my mind. Come here, look at this. I think this is my birth record."

"Huh? What?" Croix said, walking over. "Your birth record?"

"Yeah, it was in the bottom of the box," Bradley said, glancing over the information. "I guess my family's last name is Watson. It just says Baby-Boy Watson. My birth parents' names aren't listed."

"That's strange," said Croix, standing next to him.

"I know, tell me about it. Have you seen anything like this at the hospital?"

"Can't say that I have."

"It says I was born in Boston City Hospital."

"It looks like there's a number written on the post-it note."

"Yeah, it is, but…it's too faded to read what it is," Bradley said, holding it up to the light. "Well, there's nothing I can do with it. There are thousands, not mention to millions, of people with the last name Watson."

"Yeah, but how many gave their baby away."

Bradley stayed quiet, thinking.

"Why don't you get yourself some rest and deal with it later? We have to be at your parents' house by nine for the limo to pick us up."

Bradley took a deep breath and got up knowing she was right. He hadn't been sleeping well lately and a good night's sleep was probably what he needed. He turned the light out and headed upstairs to bed.

* * *

Charlotte walked into the Registry of Deeds office and up to the blonde haired woman sitting behind the desk.

"Welcome to the Registry of Deeds. How may I help you?"

"Hi, yes, I am looking for owner information regarding a particular house."

"Do you know what page in what book the information is on?"

"No, I do not. I only have the address."

"Okay, what's the address?"

"It is 465 Salem Avenue, Boston."

The woman typed the address into her computer. "Okay, the information you're looking for begins with book 10045, page 223. That book should be on the left side of the library."

"Thank you."

"You're welcome."

Charlotte walked to the back where old big books lined the shelves. She walked past them, looking at the numbers listed on the outside of each row. She found the right one and headed down the aisle, slowing her pace trying not to walk past the number. *10045*. She took the big book from the shelf and carried it out to the counter and opened it. "Page 223, page 223..." She repeated as she flipped the pages, stopping at the designated page.

"Okay," she said reading the information. "Edward J. Robinson." She looked at her watch and realized she only had 45 minutes left before her next patient. She pulled out her cell phone and speed-dialed Kenya's number.

"Hey Ken, it's me. I know you're probably busy, but I need you look up some information on Edward J. Robinson. Call me when you get this message. Bye." She hung up the phone and closed the book, taking it back and placing it on the shelf. She walked out feeling more nervous than she had when she went in.

"I think found him, Keith," Charlotte said, walking into the house and noticing Keith coming down the stairs from the bedroom. "I think found our son."

"Really? That fast?" Keith said, walking towards the kitchen. Charlotte followed suit.

"Yeah. I went to the address that my mother had given me..." Charlotte put her purse on the kitchen counter. "...and the woman there said she didn't know who lived there before her and told me to check the registry of deeds and so I did. Well, from 1980 to 1985, the house was owned by Edward J. Robinson."

"Okay, so where does Swiss Family Robinson live now?"

"I don't know. I called and left Kenya a message hoping she could find out some more information. She hasn't called me back yet."

"Are you sure you want to do this?"

"Yes, I am sure. It's either now or never."

"Well, I have a surprise for you."

"What?"

"Turn around."

She turns around. "Tyson!"

"Hi, Ma," said her six-foot-tall 19-year-old son.

"My baby. I didn't know you were coming home," said Charlotte, hugging him.

"I wanted to surprise you."

"When did you get in?"

"This morning while you were at work. Where's Dana and the baby? I want to see them."

"They're still at the hospital. Will's father should be bringing them home in a couple of hours," said Charlotte. "You hungry? You want something to eat?"

"No, Ma. I'm good. So, what's new? What's going on? Anything?" Tyson said, grabbing an apple from the bowl on the counter.

"Other than your sister having a baby, nothing," said Charlotte.

Charlotte's cell phone rang from within her purse. "Excuse me, honey." She rushed over and grabbed her phone, answering it.

"Hello? Hey, Ken." Charlotte said.

"Hi Auntie Kenya!" Tyson shouted.

"Tyson said hi. She said hi. Go ahead," Charlotte said, leaving the kitchen. "Were you able to get any information? Hold on a minute." Charlotte grabbed a piece of paper and a pen and jotted down the address. "Thank you so much Ken. I love you. I owe you one." She hung up the phone. "Thank you, thank you, thank you," she spoke towards ceiling.

DING-DONG! The doorbell rang and she got up from the couch and opened the door to Anita, Keith's secretary, holding a car seat.

"Hi." Anita smiled.

Charlotte didn't say anything as she looked her husband's mistress up and down and then cut her eyes over to the baby and then back to Anita. "Keith! Keith!"

"Yeah!" he shouted, walking out from the kitchen. "Yeah, what's up?"

"Your problem's here." Charlotte walked away as Keith walked up. He looked at Anita and the baby and stepped outside closing the door behind him.

"What are you doing here?"

"I've come to tell you I'm leaving town. I'm moving back to Maryland." The baby made a noise and Keith looked down at the bundle of joy neatly tucked in his car seat. "Yes, he's yours."

"So, that's the reason you quit."

"Yes."

"Why are you just now telling me after all this time?"

"Because once I decided to keep him, I knew telling you that day in your office wouldn't have made a difference regarding us. You weren't ever going to leave her for me. And I was beginning to want more than the dick you were giving me. So, I waited until you were completely out of my system before I told you."

Keith didn't know what to say as he stood there, just staring at her. "What's his name?"

"James. James Keith Cole."

"If you need anything, and I mean anything, call me. I want to be there for my son."

"Good." She looked down their son and then to Keith. "Well, I gotta go. My train leaves in a couple of hours."

"Call me and let me know when you get settled."

"I'll think about it."

She walked away and got into the awaiting taxi. He watched as they rode away and out of view. He turned around and went back inside.

◆ FIFTY-FOUR ◆

Charlotte walked into the Westinghouse Bank like she had every time she needed to make a deposit, smiling at the security guard, waving to a few employees, making her way to her favorite teller's window, but this time she was carrying a few empty boxes.

"Hi, Miss Watson, here to make another deposit?" The teller asked.

"No, I'm here to make a complete withdrawal."

"Oh really?"

"Yeah, I think it's about time I do so."

"Okay. Come on in the back." The teller placed her "Next Teller" sign on the counter and led Charlotte into the vault.

"How's your son?" Charlotte asked.

"Good. He's good," The teller said, taking the boxes from the safe-deposit locker.

Charlotte opened the first safe-deposit box, paused and looked at the letters. This was it. Either the day she had longed for was coming upon her or the letters were going to be burned. She took the letters from the safe-deposit boxes and placed them in the boxes she had brought, in the same order as they were originally organized.

"So, what are you going to do with all of these letters? If you don't mind me asking..." said the teller.

"I don't know. I haven't decided yet," Charlotte said, closing the boxes. "Thanks for everything."

"No problem, Miss Watson. Need some help taking those to your car?"

"No, no, I got them. Thank you so much Tiffany for everything."

"You're welcome," said the teller.

Charlotte walked out as she had many times before, but this time with the reassurance that she was never going to step foot back inside ever again.

* * *

Charlotte sat in her car looking at the house Edward J. Robinson now owned, nervous. It was a modest single family home with a wired green fence that surrounded it. She took a deep breath, trying to calm her nerves. *Do I really want to do this? Do I really want to go through this?*, she thought. She noticed her hand shaking and grabbed it. *What do I have to lose?* She opened the car door, starting to get out. *But what if he, they, had everything to lose?* She closed the car door and sighed, not knowing what to do. "Fuck it, I'm going for it."

She opened the door and stepped out, locking the door with the keyless remote. She looked in both direction and crossed the street. Her heart was beating faster and faster as she made her way to the house, up the front porch to the front door. She pushed the doorbell. It chimed in the distance. She pushed the bell once more and it again chimed in the distance. *They must not be home.* She breathed a sigh of relief as she made her way back down the front porch towards her car.

"Excuse me. Excuse me, Miss?" said the elderly woman in the yard of the house next door, catching Charlotte's attention.

"Yes."

"Are you looking for Mr. Robinson?"

"Yes. Yes, I am."

"He's not home. His wife died. She had cancer. Her funeral was today."

"Oh, I'm so sorry to hear that."

"I'm sure they'll be back later. I think they're having the repass here, if you want to come back later."

"Oh, that's okay. Thank you, Ma'am." Charlotte walked away.

"Have a nice day."

"Yeah, you too."

Charlotte felt bad as she got back in her car. "You know what Charlotte? Just leave it alone," she said to herself. She buckled her seatbelt, started the engine and drove away.

* * *

Bradley looked on from the front pew as he listened to colleagues of his mother's, nurses and doctors, get up one by one and speak kind words about her. He wrapped his arm around Junior consoling him. As he listened, the good moments with his mother that had seemed to be buried by his pain began to flood back to his mind and he started smiling, chuckling to himself. Croix looked over at him, and his smile made her smile. It had been a long time since she had seen a big smile on his face like that.

"Now a selection from our choir," said the Pastor. The chords started and Bradley began to rock side-to-side like an old southern woman as the choir stood and began singing The Lord Is My Shepherd. An elder choir member stepped to the microphone and sung lead of Psalms 23 as the choir joined in. Bradley smiled as he listened, the feeling reminding him of an old southern church. Everyone clapped as the choir finished the song as delicate and sweet as they had begun it.

"Let's bow our heads..." Everyone bowed their heads as the Pastor gave the benediction.

The home that Barbara and Eddie Sr. had shared for most of their marriage was filled with the sounds of chatter of family, friends and some of Barbara's colleagues. Bradley noticed his father walking upstairs towards the bedroom. He excused himself from the conversation he was having and followed.

Eddie Sr. sat on the side of the bed feeling more sad than he ever had. Barbara's scent tickled his nose and he smiled. Tears fell from his eyes as he thought further about her. He heard the floor creak in the distance and quickly looked in its direction and noticed Bradley standing there.

"I'm fine," he said.

"Come on, Dad. We both know you are not fine," Bradley said walking further in, sitting down. He touched his shoulder.

"I was an asshole. A true asshole to her. I treated her like shit."

"Dad…"

"I did, son. I really did. And I'm paying for it now." He cried. "She was the best thing that ever happened to me and what did I do…treated her like she was nothing. Like she didn't mean a damn thing to me." He cried. "Treated her like shit."

Bradley couldn't help but to wipe the tears from his own eyes as he felt and listened to the hurt of his father.

◆ FIFTY-FIVE ◆

Rodney stood outside of the police cruiser checking the news feed of his Facebook page on his cell phone as he waited for Bradley to return with their coffees. The day had been quiet for most of their shift, at least in their section of town anyway. He laughed as Bradley walked out carrying two coffees.

"What so funny?"

"Nothing. I was just laughing at Jackson's Facebook status," said Rodney as he took the coffee from Bradley and put his cell phone in his pocket. He took a sip of the coffee. "Good."

Bradley walked around to the passenger side and got in as did Rodney. Rodney placed his coffee in the cup holder.

"Beautiful day out."

"Yeah, it is. It was supposed to rain," Rodney said starting the engine, driving off.

"How's your dad?"

"He's good. He's hanging in there. I'm gonna stop by there after work."

"Have you made a decision about finding your birth parents?"

"Yeah, I'm not going look for them. It's not worth it. I mean I've gone this long without knowing them. I figured I can go the rest of my life without knowing them."

"Leaving well enough alone."

"Exactly."

Unit 104…, the female voice spoke over the radio.

"104…" Rodney answered.

Yeah, can you guys head over to 170 Tremont Street, we got a couple of panhandlers outside the store arguing.

"104 responding," Rodney spoke.

Rodney and Bradley slowly pulled their cruiser up to the curb, Rodney placing the gear in park.

"These two…" said Bradley.

"Frick-and motherfreakin'-Frack. Fantastic."

They got out of the car.

"Officer! Officer!" the man shouted. "She's not supposed to be here. Tell her."

"Neither one of you are supposed to be in front of this store," said Rodney. "Now, move along."

"Stupid bitch!" the man shouted at the woman.

The woman spit at him and he pushed Rodney trying to get her, but Rodney grabbed him and pushed him against the wall.

"Hey, hey, hey, what are you doing? She spit at me!"

"And you pushed me, so you're under arrest." Rodney said handcuffing him.

"This is bullshit!"

"Yup, it sure is."

The woman stuck her tongue out at him as Rodney walked him over to the cruiser and put him in the backseat, closing the door.

"You want to be arrested, too?" Rodney said turning to the woman.

"Then I suggest moving along, now," Bradley said as he got in the car, Rodney following. "That coffee came right on time."

"It sure did."

Rodney put car in gear, driving off.

* * *

Bradley pulled up in front of his parents' house and turned off the engine. It had been a month since Barbara's passing and his father was holding up well, at least for the time being. He got out of the car and walked up the stairs to the house. He rang the doorbell. Eddie Jr. opened the door, paint stains covering his clothes.

"Hey," said Junior.

"Hey," said Bradley walking in. "Is Dad home?"

"Yeah. He's in the basement. We were painting. Dad!" yelled Junior, closing the door.

"Yeah!" He responded from the basement.

"Bradley's here!"

"Ok! I'll be up in a minute!"

Bradley noticed the sheets and pillows on the couch and looked at his brother.

"Natalie and I are separating. She couldn't take me anymore, I guess." He half-smiled as Bradley touched his shoulder. "I can't stand me either sometimes."

"Hey, son," Eddie Sr. said, coming from the basement. "Uh, I mean Bradley."

"It's fine. I'm still your son." Bradley smiled, hugging him. "I was just stopping by to check on you. See how you were doing."

"I'm doing good. Let's go sit out on the deck, enjoy some of this beautiful day. Junior and I been down in the basement most of the day," Eddie said as they headed through the kitchen and out to the backyard. "Y'all want a beer?"

"I'll have some water," said Bradley.

"I'll take one, a beer," said Junior.

Eddie grabbed the beers from the refrigerator and they continued outside each taking a seat.

"Ahhh, such a beautiful day isn't it?" said Eddie Sr.

"Yeah, it is," responded Bradley.

They looked out quietly, taking in the scenic view of the trees, the neatly cut grass and the sound of the chirping birds.

"Your mother used to love sitting out here to watch the sun go down," said Eddie Sr., as he sipped his beer. "I'm sorry I didn't show you two how to be better men."

"Dad…," Bradley interjected.

"Let me finish, please. I wasn't the best role model and I

want you two to forgive me for that. Especially you, Junior. I'm sorry." He was choking up. "I've shown you wrong your whole life…and I'm sorry for that. I really am. I know you and Natalie are separating, but I want you to always be there for your family. Don't argue, don't fuss, don't fight, show them you can change, especially Bailey and Dominique. And talk to them and tell them that you're sorry and how much you love them. Do it now while they're still young. You don't want Bailey to continue what my father started and what you and I continued to do. It needs to stop, okay?"

"Okay, Dad," Junior said, wiping tears from his eyes.

"I love both of you."

"We love you, too," said Bradley grabbing his hand, his brother doing the same.

DING-DONG! The doorbell chimed in the distance.

"I'll get it. I gotta use the bathroom anyway," Eddie Sr. said getting up.

He walked inside. DING-DONG! The bell chimed again.

"Hold on, I'm coming!" He put his beer on the kitchen counter, passing through the house. He noticed the back side of a woman as he peeked out the window from behind the curtain. He opened the door. "Hello?"

"Hello. Hi, I'm looking for Edward J. Robinson," Charlotte said turning around. "Hi, my name is Dr. Charlotte Tate…"

"Nice to meet you. Are you a colleague of my wife's?"

"No. No, I'm not," Charlotte said feeling nervous. "I'm looking for some information."

"Regarding…?"

"Your former residence. Did you used to live at 465 Salem Avenue?"

"Yeah, over 20 years ago. Why? What's it to you?" he asked, concerned.

"Well, my son, he used to live there too."

Eddie felt his heart drop into the pit of his stomach. He knew exactly who she was. "Um, come inside."

"Thank you." She stepped inside. "You have a nice home, Mr. Robinson." Charlotte said looking around.

"Thank you," he said closing the door. "Have a seat." He

extended his hand towards the living room. "Can I get you something to drink?"

"No, thank you. I'm fine." She sat down on the couch.

He sat down across from her on the loveseat, nervous, knowing Bradley was in the vicinity and hoping he didn't come inside. "How did you find us? Well, me."

"Well, I looked up your former residence at the Registry of Deeds and got your name and my sister works for the D.A.'s office and that's how I was able to find you."

"How did you know we used to live in that house?"

"Well…when I gave birth to my son, a little over 30 years ago, your wife was one of the nurses in the delivery room that day and my mother had given her a note the next morning and told her to call her when he was safe and she did, giving my mother that address."

Eddie didn't say anything as he sat back, taking it all in. He knew she wasn't lying. "Why wait so long to return?"

She sighed. "Because I didn't know where he was. My mother had the baby taken from me. I was 14 when I had him."

"That young, huh?"

"Yeah."

"What's his name? Do you know his name?"

"No. My mother didn't allow me to name him."

"Some mother."

"I know tell me about it."

Eddie sat up. "So, your son could be anybody, huh? Any man you pass on the street that's about 30 years old, huh?"

"Yeah."

"So, what makes you so sure that one of my sons is yours?"

"I don't. All I know is the information I got lead me here, to your house."

"Uh-huh."

"Dad…" Bradley said walking inside. "Dad, who was that at the front…Dr. Tate?" Bradley said surprised to see her sitting in his parents' living room. "What are you doing?"

"Bradley," said an equally surprised Charlotte.

"You two know each other?" Eddie asked taken aback.

"Yeah, she's my therapist. The one I told you I was seeing.

Rodney's aunt."

"Yeah...yeah."

"Dr. Tate, what are you doing here?"

"I'm here looking for information about my son."

"Your son?"

"The child I was telling you about during one of our sessions. The big secret regarding my husband."

Eddie remained quiet looking between both of them as they spoke.

Bradley thought back. "Oh yeah, yeah. Well, what does my father have to do with your son?"

"Well, my son used to live in a house your family used to live in."

"What house?"

"The one on Salem Avenue," Eddie said knowing what was about to happen. "She's your mother, son," he said sitting back, moving his hand over his mouth, not knowing what else to say.

"What?"

"You must be mistaken, Mr. Robinson," said Charlotte. "He can't be my son."

"I was adopted."

"No, you weren't."

"Okay, where the hell did everyone go...," Junior said walking in.

"Oh my God," Charlotte said leaning back in the chair.

"Dad, what the hell are you talking about?" asked Bradley.

He sighed. "The day of your mother's retirement party, after you and her had that argument, she told me everything in the kitchen. She took you after this lady's family didn't want you in hopes that I would stop abusing her. Since I never hit her when she was pregnant."

"So, mom lied to me again."

"Yeah. I thought you knew."

"No, she didn't tell me." He hit his hand against the wall, angry. "I need to step outside." He swung out the front door, walking outside.

"Bradley..."

"I got him," said Junior.

240

Charlotte and Eddie sat in the living room, silent, nervous, making eye contact every few glances or so. Charlotte dreamed of the day she would meet her son, but never thought it would be like this.

"I'm...I'm going to leave now." She got up and headed for the door. "Sorry to hear about your wife, Mr. Robinson."

"Why didn't you want him?" he asked.

"I did, but my mother didn't."

She walked outside and noticed Junior sitting in the distance talking to Bradley. Having made eye contact, she wanted to walk over to him and counsel him, but their sessions had ended moments ago; for he was now no longer her patient, but her son. She walked to her car and got in and drove off.

♦ FIFTY-SIX ♦

"So, you really think this guy, your patient Bradley, is our son?" said Keith, grabbing the bottle of wine from the table pouring himself a glass.

"Yes," Charlotte said finishing her glass, wanting the bottle back to refill it.

"Are you sure about this?" Keith asked sitting down across from her in the living room.

"Yes, he is our son. I mean if he wants a DNA test to prove it, I'll get one, but he is our son."

"That young man I dragged in here that night?"

"Yes, Keith," she said drinking wine. "Everything adds up: his mother Barbara was the nurse that was in the delivery room when he was born; my mother had the address of where they used to live…it just makes sense."

"Have you told your mother yet?"

"No, I haven't said anything to anybody yet. Just you."

"Well, if this man is our son, you're still not going to counsel him?"

"No, I'll just refer him to someone else, if he still thinks he needs counseling."

Tyson and Dana walked in carrying the baby in the car seat. "Hey," she huffed closing the door.

"Here's Nanna's baby," Charlotte said putting down the

242

glass and taking the car seat from Dana. "Come here, precious." She unfastened the strap, slowly taking the baby from the seat. "Ya'll two had fun at the mall?"

"He did," said Dana.

"You got the stuff you wanted to take back to school?" asked Charlotte

"Yeah," said Tyson. "I'm gonna put it in my suitcase."

"Okay."

Tyson ran upstairs to his room.

"You didn't give your mother too much trouble at the mall, I hope," Charlotte said to her granddaughter.

"Not really. I only had to change her a few times. Other than that she was quiet."

"I'm a good baby Nanna, that's right." Charlotte said playfully.

"I'm gonna take her upstairs and change her for bed. Come here," Dana said taking her. "Let's get so fresh and so clean, babycakes."

"Don't forget to use the no-fragrance wipes."

"I won't, Ma," Dana said walking upstairs.

Charlotte sipped her wine. "I don't know what I'm gonna do, Keith."

"About what?"

"About our son."

"What else is left there for you to do? He knows. You know. What else is there for you to do except to just let it be? Let it be what it is. You can't fix everything. I'm sure, he'll come to you."

* * *

The thunder rumbled and lightning flashed as Bradley and Croix sat in the kitchen at the table drinking coffee. Croix, still stunned by the revelation Bradley had disclosed to her hours before when she got home from work.

"I still can't believe it. I've heard a lot of stories from the people that come in and out of the emergency room, but this one takes the cake."

"Tell me about it," said Bradley staring at his cup of coffee.

"So, Dr. Tate, the therapist you've been seeing all this time, is your mother?"

"That's the way it seems."

"Wow."

"Yup."

Are you sure?"

"From what my father told me about what my mother said to him, and the hospital record in the bottom of that box, it all makes sense. Why would my mother keep and hide that record if wasn't true?"

"So, what are you gonna do? Are you still going to see her as a therapist? I mean it will feel kind of awkward, don't you think?"

"I have no clue what I'm going to do. I really don't." Bradley sighed. "I know my father must be beside himself right now."

"I know. Well, at least Junior's there with him."

"I know. I just hope Junior doesn't upset him with his bullshit."

Croix wondered what was going through her husband's mind as he stared at his coffee like a lost child. "Hey."

He looked up.

"I love you," she said reaching across the table touching his hand.

He smiled half-heartily as he tapped her hand and got up from the table. "I'm gonna head to bed."

"Okay. I'll be up after I finished this."

"Okay." He said as he left the kitchen and headed upstairs.

♦ FIFTY-SEVEN ♦

Charlotte played with the pearls around her neck as she looked out the window of her office at the view of the city, replaying what had happened at Bradley's parent's home. Was he really her son? That baby boy she had had so many years prior, or was God playing a cruel trick on her?

She looked down at her watch. One o'clock. She wondered if Bradley was going to show up to their already scheduled meeting. If he didn't she'd understand, just the thought of it made her feel uncomfortable.

"So when can we get a blood test?"

She turned around, startled, seeing him standing there in the doorway. "You scared me."

"Sorry. So, when can we get a blood test?" he asked.

"I can, um, call a friend of mine who works at the clinic and set that up," she said walking his direction. "I can do that right now if you'd like."

"Could you?"

"Sure." She walked over to her desk and picked up the phone, wanting to address the awkwardness between them, but flipped through her rolodex and dialed her friend's number. "Hi Andrew, it's Charlotte, long time no hear. I'm good. How are you? Good. Listen, can you setup an appointment for a friend and I? A swab test, yes. Tomorrow." She covered the receiver

with her hand. "Is tomorrow good for you? This time
tomorrow?"

"Perfect."

"Tomorrow at one is a go. Thanks, Andrew. See you then.
Bye-bye." She hung up the phone. "So, tomorrow at one
o'clock."

"Okay." Bradley started to leave...

"Bradley..."

He turned back around.

"You know I wanted you, right."

"Yeah...I know. Tomorrow at one."

"Tomorrow at one."

Bradley had driven around for hours after he left Charlotte's
office, still trying to come to terms with what had happened. As
a cop, he witnessed and heard a lot of stories, but his life really
did take the cake like Croix said. He laid his back against the
driver's seat as he placed the car in park. He got out of the car
and walked across the grass, passing the pieces of stone that had
the names and the dates of people who had once lived, arriving
at Barbara's, who was the last one in the row. He looked up.

"You know I could be bitter right now. I could, but I can't,"
he said as he looked down at her grave. "I understand why you
did what you did, even if it was selfish. But what I don't
understand is why didn't you just tell me the truth, the whole
truth, and nothing but the truth since the beginning. You only
gave me fragments, pieces of the truth. Pieces that I now have to
learn how to put together so the puzzle of my life can work."

He looked off into the horizon. "You treated me like
shit...like shit. Like I was nothing to you." Tears streamed down
his face. "You took an innocent child and used me like I was
nothing...but I forgive you. I do. For every slap, for every time
you pulled me upstairs and made me strip; for every...for every
time...you slapped that belt against my skin as a punishment for
something I never did. I never hit you. Not once did I ever put
my hands on you. Not even when I was a teenager and could, I
didn't.

But unlike Dad, you never apologized after your hits, you just moved on like it was nothing...but I forgive you. Both of you, you and Dad, for being cowards. The one thing I learned from being a police officer is that cowards hit and abuse other people," he said looking back down at Barbara's grave. "But I...forgive you...not for you, but for me." He cried, beating his hand across his chest. "And I forgive myself...for running away for so long. Away from you and from myself. It's because of you, I'm here." He smiled wiping the tears from his cheeks. "No matter how broken I am, or was, I'm here. And that's gotta mean something."

He took a deep breath as a breeze flowed by. "Take care, Barbara." He walked away.

♦ FIFTY-EIGHT ♦

"Have you been waiting long?" Charlotte asked, walking up and sitting down next to Bradley. It had been three days since their mouths had been swabbed for the maternity test and now they both sat in the waiting area of the clinic waiting for Charlotte's associate to call them into the office.

"No. Just got here a little before you did."

"Okay," Charlotte said, letting out a breath. She started fanning herself trying to calm her anxiety. "Are you nervous?" she asked.

"Not really. Are you?"

"A little bit," she said, grabbing a magazine from the nearby table for a much larger breeze.

"If it turns out that we're not related, will you see me as a patient?" Bradley asked, closing the TIME magazine he was reading.

"Of course."

"And if we are related…"

"Well, it depends…"

"Depends on what?"

"How comfortable you'll be with seeing me as your therapist and your mother…"

"Hey, Charlotte," said Dr. Andrew Cassidy, her associate and friend.

"Hey."

"You two can come into my office."

Charlotte put the magazine down and followed Andrew, along with Bradley, into the office. She took a deep breath trying calm down her rapidly pulsating heart.

"Have a seat," said the doctor, closing the door.

Charlotte and Bradley sat down. He grabbed her hand trying to ease the nervousness he knew she was feeling.

"Okay…," Dr. Cassidy started, sitting down behind his desk. "So, the results are in. Now, I didn't look at them. I wanted to wait. So, you two ready for this?"

"Oh, I've been ready," Charlotte said, putting her other hand on top of Bradley's, her heart ready to explode as Dr. Cassidy took his letter opener and cut open the envelope. Charlotte grabbed Bradley's hand tighter. He looked at her and smiled.

"Stop! Just…," Charlotte said, getting up, pacing the floor.

"Charlotte…," said Dr. Cassidy.

"Is everything okay, Dr. Tate?" Bradley asked.

"Maybe we shouldn't do this. What if my husband's right. Maybe you're not my son and I'm just making this all up because I want to find my son."

"We don't have to do this if you don't want to," said Bradley. "I'm perfectly fine without knowing. I'm content with everything as it is now."

"If you don't want me to read the results I won't," said Dr. Cassidy.

She was shaking as she nervously continued to pace. "I don't know. I don't know. It just all seems too good to be true. Everything just seems like it's happening so fast. My mother giving the information of where my son grew up; me finding your father and then learning it's you…it's just… I don't know."

"Charlotte, have a seat, you're beginning to freak out," said Dr. Cassidy.

"Okay." She sat down.

"Now take a deep breath," said Dr. Cassidy. "And now another one."

She did, calming herself. "I'm sorry for freaking out."

"It's okay. It happens all the time. I'm used to it."

"I'm just nervous."

"I know. You okay now?"

"Yeah, I'm good."

"Do you want me to read the results?"

"Yes."

"You sure now? 'Cause we don't have to do this."

"Yes, I'm sure." She grabbed Bradley's hand. "Go ahead."

"Okay. The following is the results of the maternity test performed on mouth swabs taken from Charlotte Watson-Tate and Bradley Avery Robinson. The completed test confirms Mrs. Charlotte Watson-Tate is not excluded as the biological mother of Mr. Bradley Avery Robinson."

"So, you're saying…"

"Yes, he is your biological son."

Charlotte lowered her head on top of her and Bradley's joined hands and cried. Bradley wiped the tears from his cheeks, not really knowing how to feel. He took the tissue from the doctor. "Thank you."

This was the moment Charlotte had been waiting for all of her life and Bradley felt that, giving her the tissue to wipe her face.

"Thank you so much, Andrew," Charlotte said, lifting her head and wiping her face.

"No problem. I'm glad I could help." He stood up as Charlotte walked to him and hugged him.

"Thank you, thank you."

"No problem." They released from the embrace. "If you need anything else, call me, okay?"

"I will. Thank you. May I keep the letter?"

"Sure. You take it. It's yours."

He handed Charlotte the results letter. She walked back around and grabbed her purse as Bradley stood up ready to go.

"Thanks again, Andrew."

"You're welcome. And tell Keith I said hello."

"I will."

"Nice to meet you. And thank you," Bradley said, extending his hand.

"You're welcome."

Charlotte could barely contain the joy she was feeling inside as they left the doctor's office, walking past the waiting area and onto the elevator. The day she had wanted for 30 years had finally arrived. Nothing else mattered to her now. Not her career, Keith's affair, her broken relationship with her mother, nothing. She put her purse on her shoulder and grabbed Bradley's hand. He looked at her and smiled.

"You okay?" she asked.

"Yeah, I'm fine. I'm just…taking everything in."

The elevator doors opens and they walked outside.

"How are you?"

"Um…happy." She smiled with tears streaming down her cheeks.

They stopped and he wiped the tears from her face.

"Thank you for listening me, taking me on at the last minute, for helping me and for making me face and talk about things I was afraid to talk about. I thank you for that."

"You leaving town or something?" Charlotte asked, smiling.

"No, no. Things have now obviously changed since we know the truth and I wanted to thank you as a patient."

"Okay. Well, you're welcome." She laughed.

The tiny bell above the front doors of the Coldstone ice cream shop chimed as a few customers exited. "You want to get some ice cream?"

"Sure, why not?"

Bradley caught the door before it closed and they walked in.

"Can I help you?" asked the young man behind the counter.

"Yeah, let me get a medium cup of French vanilla ice cream with Reese's peanut butter cups."

"Okay. And you Miss…?"

"I'll have medium cup of strawberry ice cream, please. Thank you."

The young man scooped and prepared their orders. Bradley paid and they walked out tasting the flavorful cool dessert.

"Oh my God, this is so good," Charlotte praised as the ice cream hit her lips and then her taste buds. "Thank you."

"No problem."

Silence began to grow between them as they walked down the street, enjoying their ice cream.

"So, when do I get to meet everyone else?"

"How about this evening? I can get Keith to throw some food on the grill and I can see about getting everyone over to the house."

"Okay. And I'll tell Croix and the girls."

"Sounds like a plan."

"A plan it is, Dr. Tate." Bradley laughed.

"Charlotte."

"Whatever you say…Mom."

They laughed.

"Do you have any place to be after this?" Charlotte asked.

"No. Why?"

"Would you mind going somewhere with me? It's very important."

"Sure, I don't mind."

♦ FIFTY-NINE ♦

Charlotte noticed her mother's black Buick in the driveway as she pulled up in front of the house. She hadn't spoken to her since their field trip and she was feeling a little anxious, putting the car gear in park and shutting off the engine. She took a deep breath.

"You okay?" Bradley asked.

"I'm fine. Let's go."

She got out of the car, as did he. They made their way towards Carol's front door and she pushed the doorbell. Charlotte rubbed her hands together, nervously.

"Who is it?"

"It's me, Ma. It's Charlotte."

Carol opened the door.

"Surprise," Charlotte said unenthusiastically.

"I didn't know you were coming over," Carol said as Charlotte and Bradley stepped inside.

"Don't worry, we're not saying long," said Charlotte.

"I would have dressed better if I had known you were bringing company. How are you doing young man?" Carol said shutting the door.

"Hi," said Bradley.

"Ma, this is Bradley. Bradley, my mother."

"Nice to meet you, Bradley," Carol said shaking his hand.

"Y'all have a seat."

"Yeah, let's do that," Charlotte said sitting down on the couch, Bradley sitting next to her.

"So, what brought you on this visit?" Carol asked.

"Ma, do you know who this is?"

"No. I have no idea," Carol answered, feeling uncomfortable.

"You should. You used to watch him when he was a kid…remember…?"

Carol's eyes welled with tears. "Excuse me for a second, I have to get some tissues."

"Where you going? I got some right here in my bag," Charlotte said opening her purse and pulling out some tissues. "I'm a therapist, so I have to them handy. There you go."

Carol took them, reluctantly, and wiped her eyes.

"What are you crying for, Ma? Come on, let's talk about it," Charlotte said placing her purse on the floor. "Since you're my mother, I won't charge you for the session."

Carol didn't say anything, just kept her eyes on Bradley as the tears fell.

"Let's see, where do you want to begin? Hey!" Charlotte clapped her hands, getting her mother's attention. "Get your head out of the clouds."

Carol, once again, didn't speak as she looked at Charlotte, wiping her eyes.

"Handsome, isn't he?" Charlotte said rubbing Bradley's knee, looking at him.

"I'm sorry," Carol said spoke softly through the tears.

"Excuse me, what? Did you say something? I didn't hear you. Come again," Charlotte said holding her ear in her direction.

"I said I'm sorry." Carol spoke a little louder.

"To him? Me?"

"To both of you. I'm sorry. Bradley, I did what I thought was best for my family."

"No, Ma, you did what you thought was best for you. You shamed me so you could hide your own shame. And that's something I refuse to do to my own daughter or my granddaughter. That ends today. Now, if your grandson wants to have a relationship with you, that's up to him, but I thought you should meet him," Charlotte said standing up. "Bradley, let's go." He stood up.

"Charlotte, Bradley..." Carol said standing up. "...I'm asking for your forgiveness. Please forgive me."

"I have nothing to forgive you for," said Bradley. "You didn't hurt me, you hurt her."

"Charlotte..."

"You know Ma, it's the only thing I've been waiting all these years to receive from you and right now...I just..."

Charlotte and Bradley headed for the door.

"Charlotte...I love you," said Carol.

"Yeah, I know, Ma."

Charlotte closed the door.

EPILOGUE

A couple of hours had passed since Bradley, Croix and the girls had arrived at Charlotte's home and were introduced to a new side of their family. Bradley listened to the laughter and chatter in the backyard as he walked around the living room admiring the décor of Charlotte's home and the pictures of his new biological family. He was still little unsure about everything, but it all was beginning to settle down.

He smiled to himself at the amazement of it all, his life now and wondered if it was all just too good to be true. If this was all just a dream and he would wake up at any moment. He pinched himself hard. It wasn't a dream. He was awake. This was for real.

"There you are," said Charlotte, walking in with a few boxes. "You okay?"

"Yeah, I'm fine. Just admiring the pictures. You really do have a nice home, Dr. Tate."

"Charlotte. And thank you."

"Sorry," he chuckled, "I'm just still trying to wrap my head around all this."

"Yeah, me too. It's going to take a while. My family can be a little overwhelming sometimes."

"It's mine now, too," he laughed.

She smiled. "Bradley, sit down, if you don't mind. I have something to give you." He sat down as did she. "In these boxes, is everything you need to know about me." She handed the top box to him and he opened it.

"What are these?"

"They're letters. One for each day of my life since the time you were born. Well, almost every day. I might have missed a few."

"You wrote all these?"

"Yep. And they're in order by date."

"Wow. I don't know what…I don't what to say."

"Don't say anything. Just read them when you get ready," she said, trying to catch the tears before they fell.

Bradley didn't know what else to say, feeling very overwhelmed by the envelopes upon envelopes that filled the boxes. "Do you mind if I read one?"

"Sure. They're yours now."

He pulled an envelope from the second box and opened it.

July 1, 1982

Dear Baby Boy,

It's been almost two years since you've been gone, and I still miss you. I'll be 16 in a few months. Can you believe it? Mama doesn't talk about you, but I know she misses you, too. Anyway, you would not believe what happened last week. Miranda and I were walking down the street headed to Pam's house…

Charlotte just watched him as he read. He was handsome, just as she had imagined him to be. She rubbed his head, he looked back, smiling. She was amazed at the fact that she was now living the moment she had dreamt about for most her life…the moment her son came home.

A SEQUEL? MAYBE…

I'D LIKE TO HEAR FROM YOU.
FOLLOW ME AND COMMENT USING #JOHNDOE
ON EITHER…

TWITTER: @terrelhicks

or

THE JOHN DOE FACEBOOK PAGE

Made in the USA
Columbia, SC
17 October 2018